Also by Lilja Sigurðardóttir and available from Orenda Books

The Reykjavík Noir trilogy
Snare
Trap
Cage

Betrayal

The Áróra Investigation Series
Cold as Hell
Red as Blood

ABOUT THE AUTHOR

Icelandic crime-writer Lilja Sigurðardóttir was born in the town of Akranes in 1972 and raised in Mexico, Sweden, Spain and Iceland. An award-winning playwright, Lilja has written ten crime novels, including *Snare*, *Trap* and *Cage*, making up the Reykjavík Noir trilogy, and her standalone thriller *Betrayal*, all of which have hit bestseller lists worldwide. *Snare* was longlisted for the CWA International Dagger, *Cage* won Best Icelandic Crime Novel of the Year and was a *Guardian* Book of the Year, and *Betrayal* was shortlisted for the prestigious Glass Key Award and won Icelandic Crime Novel of the Year. The film rights for the Reykjavík Noir trilogy have been bought by Palomar Pictures in California. *Cold as Hell*, the first book in the An Áróra Investigation series, was published in the UK in 2021 and was followed by *Red as Blood* in 2022.

Lilja lives in Reykjavík with her partner. You'll find Lilja on Twitter @lilja1972, Instagram @sigurdardottirlilja, on facebook.com/liljawriter and on her website, liljawriter.com.

ABOUT THE TRANSLATOR

A series of unlikely coincidences allowed Quentin Bates to escape English suburbia as a teenager with the chance of a gap year working in Iceland. For a variety of reasons, the year stretched to become a gap decade, during which time he went native in the north of Iceland, acquiring a new language, a new profession and a family.

He is the author of a series of crime novels set in present-day Iceland. His translations include works by Guðlaugur Arason, Ragnar Jónasson, Einar Kárason and Sólveig Pálsdóttir, as well as Lilja Sigurðardóttir's Reykjavík Noir trilogy, standalone novel *Betrayal* and the Áróra series. Follow Quentin on Twitter @graskeggur.

WHITE AS SNOW

Lilja Sigurðardóttir

Translated by Quentin Bates

ORENDA
BOOKS

Orenda Books
16 Carson Road
West Dulwich
London SE21 8HU
www.orendabooks.co.uk

First published in Icelandic as *Náhvít jörð* by Forlagið, 2021
First published in English by Orenda Books, 2023
Copyright © Lilja Sigurðardóttir, 2021
English translation copyright © Quentin Bates, 2023

A catalogue record for this book is available from the British Library.

B-format paperback ISBN 978-1-914585-84-5
eISBN 978-1-914585-85-2

The publication of this translation has been made possible through the financial
support of

ICELANDIC LITERATURE CENTER

Typeset in Garamond by typesetter.org.uk

MIX
Paper | Supporting
responsible forestry
FSC
www.fsc.org   FSC® C171272

Printed and bound by CPI Group (UK) Ltd, Croydon CR0 4YY

WHITE AS SNOW

PRONUNCIATION GUIDE

Icelandic has a couple of letters that don't exist in other European languages and which are not always easy to replicate. The letter ð is generally replaced with a d in English, but we have decided to use the Icelandic letter to remain closer to the original names. Its sound is closest to the hard th in English, as found in *thus* and *bathe*.

The letter r is generally rolled hard with the tongue against the roof of the mouth. In pronouncing Icelandic personal and place names, the emphasis is placed on the first syllable.

Aktu-Taktu – Aktou-Taktou
Áróra – Ow-row-ra
Auðbrekka – Oyth-brekka
Baldvin – Bal-dvin
Elín – El-yn
Elliðavatn – Etli-tha-vatn
Garðabær – Gar-that-byre
Gylfi – Gil-fee
Gufunes – Gou-fou-ness
Gurrí – Gou-ree
Hólmsheiði – Holms-haythi
Ísafold – Ysa-fold
Jahérnahér – Ya-her-tna-hyer
Jóna – Yoe-wna
Keflavík – Kep-la-viek
Kópavogur – Koe-pa-voe-goor
Kristján – Krist-tyown
Lárentínus – Low-ren-tien-us
Leirvogstunga – Leyr-vogs-tou-nga

Mosfellsbær – Mos-fels-byre
Oddsteinn – Odd-stay-tn
Rauðhólar – Royth-hoe-lar
Sæbraut –Sey-broyt
Skeifan – Skay-fan
Smiðja –Smith-ya
Valur – Va-lour

Cold. It menaces her, forcing itself on her from every direction, searching for any way to get to her, slipping inside clothes, gnawing at flesh. It catches hold of extremities, fingers, hands, feet, legs as far as the knee. She fights back, shifting her legs. She gets to her feet and jumps, kicks into the darkness until she's too weak to stay on her feet. That's when she huddles into a ball and rubs her hands together, pushing them between her legs or into her armpits, and shivers. When she stops shivering is when she feels the numbness in her feet. It's like they are gone, that they no longer belong to her. She can still move her feet, but has no feeling in them.

But cold is a liar. The numbness fades and the piercing pain that comes from inside, all the way from the bone, makes her again aware of her feet. She weeps, sees double so that the glimmer of light that comes through the grille appears multiplied and for a moment it's as if she's in her own bed at home, waking up to see the sunrise, and before long she'll hear the cock crow and get up, go to the doorway and warm herself in the morning sun, listen to the news on the radio and drink coffee spiced with cardamom.

That's how deceptive cold can be. It pretends to be warmth. It pretends that it's warming her all the way through, and it's such a joy to be warm that she loosens her clothing at the throat. But she's too weak to undress. Clara lies half across her and she's too heavy to be moved. So she just lies there and delights in finally being warm again, allowing herself to rest, to relax, to forget the nightmare of the last few days.

When she comes to her senses, the cold is everywhere. The deception is no more and she's back in this wretched reality of a steel container that's shaking. It rocks and rattles and shivers so that Clara is shaken off her, rolling to the floor where Marsela lies.

In the air there's no sign of the newly risen sun or aroma of hot coffee, but just the merciless stench of fear and cold steel. With a struggle, she opens her eyes, but shuts them again as the white light flooding the container stings them.

TUESDAY

1

There was complete darkness in the room when Elín awoke. From the window, open just a crack behind the heavy curtain, she could hear a murmur, as if the wind played over the gap, producing a constant, monotonous whine that occasionally rose to a whistle. But it wasn't the whine of the wind that had woken her, but Sergei's voice from somewhere in the flat. He was on the phone, and she could tell from his tone of voice that he was speaking to the woman – the one who could call at any time of the day or night and who he said was his mother in Russia. That might be true, but there was still something odd about it – the way he left the room whenever she called and shut himself away. Why did he need to be in another room to speak to his mother? And anyway, Elín didn't speak Russian, so he could be talking right in front of her, and she'd have no idea what it was about.

Elín stretched out a hand, felt on the bedside table for her phone, and was dazzled for a moment when the screen lit up bright blue, and she had to squint to see the time. It was getting on for six-thirty, so she might as well get up rather than try to go back to sleep. She was used to being up early and going down to her workshop, and had often been at work for two hours by the time Sergei knocked to let her know that he was awake and had made tea. It always took him a while to brew tea, as he followed a strict set of steps, adamant that it had to be done in a particular way. He started by making tea as dark as ink in a pot, then let it stand for a good while before decanting it into a small flask. Then he filled a large flask with hot water and sliced a lemon, putting the slices in their cups. By the time she came up, he was usually pouring the tea from the little flask into the cups – half a cup for him and just enough in hers to cover the bottom because she didn't like it too strong – and then he filled the cups with water from the large flask. This was what he called 'caravan tea', and he was clearly convinced it was worth the trouble he took over it. She could just as well have dunked a tea bag in hot water and not noticed the difference.

Elín sat up, feeling with her toes for her thick woollen socks and pulling on her clothes in the darkness. She hadn't exactly intended to eavesdrop on Sergei's conversation, but found herself, almost without realising it, in the corridor, her ear to the bathroom door, listening to his strangely gentle tone. He had taught her a few Russian words, so she could pronounce them and understood whenever he said them to her, but when he spoke at his usual speed with other Russians, she couldn't even tell one word from the next. His speech was just a string of strange syllables that all sounded much the same to her.

Tsya-tsya-sne-sne-minya-privnya-sne-sne.

It wasn't the words that made her so heartsick, but his tone of voice, the gentleness of it. It was the tenderness that had captivated her because it was so diametrically at odds with his usual manner. Sergei was a big man, and looked to have some rough edges, although he was a good-looking guy, normally dressed in sports gear, with a gold chain dangling from his thick neck onto his chest, which he shaved in the shower at the same time as his head. When Elín suggested he wear a smarter shirt and a pair of jeans, he just laughed and told her that was the age difference talking. That Elín didn't know anything about current street fashion and that he wouldn't be putting on a shirt and tie, even though he was approaching thirty. When he reminded her, like this, of the almost twenty-year age difference between them, he left her with the lingering feeling that it was foolish for a woman of almost fifty to be so smitten.

This was the feeling that overwhelmed her now as she stood by the bathroom door and listened to him speak. *Tsya-tsya-sne-sne.* She felt, deep in her chest, that a hole had opened up in her heart, and the hot blood began to flood her belly, which stung with pain as she made out a familiar word. *Baby*, he had said into the phone. *Come on, baby*, as so often he said to her. When he needed to cajole her, get her to do something, take her out dancing, lend him money, get her between the sheets. Elín leaned against the door frame and hardly dared draw breath for fear of missing some word that she might know, some kind of clue. Who was he speaking to in this tone of voice? Wasn't this the tender tone he kept for her alone?

Come on, baby. Come on, Sofía. Sne-sne. Tsya-tsya-sne.

2

The rust-red earth of the pseudocraters seemed brighter now that the ground was mostly covered in a thin layer of snow, which also seemed to have settled on the northern-facing slopes, as well as on the fence posts and the container itself, which was out of sight of the road. Daníel had parked at the side of the main road so as to not disturb any potential tyre tracks on the rarely used Heiðmörk road or on the track leading into the reddish gravel that gave the hills of the Rauðhólar district their name. Helena was on her way with the forensics team, and they too would leave their vehicles by the road – not sure yet whether it was safe to drive up here without comprising the evidence – and walk the rest of the way to the container, carrying any equipment they needed.

The snow had settled on the city during the night, melting almost immediately in the low-lying districts; but up here, according to the car's temperature gauge, it was a couple of degrees colder. It was starting to get light as Daníel walked up the track, although it would be a little while before the pale March sun raised itself into the sky. He wasn't exactly cold, but he zipped his coat up to the neck, as he felt a kind of a chill inside him. This had to be simple apprehension about what was to come. The message from the emergency call centre hadn't sounded good. In fact, it had sounded horrific.

A jogger with a dog had come across the container first. The man made a habit of jogging here before eight every morning and had called the city's environmental department, demanding to know what a twenty-foot shipping container was doing out here in this protected natural paradise.

The guy from the city council who'd turned up to take a look had opened the container and promptly vomited over his orange overalls. The two police officers who had been next on the scene had struggled to describe the sight that met their eyes. 'A stack of corpses,' they had said. A stack.

The officers stood some distance away from the container, one with his hands in his pockets, stiffly shuffling his feet. The other jogged on the spot, beating his shoulders with gloved hands to keep himself warm. Daníel thought he knew one of them but wasn't sure. They had to be from the Dalvegur station. He fished out his ID, which hung from a lanyard around his neck, and held it up.

'Daníel Hansson from CID,' he said, and the two uniformed officers nodded at the same moment, neither of them bothering to glance at his card. Both of them had stiff, shocked expressions on their faces, and it seemed to Daníel that they were holding back tears.

'We let the city council guy go home. He was ill at the sight of it.'

'You took his details?' Daníel said as he pulled latex gloves from his pocket.

'I did,' one of the officers said. 'And I took a short statement from him covering why he came up here and opened the container, and what he saw inside.'

He held up a notebook, and Daníel nodded.

'That's good. You can write it up when you get back to the station and send it to me. What about the jogger who found the container?'

'It seems the city council's switchboard forgot to note down his name, but I guess CID can trace the number?'

Daníel gave a quick smile. Officers in uniform sometimes had strange ideas about CID's priorities in the initial stages of an investigation.

'We won't worry about that right away.' He pulled on one

glove and looked at the two officers in turn. 'What are we looking at, exactly, inside the container?'

'I counted,' the other officer said, the one who had been jogging on the spot. 'There are five of them.'

'All women?' Daníel asked.

'I think so.'

'You think so?' Daníel asked with a searching look.

'Yeah. Well. It's dark in there and, well ... I don't know. The city council guy threw up over the scene and I had to get him out of the way, and Jonni here went to call in for assistance and ... well. I pretty much got out as quick as I could, and reckoned you'd check it out properly when you got here.'

Daníel had the second glove on.

'Did you check all five for signs of life?'

'Signs of life?'

'Yes. Pulse, breathing.'

The officer stared at him in disbelief.

'It's not like that,' he said. 'You'll see when you look inside. The smell, man. There's a terrible stink. Just like at the apartment where that old guy was found after a month...'

'Understood,' Daníel said. 'All the same, it's a rule to always check for signs of life.'

He set off towards the container and slipped off one glove as he walked. He took a jar of tiger balm from his pocket and applied a generous amount under his nose. This wasn't something he often needed to do, but having encountered the smell of someone long dead, he knew the instinctive reaction would be to retch, and going by the initial information, he would need to be in control.

If it was correct that there were the corpses of five women in the container, then the crime scene and the structure of the investigation would be an organisational nightmare. Daníel felt a weariness settle on his mind at the thought of it, but this vanished as he approached the open door of the container. There wasn't so much a stench of death in the container. It was a smell of pure desperation. The sensation that sometimes came over him at a crime scene began – it was like a spark of light at the back of his mind, moving to his forehead until it interrupted his vision for a moment, then becoming a whirlwind that spun through his head while a voice hissed in his ear that death had come calling here, ice cold and ruthless.

3

The kettle was boiling when Elín heard the bathroom door open. Sergei came out. He wore boxers and a T-shirt and smelled as if he had just shaved. Had he locked himself away because he was shaving?

'I'll make caravan tea,' he said, laying an arm across her shoulders and quickly squeezing her against him as he planted a kiss on her neck. Elín felt a wave of delight, but also a touch of disappointment as bristles rasped against her skin. He wasn't freshly shaved, so that wasn't the reason he had locked himself away in the bathroom.

'Who called?' she asked, looking at him enquiringly, trying to assess whether or not he was telling the truth.

'It was my mother,' he said, quickly glancing up before going back to the tea procedure.

It seemed to Elín that he was telling the truth. But that was her all over. She always believed him – mainly because she wanted to believe him. She longed to believe in the rightness of old-fashioned romance, and that everything really could turn out for the best; that Sergei was as in love with her as she was with him, that they could have a bright future together filled with joy and happiness. She wanted to believe that the woman he hid away to speak to really was his mother.

He carried the tea cups to the little table under the kitchen window and sat down. Elín took a seat facing him.

'What did your mother have to say?' she asked.

'The same as usual,' he said. 'She's short of money. Things are tough in Russia. Especially for old people, for old ladies. She has no savings. But I told her she would have to make it through to next week. There's a guy I've been doing a lot of work for who owes me quite a bit, so she'll have to wait until he's paid me.' Sergei paused, and Elín knew what was coming. 'Unless you … No, nothing. Forget it.'

Sergei gazed at her with what she thought of as puppy-dog eyes. He looked awkward, and his brown eyes seemed to become wider.

'Yeah,' Elín muttered. 'I can give you something to tide her over.'

She reached for the handbag that lay on the kitchen windowsill.

'No, no. Forget it,' Sergei repeated, but she knew he didn't mean it. He feigned reluctance to accept money because she had already loaned him some, but she was aware that he had few other options. He had no regular income – only what he picked up working the odd shift as a doorman at various clubs, or doing removals or whatever else came up that called for strength and was paid cash in hand. And anyway there was nothing wrong with lending him money. She had often done it and he had repaid her quite a few times. Not that she kept a precise tally. There wasn't much point in that, considering they lived together.

She opened her wallet, counted out a few five-thousand-krónur notes and handed them to him. A quick smile appeared on his face, he nodded and took the cash.

'Thanks, Elín,' he said. 'I'll pay you back as soon as I get some money.'

'Don't worry about it,' she said, and sipped the hot tea. For a moment she basked in the sense of bliss that came from being in Sergei's proximity. The tea warmed her inside, and the smell of his aftershave was good. She could spend an age sitting like this, admiring his musclebound arms and taking deep breaths of his aroma. She could revel in the domestic routines they had so easily slipped into, sink herself into the love that she felt enveloped them like a cloud whenever they were together.

But then the disquiet sought her out once more, along with the questions that multiplied every time this woman phoned. Why did Sergei hide away like this if it was his mother calling? Before Elín knew what was happening, she once again found herself deep in the cold loneliness of jealousy.

'What's your mother's name?' she asked, surprised at herself for never having asked this before. Sergei looked back at her and narrowed his eyes, the puppy-dog expression gone now.

'Why do you ask?' he said, no warmth in his voice.

'Just because,' Elín replied, trying to sound unconcerned. 'I was just wondering what her name is.'

'Her name is Galina,' Sergei said. There was a sharp look on his face, as if he were waiting for an argument. As if he was waiting for her to ask more questions, to accuse him of something; and he was right.

'Oh? I thought her name was Sofia,' Elín said, wishing as she spoke that she could have bitten her tongue, because Sergei rose to his feet so fast that he sent the kitchen chair flying to the floor and then kicked it halfway into the living room.

'Sofia?' he snapped. 'Why do you say that?'

'I heard you say something on the phone that sounded like Sofia,' she said humbly, longing now to throw herself at his feet and beg his forgiveness; to make it all good again, to beg him to sit down, make more tea and look at her once more with those puppy-dog eyes and not this hard, cold glare.

'Are you listening to my calls...? Are you spying when I'm on the phone, thinking you hear the names of other women? Is your Russian so good that you can hear me say other women's names? That's fantastic!' He picked up the notes from the table and flung them at her. 'Keep your money. I'll find some other way to support my mother. I can't live with this suspicion.'

He snatched his coat from its hook and stormed out. Elín started as he slammed the door behind him.

4

Helena slowed down and brought the car to a halt by the gravel track leading up to Rauðhólar, giving way to the ambulance, which was turning onto the main road. She drove along the track and parked on the verge at the top, and as she got out of the car, she could hear the wail of the ambulance's siren down on Suður-landsvegur. That would get them through the morning rush hour, which was now at its peak and which would stay busy until after nine. The number of cars that had collected by the side of the main road was a concern – a patrol car made its way through the middle of them, its blue lights flashing. This would attract the attention of the hundreds of people heading either into the city or out of it, up to the heath, and sooner or later someone would tip off the media. It was as well that the container itself was out of sight of the road, and that the forensic team had decided to park further along, so their white van wasn't easily visible from the road and was still some way from the container.

The red gravel crunched under Helena's feet, and she recalled when it had been a common sight on pavements and drives throughout the city. There was something enchanting about its colour, and back then people had no idea of the geological importance of the area it came from, so removing a trailer of dirt from this or that mound wasn't seen as anything to be concerned about. They knew better now, and it had slipped out of use.

She took care to walk on the verge, although there was no need to, as the ambulance had most likely eradicated any tyre marks – if there had been any – and as she approached the container she saw the tangle of footprints in the thin layer of snow that covered the red gravel. There was something Christmassy in the juxtaposition of these colours and the green of the moss that peeked here and there from beneath the snow, now that the morning sun had made a late appearance and was picking out every detail.

This pleasant feeling quickly vanished when Helena spotted Daníel on his knees in the heather, shivering. She sent an enquiring glance to the uniformed officer who stood not far from the container, but he stared back with dazed eyes. She knew that look. The man's mind was elsewhere; more than likely he was thinking about something mundane and ordinary, something that he meant to fix in the garage at home or the TV series he was currently watching. This was the soul's defence mechanism at work, protecting him against the ugly parts of life.

She clambered over the tussocks and into the heather to crouch at Daníel's side. His breath came in heavy gasps and he growled from between clenched teeth, as if his powerful jaw and teeth struggled to hold back a colossal flood of sorrow.

'There was one still alive,' he gasped. 'She was still alive in the middle of the pile. The bodies of the others must have been just enough to keep her warm.'

Helena placed a hand on his back and gave him a couple of firm strokes.

'I heard at the station,' she said, 'that she's regained consciousness.'

Daníel snorted, apparently dismissive, but Helena knew him well enough to know the sound indicated surprise or astonishment.

'I don't know if I'd call it conscious, exactly,' he said. 'I could hardly believe she had a pulse, so I pressed harder to make sure and she jumped to her feet and rushed out onto the moor, howling in terror.' He took a couple of deep breaths. 'I tried to tell her again and again that I'm from the police. I've no idea if she understood me, but in the end she let me wrap my coat around her. Maybe she was just too exhausted and cold to protest.'

'Christ, Daníel,' Helena said. 'Unbelievable.'

Daníel lifted himself up, got to his feet, shivered, and stared in fury at the container. Helena felt a jolt of surprise when he let out a heartfelt howl of rage; but it failed to carry far – it was swallowed up by the mutter of traffic on Suðurlandsvegur and muffled by Rauðhólar's snow-speckled moss.

'Never seen anything so totally fucking revolting.'

5

Elín was still trembling inside as she went down to her workshop, wondering whether to forget work and just go back up to the flat and spend the day watching television. But today not even a crime series was going to be enough to capture her attention, let alone one of the soap operas she and Sergei usually watched. Every argument with Sergei left her feeling like this – with her nerves shredded; that, or dissatisfied. Dissatisfaction was hardly the word; distressed was better. The pattern had always been a sharp exchange, followed by Sergei storming out. Elín had found it so distressing the first time it happened, she hadn't been able to get it out of her mind. She had even wondered if he had gone for good, abandoned her, so by the time he returned, she had cried all the tears she had to shed. Now that she'd seen him storm out and return more than once, she knew that this was his way of cooling off – calming himself down and regaining his composure. He'd return, placid and sensible. Normally he'd apologise and they would be friends again.

Even though she knew that he would come back and that they would quietly make up in peace and quiet, she still felt disturbed. There was a knot of tension deep inside her, she felt nauseous and every nerve in her body felt as taut as a violin string. She was sure that if she were to put a microphone to her skin, she would hear the sound of these overstretched nerves – a painful chorus of anxiety, almost clear enough to call Sergei home to comfort her. No, it would more likely be her role to comfort him, to ask his forgiveness and apologise for her jealousy. Now, down here among her paintings, she couldn't imagine what she had been thinking, what kind of suspicion had taken root inside her.

Elín looked around the little studio she had installed in the garage on the ground floor of her terraced house and suddenly felt that the place was a mess. In truth, it was no more disordered than usual; it must be her state of mind that was making her think this way.

She was about to give up for the day on the painting she was working on, and had started preparing a new blank canvas when her phone rang. She snatched it up and rushed to answer, certain it was Sergei, but it turned out to be her father.

'Well, sweetheart,' he said cheerfully. 'What's new in the art world?'

This was his standard opening question whenever he called or visited. She never failed to reply in the same way, that there was precious little to report. It was true in a way: in terms of her work one day was much like the one before. She stretched canvases, put down a base wash, sketched outlines with a pencil and then began to paint – and she couldn't talk about paintings while she worked on them. If she tried to explain what lay behind them or how they had developed, it was as if the flow had been interrupted and she would lose interest. Maybe this was something akin to writer's block. She never spoke about a work until it was complete, which meant she rarely had much to tell her father. Throughout her career she had exhibited every second year, but recently, she'd begun to feel that she didn't have a body of work strong enough for an exhibition, so the paintings had begun to stack up. She wondered if she was losing the self-confidence an artist needed to put on an exhibition. There was certainly some kind of internal obstacle preventing her from producing the right material. Occasionally she would sell a work straight from the studio, but that was rare these days. She lived mainly on the rent she earned from another apartment, which she had bought when her father had paid out her inheritance in advance. It provided her with a decent income as she had already paid off her mortgage on her own place.

'I'm stretching a canvas,' she told her father.

'Well, love,' he said, and she could imagine him in his wheel-chair by the living-room window, looking out over the burger joint and the slipway across the street.

'What ship is out of the water now?' she asked, and heard as he sat up in his chair, relieved to have something to tell her.

'*Saltvík*,' he said, and she scrawled it at the bottom of the list of ship names she had been collecting on one of the studio walls. This had become a game for them over the years, ever since her father had bought a flat overlooking the slipway. She liked collecting the names and was sure that one day something linked to this would become a painting. That was where ideas came from – something insignificant, often a trivial detail. A routine or some habit would take root, and at some point would ignite the fuse of inspiration, like a spark in a powder keg.

'Well,' her father said, and Elín knew what was coming next: 'Your Russian's being good to you, is he?' he asked.

She sighed.

'Yes, Dad. Sergei's fine.'

Her father never referred to Sergei by name, always as the Russian, and Elín could tell that he was not fond of this choice of hers, although he was unfailingly courteous whenever he met Sergei.

'He hasn't been talking about a wedding again?'

'He has, actually,' she said slowly. This wasn't something she wanted to discuss with her father, especially now, in the middle of a disagreement with Sergei. 'He needs a residence permit and a work permit, and getting married is the easiest way to fix that.'

She had already explained this to her father more than once, but he never seemed to take notice and every time it was as if this was something new.

'Well, now.' Her father hummed over the phone, and Elín hummed back, as if their conversation had suddenly run aground and neither of them quite knew how to get it afloat again.

Her father was the first to break the ice. 'Remember what I said to you the other day about a pre-nup,' he said. 'Because you have assets, and he doesn't. So you'll have to have a pre-nuptial agreement if you get married. Which you know I think is complete madness.'

6

'I've only been ready to quit once in my whole career,' Daníel said to the commissioner, who drew up one of the red armchairs that were arranged in her office, and sat down facing him, so close that their knees almost touched. 'That was an investigation into a house fire in which someone died and I ... I've never been able to clear my mind of the image of that person's body, or the smell. The smell was the worst part.'

'Drink this,' the commissioner said and passed him a cup she had filled with Coke. 'The sugar will pick you up.'

Daníel took the cup, drank half the sweet pop and almost took comfort in the feeling that his taste buds were being wiped clean, even though all his other senses were still shackled to the woman who, only two hours ago, he had cradled in his arms and covered with his coat, and to whom he had muttered that he was from the police and was there to help her, faintly hoping that his words would make it through the terror in her eyes and her chilled-through body, and that if they did make it through, they would have some meaning for her.

'I feel I'm ready to burst,' he said. 'I want to go down to the docks and yell at Customs that they need to check every single container that gets shipped to Iceland. They need to open every single one and...' His words faded away as the memory of the contents of the container up at Rauðhólar appeared again in sharp relief before his eyes – the bodies of women wrapped in clothes and blankets that were nowhere near enough to cope with the cold of winter up here in the north.

'That would be the ideal situation, but even if funding for the Customs service was ten times what it is now, doing that still wouldn't be realistic,' the commissioner said. 'They only manage to check a tiny fraction of the containers that arrive here. That's why our work is so important. We have to nail whoever was behind this horror.'

Daniel shook his head, not sure if it was the commissioner's words he wanted to shake off, or the memory of the curly, foul-smelling hair on the head he had held tight, in the desperate hope the woman would sense some warmth from him, even a little humanity and goodwill.

'The smell...' he said, looking up to meet the commissioner's eyes. 'Her smell, and the look in her eyes ... I can't do this. I can't work on this case.'

The commissioner sat a little straighter.

'You are one of my most experienced officers,' she said. 'This is going to call for a large team, but I can ask the chief superintendent to keep you away from any major responsibilities – you had asked for time off to look after your children before this, anyway. We do need someone of your calibre on this, though. Someone who can read people. Someone with your deep understanding – your insight and sympathy.'

'What you call insight is really working against me right now,' Daniel said. 'The whole world is somehow becoming too ... too *something* for me. After all these years of all kinds of investigations, I've hit my limits. I can't handle my job if it's going to get any worse.'

The commissioner placed a hand on his arm and squeezed.

'Daniel,' she said, and tried to catch his eye. 'It can't get worse than this. This is as bad as it gets.'

7

Helena was startled when she entered the large room: it was packed with people, some of them on their feet, as there were not enough chairs for everyone. It was clear that everything was being thrown at this investigation: representatives of every branch of the force, support departments included, were present. She slipped between the bodies and found a perch on the end of a table from which she could look around the room. The atmosphere was subdued, people speaking in low voices, and from what she could make out from the whispers, they were mostly questions. Apart from her and Daníel, it seemed likely that few people knew what this was about.

She looked for him, but he was nowhere to be seen; however when the commissioner entered the room, accompanied by Gylfi, the chief superintendent responsible for CID, Daníel was with them. For a moment she wondered if the unhappy look on his face meant that he had been given responsibility for this investigation. She saw him searching the faces, then he caught her eye and gave her a quick wink – to her relief. This was the signal they kept for each other, an indication that things were fine, so she now felt sure that he wouldn't have to shoulder the burden of this horrific case.

Helena thought of him this morning, kneeling in the peat, overcome with despair, and she was glad that he wouldn't be under the yoke of this investigation. She had seen how people struggled with serious criminal cases and how personally they took it when the cases remained unsolved.

The commissioner cleared her throat and a silence fell across the room. Chief Superintendent Gylfi glanced at her, nodded, looked over the assembled throng, and nodded again before speaking. This was a habit of his that some people found endlessly irritating. Helena found it a rather amusing mannerism, and enjoyed seeing it made fun of so often at the station. Opinion was that the number of times he nodded his head before speaking was an indicator of how serious the case would turn out to be. This certainly applied now, as she reckoned that he had nodded his head no less than seven times before saying a word.

'Just before eight this morning the emergency line had a call informing them that a twenty-foot shipping container had been found in the Rauðhólar park, south of Suðurlandsvegur, and in it were several bodies. Police officers established that in the container were five women, of whom one was alive and four were dead. The suspicion is that they died of hypothermia or from the effects of the poor conditions inside the container. It was clear that the women had been in it for some time. The nationality of the victims is unknown, although the indications are that they are of foreign origin. We are assuming that they were brought to Iceland in the container. The fact that these women were not simply doped and put on a plane, as we have seen happen before, indicates that they are from countries that do not have access to the Schengen agreement, or that they would require visas to enter Iceland.'

'Are we talking about people trafficking?' Kristján asked from where he stood in a corner.

Gylfi nodded gravely twice.

'It's a strong possibility, so it's a scenario we will examine.' He nodded again a couple of times, as if fumbling around for the thread he had lost when Kristján interrupted him. Then he continued: 'The survivor is suffering from extreme hypothermia and is being treated at the National Hospital. She's lost consciousness again. The doctors say that they will be able to tell in the next couple of hours if she's likely to regain consciousness anytime soon.'

Gylfi gazed over the group in front of him, his head rising and falling as if he was registering the reactions of those present. Most seemed appalled.

'This investigation has been given top priority, which is why you have all been called in to work on it,' he said. 'The commissioner and I have decided that it calls for a substantial response, which can be scaled back if necessary, rather than the opposite approach. From this moment this is the only case you are working on. I'd like you all to list your current active cases and send them to me. I'll assign them to other teams.'

For the first time since Gylfi had starting speaking, a low murmur went around the room. People could get close to a case, even becoming emotionally attached, or, as the chief superintendent had been known to describe it, hanging on to it like a dog with a bone.

'I will manage this investigation personally,' he continued, 'and will handle the media myself. I don't need to emphasise to you the importance of maintaining discretion and sending any media questions in the right direction. There's no doubt that news of the container will soon hit the front pages, but the fact that one of these women is alive is something we'll keep to ourselves for as long as possible.' Now almost everyone in the room was nodding in agreement. 'The nature of this case means that there's going to be all kinds of rumour and speculation, so we all need to take care not to add to the media madness.'

The chief superintendent fell silent and stepped aside, and the commissioner took his place.

'I want to introduce our colleagues from the support departments,' she said. 'Most of you know each other already, but it's as well to be clear about who does what. First is Jóna, who is the forensic pathologist.' The commissioner gestured to an older woman with a bun of grey hair who was sitting to one side. 'Her role, as usual, is to establish the cause of death, and in this instance there is the task of identifying the deceased. She will be supported by the national police commissioner's International Division, so I'd like to introduce Ari Benz Liu, chief superintendent of the International Division.'

Ari Benz stood up from his chair and raised a hand to indicate who he was, which was hardly necessary as literally everyone in the room knew him. He had started as a young officer in uniform at the Hverfisgata station, and had climbed rapidly through the hierarchy; but he was best known for repeatedly changing his name. He had managed to stretch Iceland's strict laws around names more than anyone else Helena knew, and while he had met with a decisive refusal on the most recent occasion, he had got around it by simply informing his superiors and colleagues that he had taken the middle name Benz. The commissioner had decided that the force should be sympathetic to its officers' cultural backgrounds, so allowed him to use the new name and to abandon the old one that Ari's family were convinced came with a curse attached.

'Oddsteinn from the prosecutor's office will be with us from the word go,' said the commissioner, pointing to where Oddsteinn stood, by the wall at the back of the room. 'He'll provide advice on any suspects you have in mind, but make full use of him – go to him if there's anything you're unsure of. We need to build a case that's bullet-proof so there can't be any holes in the investigation, or procedural errors.'

Oddsteinn smiled, briefly and stiffly, and adjusted the knot of his tie.

'There's a huge amount at stake here,' he said. 'Please ensure that every detail is recorded in the LÖKE system, and if you're in the slightest doubt, call me. My number's on the board.' He adjusted his tie again, as if this was a signal that he had no more to say, and the commissioner continued.

'You can have all the officers you need for arrests, for on-scene presence, for door-to-door enquiries, and for anything else,' she said. 'We'll also have staff resources in the records department, to ensure that all documentation is up to date and to answer the phones. Jean-Christophe and his forensics team have already carried out the initial examination of the scene, and the container is now being taken to a secure location where they will go over it in fine detail, which is why they aren't with us here. Rannveig, where are you?'

The commissioner lifted herself onto her toes and peered into the room. Rannveig raised a hand.

'Rannveig from the cybercrime division is your best friend right now, as the moment this meeting ends she'll be focused on checking the traffic cameras around Rauðhólar, as well as data from all the CCTV from the ports around the capital region, which we have already requested. Once we find whoever moved that container out to Rauðhólar, the ball starts rolling.'

Gylfi again stepped forward, almost as if this had all been choreographed. He nodded quickly and began the announcements that Helena and the others from CID had been waiting for with trepidation.

'Baldvin is my deputy,' he said, and Baldvin stood up, going over to stand next to him.

There was no doubt that he had been given this information in advance, as it didn't seem to take him by surprise – although it did the others present. Most of them had undoubtedly hoped that this role would go to Daníel, but they managed to conceal their disappointment.

'Baldvin will manage all aspects of the investigation, will prioritise assignments, listen to all statements that are taken and read through everything recorded on the LÖKE system, so please take care.'

Gylfi pointed a finger at the group, like a strict teacher scolding schoolchildren.

'Kristján, you're the incident-room manager: prepare the

facilities and keep an overview of what manpower is needed and issue whatever equipment is required.'

Kristján nodded briefly. This was his usual role, and there was nothing about him that indicated he was unhappy with it.

'Daníel liaises with the survivor, as he found her in the container and there's already a connection there.'

Daníel put up a hand, and Gylfi raised a questioning eyebrow.

'Could I have Helena with me on this? I believe it would be useful having a female presence.'

Gylfi agreed immediately.

'Any further questions?' he said, and everyone shook their heads. He nodded a couple more times as he scanned the team. Then he clapped his hands to indicate that the meeting was at an end.

'Good luck,' the commissioner said as the meeting dissolved.

8

Sergei knew how to appreciate a dinner, even though Elín had been in no mood for cooking. She had just thrown bits and pieces from the fridge together with pesto and poured the mix over pasta. They were reconciled. He had come home and taken her in his arms, holding her tight for a long time, and she had whispered words of apology into his ear, and that had settled things. Quarrel over. There was no outward sign that he was in any way upset, although she still felt raw inside, her nerves still jangling occasionally, like aftershocks.

'Dad called today,' she said, and he looked up. He slowly chewed his mouthful of food as he sent her a questioning gaze.

'What did he want?' Sergei asked once he had swallowed.

Elín hoped this wouldn't lead to yet another disagreement, but it was as well to get it over with. And there was a certain benefit in being able to hide behind her father's concerns, as, if she were completely honest with herself, they reflected her own.

'He says we should have a pre-nuptial agreement if we get married,' she said, maybe in a quieter voice than she would normally use.

Sergei rumbled something incomprehensible, took another mouthful and chewed slowly.

'Dad has a right to have his say about it,' she continued. 'He did pay out my inheritance while he's still alive, and I used it to buy the rental flat and to finish paying off the mortgage on this flat.'

Sergei nodded and continued to eat, and for a moment Elín felt that he concurred with what she had said, that he had thought things over and had seen the good sense in such an agreement – thought that it was the correct course of action.

Any marriage would have to ensure the wellbeing of them both. She needed to protect her assets just as much as he needed a residence permit.

'Darling,' Sergei said, wiping his mouth with a square of kitchen roll and extending a hand across the table to her.

She placed her hand in his and felt a rush of joy pass through her as he wrapped his warm palms around her hand and pressed it gently. There was always a warmth to him. It was as if there was some kind of unquenchable heat source deep inside him that was never switched off.

'Baby, people can't understand a relationship with an age difference,' he said, and looked directly at her, deep into her eyes so that she felt herself melting. 'People have prejudices, and your dad is no exception. People can't figure out how a chunky middle-aged woman like you could have hooked a cool guy like me.'

This stung a little, but the words were typical of Sergei. He didn't beat about the bush. Perhaps it was because his English skills didn't allow much by the way of fancy expressions and compliments. And in some ways it was refreshing that he said exactly what he meant, instead of tiptoeing around like a cat around a hot dish. Elín knew that he spoke the truth. Most people couldn't understand the relationship she had with Sergei. She noticed how they were stared at in shops and even on the street, and if they ran into people she knew, she could see they were literally dumbstruck. Sergei's Russian friends were more tolerant. At any rate, the two she knew were. Sometimes they came around to have a beer with Sergei and were never anything but warm and courteous.

'I love you, and you love me, and that's all there is to it. Just book an appointment with the sheriff tomorrow, OK?' Elín nodded, but Sergei appeared to feel that she wasn't as enthusiastic as she could have been. 'It can take a long time to get an appointment,' he went on. 'And I need to get a residence permit so I can start to work properly. So you don't have to support both of us. Come on, baby, be a good girl and do as Sergei says.'

He winked and grinned, and Elín couldn't stop herself from laughing out loud. Sergei stood up and took her in his arms, and burying his face in her neck, blew raspberries so that it tickled, and she shrieked and giggled as he carried her into the bedroom.

9

As he sometimes did around midnight, Daníel opened the door to the garden and padded barefoot over the frost-crusted grass to where Lady Gúgúlú lived in her converted garage. His insomnia generally seemed to chime with the sleep patterns of the drag queen, for whom the early part of the night was the best part of the day.

'I come bearing gifts,' Daníel said, looking for a space on the table to put down his pack of beers, but ending up pulling one from the plastic strip and handing Lady Gúgúlú the other five. She took one from the strip herself and put the rest in the little fridge under the bench.

'What are you making?' Daníel asked as he sat down. He had no great interest in dressmaking, but right now he was happy to listen to long, involved explanations of practically anything – any subject that would distract his thoughts from the abject terror he had witnessed in the woman that day, and from the huge task ahead.

'It's an angel costume. The inner section is made from elasticated material that moulds itself to the body, so I can move comfortably on stage. Then there's a layer of thin silk that produces the deep glimmer you see when the light hits it. Look.'

Lady held out a piece of cloth to show him.

'You're right,' Daníel said, taking a gulp of beer. 'It shines.'

'Exactly,' Lady said. 'There's a layer of fine chiffon that will lie over the silk in a couple of random waves. I'll tack it here and fix it just like this, see?'

'Hmm.' Daníel tried to visualise Lady as an angel. He had twice been persuaded to accept tickets to her drag shows, and had enjoyed himself on both occasions, although he much preferred these quiet late-night chats in her garage.

'Then I'm going to thread a tiny strip of lights through the chiffon so that the silk reflects them and the whole costume lights up and makes it look like there's some kind of a halo around me.'

'I'm sure it'll be beautiful.'

'Absolutely!' Lady said. 'Beauty is exactly what I'm looking for this time. In the previous shows I've interpreted Death, Fear and Misunderstanding, and now it's Beauty that's in the spotlight. Along with the element of surprise that the audience always gets as well, of course.'

'Of course,' Daníel said, smiling.

'What's up, my dear? Can't sleep?'

'Hmm. Yep.'

'Something to do with work?' Lady looked at him hard, and Daníel nodded. He would have preferred to not talk about work right now though. He absolutely didn't want to have to think about the next day and how he was going to tell his children that he wouldn't be able to take as much time off as had been promised.

'The kids are coming tomorrow, just as we have a massive case that I can't avoid being part of – although I'm doing everything I can to keep my involvement to a minimum.'

'Oh, darling. You know I'm always here for you and can babysit. Except mornings, of course, and late evenings. I like those little worms of yours.'

'Thanks,' Daníel said. 'It's not easy to explain – but it's not so much a matter of time as of going back and forth, you know: from the horrors of it all, then straight home to the children.'

Lady looked at him thoughtfully.

'Sometimes, when I'm going through a bad patch – believe it or not, it happens – I go out into the garden, put my hand on the elf stone and ask for help. I know that you, in your pigheadedness and with your failure to grasp physics, refuse to admit that there are other planes of existence, but sometimes it doesn't do any harm to take a pot-shot and hope for the best.'

Daníel grinned.

'Asking your weed elves for help would be my last resort, but if ever I've come close to it, it's now,' he said. 'I have the feeling that over the next few weeks I'm going to need all the help I can get, from whatever plane of existence.'

Lady watched him carefully, then leaned forward, placed a hand on his shoulder and squeezed.

'I'll ask our friends in the rocks for help. They owe me for a hundred or so good turns.'

'Is that how business is done in the elf world?' Daníel asked, and laughed. 'One hand scratches the other?'

'That's how business is done everywhere,' Lady replied. 'Whether you can see it or not, it's a basic law of the universe. Yin and yang, plus and minus, in and out.'

Daníel drained his can of beer, crushed it in his hands and passed it to Lady in exchange for a full one from the fridge. Lady lobbed the empty into a corner, but managed to miss the black rubbish bag, which was overflowing with empty cans.

'Now you'll have to go to the recycling centre,' Daníel said.

'Nope. I'm going to make myself a beer-can dress for the spring show,' Lady said. 'You'll have to make an effort to keep me supplied.'

Daníel laughed at the thought of Lady Gúgúlú in a dress decorated with beer cans. That would be a show he'd have to go and see. Maybe he ought to go to the angel show as well. He had promised himself that he'd make more of an effort to be sociable, and to be a better friend to this odd tenant of his.

'What about wings?' Daníel asked, opening the new can. 'Angels need wings, don't they?'

'So glad you asked, darling,' Lady said, a look of expectation on her face.

Daníel leaned back in his chair and waited for a detailed explanation of the angel-wing design. The knot of worry inside him was starting to soften.

WEDNESDAY

10

Áróra was on her knees on the floor, engrossed in a map of the west of Iceland, dividing it into manageable search areas, so it took her a while to work out what the woman on the phone wanted. Áróra needed to be fully prepared, because the days were getting longer, the snow was melting away, and soon there would be calm days that would allow her to search with the drone. She had spent most of the previous summer, and well into the autumn, doing exactly this, and she'd covered most of the south-western part of the country. She'd decided that the western area and the Snæfellsnes peninsula would be next. She had resolved to drive every one of the lanes, paths and tracks that criss-crossed the country, with the drone cruising above the car at a height that would cover a respectable swathe each side. Scanning the places where someone would be most likely to have dumped a body.

Her mother called regularly from England, wanting her to come home, telling her that this search was an obsession, that her sister would never be found. The country was so wide and rugged, and there was no telling if Björn had disposed of her in the sea or in a lake. And how would she search there? That was something Áróra couldn't answer except by saying that she was determined to try. She had to search for the answer, and couldn't stop until she had found her sister's final resting place.

Áróra understood her mother's concerns but it wasn't as if she was badly off in Reykjavík. She had bought a flat and furnished it, and had taken on quite a few assignments since moving to Iceland, so money wasn't a concern – and wouldn't be for a while, considering she charged high prices for her work and had substantial savings. She suspected that her mother hoped, deep inside, that her sister's body would never be found, because if it was, her last hope would be extinguished. Her hope was that the police in Reykjavík had got it wrong, and that Ísafold wasn't dead after all, but had disappeared with her husband Björn to start a new life in Canada. It was true that Björn had fled to Canada, escaping justice, so why shouldn't Ísafold have gone to be there with him? Áróra suspected that this is what her mother thought, although she never actually said as much.

But now another part of Áróra's past had come knocking – and it was nothing to do with her mother or Ísafold. It was Daníel. He had advised this woman on the phone to call Áróra.

'Daníel said you were some sort of private investigator,' the woman said.

'Yes, I specialise in tracking down hidden money. I mainly work for tax authorities and banks,' Áróra said, still not clear what the woman wanted from her.

'Well, y'see, Daníel said that you could investigate finance and that kind of stuff, quietly, and better than the police do,' the woman said in an apologetic tone. 'I need to know more about the man I'm thinking of marrying.'

Áróra got to her feet and sighed. Roughly every third call she took came from someone who didn't understand what she did; they often asked for the strangest things.

But on this occasion the woman had come to her through Daníel, which gave Áróra a reason to get in touch with him. She still hadn't got over how they had parted the last time she'd seen him, how she had marched out with her nose in the air. And when she had called and made a clumsy apology, it had only made things worse. It felt as if anything to do with Daníel was inflammable, or maybe delicate, or perhaps even just silly. But now, here was this woman with her enquiry. If Áróra were to respond positively to her, it would give her a pretext to speak to him and fix things between them. There might even be a chance to meet him. Áróra felt the blood rush through her veins at the thought of meeting Daníel face to face – to see him, look into his eyes and listen to that warm, measured voice.

'You said your name's Elín, yes, and you're my cousin?' Áróra said.

'That's right, but you won't remember me. You would have been too young the last time we met. But your father and I were first cousins. The family always called me Didda, although I never liked the name. I went to Daníel because he's a police officer; I thought he might know how to look into someone's past – a foreigner's past, that is. But he said it wasn't a job for the police, and pointed me towards you. He said that you're someone I can trust.'

Things were starting to take shape in Áróra's mind, but there was one piece of the puzzle missing.

'So how do you know Daníel?' she asked.

'Ah, sorry. I should have said straight away,' the woman replied, laughing awkwardly. 'It may sound weird that I went to him about my boyfriend, but I didn't know where else to turn. You see, Daníel's my ex-husband.'

11

Daníel and Helena stood in the corridor, quietly waiting at the door to the National Hospital's intensive care unit. Helena had managed to get a haircut the previous day; Daníel noticed her dark hair was shorter than before, cropped close at the sides, leaving just enough on top for it to be forced into place by a generous helping of gel, leaving a dead-straight parting, like a boy at some English public school. In fact, everything about Helena was boyish. She was of average height, slim but not skinny, always turned out neatly, like a young salaryman. Her shirt was tucked tidily into her trousers and buttoned to the throat. Her shoes gleamed and her jacket was pressed. Daníel somehow felt that he was scruffy in comparison, as his shirts instantly creased when he put them on, and he rarely wore anything smarter than jeans. One thing they had in common was that they both missed wearing a uniform – she because it was smart and gender-neutral, and he because when he was in uniform there was never any question about what to wear.

They had been given a quick report on the condition of the woman from the container. Immediately after being admitted, her body temperature had been raised, and then she been brought to intensive care, where she had now regained consciousness. Daníel had always disliked the smell of hospitals – or maybe it was the lack of a smell in a hospital. The antiseptic and slightly too-cold atmosphere were disagreeable to him – no doubt because of the many visits he'd had to pay to crime victims, and because of the pain and fear, from which he made every effort to retain a dispassionate distance so that he could maintain the clear and objective thinking that investigations demanded.

Helena seemed impatient, repeatedly lifting herself onto her toes, as if standing still was too much of an effort and she needed to release some internal tension. He wasn't sure, but he thought that she was humming a Christmas tune under her breath.

'Didn't you know that Christmas is over?' he said. 'Quite a while ago.'

Helena laughed.

'Ach, yes. I've no idea why I do this. It always happens when I'm stressed. I get this Christmas stuff running through my head.'

Daníel smiled to himself. They were both tense, and for the same reason: they were dreading seeing the victim. There was no guarantee she would co-operate with the police. People who had been through such a turbulent experience were often confused, not knowing who to trust, and that was particularly true of the victims of organised-crime gangs, which at first glance, was what she seemed to be.

The doors to the intensive care unit swung open, and a young woman in a white coat came out. She held a clipboard in her left hand and extended her right in greeting.

'Sóla. I'm a doctor in intensive care,' she said.

Daníel and Helena muttered their names and proffered the ID cards that hung on lanyards around their necks. Then they followed the doctor along the intensive care unit's corridor to a large room that appeared to be some kind of waiting area.

'We're full right now,' she said apologetically, and gestured to a sofa in one corner. 'So we'll have to use this – the relatives' room.'

Daníel and Helena sat on the sofa, while the doctor fetched a kitchen chair from the other end of the room and sat down on it. She scanned the paperwork on the clipboard in her hand, looked up and spoke as if she had just memorised every detail.

'Yesterday morning a young woman was admitted, aged between twenty and thirty, in a serious hypothermic state after a long period under hostile conditions.' Daníel's thoughts immediately went to the dark, foul-smelling, ice-cold container. 'Body temperature was thirty-two degrees on arrival, and she had limited consciousness. She had lost a great deal of fluid and showed symptoms of frostbite on her fingers and toes. As the A&E staff have minimal experience of treating frostbite on people with darker skin, a consultant dermatologist was brought in. As the patient was warmed up in A&E, she began to hyperventilate, her heart rate became very rapid and she became extremely restless, calling out in a foreign language. She was sedated and became calm enough for her extremities to be treated, and these appeared less serious than had been initially diagnosed, so the consultant's conclusion was that she's suffering from second-degree frostbite, which results in blisters forming and a great deal of pain. The patient was given a strong painkiller. After treatment in A&E, the patient was moved up here to intensive care and has been under observation overnight.'

The doctor let the clipboard drop and looked expectant, waiting for their questions.

'What's her condition now?' Helena asked.

'She's fully conscious but weak – took some nourishment this morning but hasn't spoken. Neither her name nor any other information. We suspect she understands neither Icelandic nor English.'

'What's next for her?' Daníel asked.

'Her condition is considered stable, so later today she'll be transferred to A4, which is the ward for ear, nose, throat, burns and arterial surgery. That's where the treatment for the damage to her extremities will be carried out.'

'We need to speak to her. Or at least find out what language she speaks so we can find an interpreter,' Helena said.

The doctor stood up, deftly swinging the kitchen chair aside.

'Please keep it short and be considerate to other patients.

You'll have to wait until she's on a regular ward before you can question her properly.'

Daníel and Helena nodded at the same time and followed Sóla along the corridor.

12

The woman's face seemed almost completely black, her head resting against the white pillow. Her face was swollen, and her hair was bedraggled. She was hooked up to sensors, presumably monitoring her heart, and there was a saline drip in her arm. She looked up as Helena and Daníel stepped inside the curtains that encircled the bed, and Helena saw her eyes immediately fill with fear. Helena quickly held up her warrant card.

'Police,' she said. 'You are safe.'

This appeared to have little effect on the woman, who continued to stare at Daníel as he fidgeted awkwardly behind Helena, his ID held up too. Helena turned, gestured for Daníel to back away, and sat on a chair by the side of the bed. It was obvious from the line that rose and fell on the monitor's screen, that the woman's heart rate had risen.

A nurse bustled in and placed a hand on the patient's arm. 'OK?' she asked gently, and the woman seemed comforted by her presence, as she smiled faintly and nodded.

The nurse was about to turn and leave when the woman in the bed emitted a whining sound that could have meant *no*, and grabbed her arm with hands bandaged so that they resembled boxing gloves.

'Could you maybe stay with us for a moment?' Helena asked, and the nurse nodded quietly, and stayed standing by the bed, a friendly hand on the patient's arm.

After introducing herself and Daníel formally, and seeing that this made no impression on the terrified woman, Helena placed a hand on her own chest and said slowly and clearly 'Helena.' She half turned, pointed at Daníel and said clearly, 'Daníel.'

The woman's eyes flickered from one to the other, and Helena couldn't be sure if the look in them reflected fear or suspicion. Helena pointed to the nurse, with an exaggerated look of enquiry, and she responded immediately with 'Eva,' pointing at the same time at the badge displaying her name. Helena then pointed to the woman in the bed, and she replied immediately, but so quietly that her voice was indistinct.

'Bisi,' she whispered. 'Bisi Babalola.'

Helena wanted to let out a sigh of relief, but held it back. This brief exchange had broken down the first barrier. These were the first indications of trust. Helena gave the woman a warm smile. She could hear Daníel behind her, tapping something into his phone.

'That's a Nigerian name,' he muttered.

'Nigeria?' Helena asked, and the fear returned to the woman's eyes as she shook her head.

'France,' she said.

Daníel tapped at his phone again and passed it to Helena so that she could see the screen and read it with what could pass for French pronunciation.

'*Nous embauchons un interpréte Français pour vous,*' she intoned, and hoped that Google had correctly translated 'We will bring a French interpreter for you'.

Bisi stared at her with a look of surprise on her face.

'Do you not speak English?' she asked, and Helena had to bite her lip to not laugh at her own stupidity. She could have tried that first, before assuming that Bisi spoke no English.

'Yes. It makes everything easier if you speak English,' she said, and smiled.

The nurse looked astonished.

'She hasn't said a word up to now,' she whispered in Icelandic. 'So we didn't know if she understood anything – even in English.'

'We want you to know that you are safe here in Iceland and

we will do everything we can to help you,' Helena continued in English, and the fear returned to the woman's dark eyes.

'Iceland?' Bisi said. 'I'm in Iceland?'

13

Bisi felt her heart rate slow and she seemed to be sinking deep into the hospital bed as the medication the nurse injected into her arm flowed through her. To begin with, it was a relief. She saw the people from the police were further away now, behind the doctor and the nurse who held her down. This restraint was not so bad, because she knew that they meant well, that they wanted to keep her in bed; the doctor had explained it was important at this point. She was to stay calm, rest and relax, and she would shortly be moved to another ward, where she would be able to move about more freely.

Despite the drugs and the soft hands pushing her down into the bed, holding her with increasing force, she resisted. Her body seemed to see this as its duty, deciding to fight its own battle, regardless of what she wanted or thought. But gradually, her body became calmer, and with her heart no longer pumping blood through her at high pressure, her limbs became limp and she sank down, first into the bed and then into a dreamworld.

It began well, she felt a sense of wellbeing and even a little joy as she recalled sitting in the hotel room in Paris looking at the packed suitcases, filled with perfumes, silk scarves, watches and the other luxury goods she had purchased as she had gone through the family's shopping list. She looked forward to arriving home with all the goods and distributing them to everyone. Then she sank further, and the dream gradually began to sour, because somewhere above and beyond this dream she knew that the phone would ring and the version of Bisi who sat in a hotel room looking happily at all the good stuff would no longer exist. The nightmare would be about to begin – and it began with that phone call, the call that changed everything.

She hoped that the people from the police would believe that she was from France. French citizens had more rights than Africans. It would hopefully take them a while to figure out that she wasn't French, and that would give her time to figure out what to do next. Where could she go? How could she get to...? Her thoughts hesitated, despite the drugged fog. Where should she head for? Where *could* she go? Where in the world would she be welcome? Had those people really said that she was in Iceland? What the hell was she doing there?

The ringing phone echoed in her ears, first a quiet, sinister chime, then louder and louder, until it filled the hotel room, stabbing at her ears and then right through her head so it seemed about to split open under the onslaught of this deafening, incessant noise, until she answered, put the phone to her ear, and the nightmare began.

14

Daníel was reluctant to leave the woman in intensive care, but the nurse told him that she'd had enough; now what she needed was a sedative to help her through the shock of finding out that she was on an island in the far north. They would have an opportunity to speak to her once she had been transferred to a general ward. Daníel had his concerns about this and said on the way out that they should call in at Ward A4 and have a word with the staff there.

Helena followed him without saying a word, assuming that they were thinking along the same lines: those responsible for bringing these women into Iceland must have a network here, ready to receive them. Anyone who trafficked women in shipping containers was dangerous, so it was important to ensure that the news one of them had survived did not leak out. The people who had dumped the container at Rauðhólar must have been certain that all the women were dead, so to keep Bisi safe, it would be best to let them continue thinking that.

They stood for a while in the corridor outside the ear, nose, throat, burns and arterial surgery ward, as it was referred to, and Daníel wondered if all these various ailments had something in common, or whether having just a few patients in each category was a good reason for them to be brought together in one place. A woman in a white overall marched along the corridor towards them, and turned out to be precisely the person they needed to speak to.

'Brynja, lead practitioner,' she said, a questioning look on her face.

Daníel and Helena introduced themselves, holding up their ID.

'Could we have a word in private?' Daníel asked, and Brynja

glanced around quickly, before pointing them towards doors leading off the ward.

'All the offices and storage areas have been converted into spaces for patients, so we'd better go out there.'

In fact, the lobby outside was no less busy, but this was a larger space, and they went over to one of the windows overlooking the hospital car park.

'You have a new patient arriving on the ward later today,' Daníel said. 'We need to talk about her.'

Brynja nodded.

'We've been told there's an unnamed foreign national who has been admitted,' she said. 'I guess she's the one. It's not often we get a patient without a name.'

'Actually we know what her name is, but it's important that as far as anyone else is concerned, she remains an unnamed foreigner,' Daníel said. 'She's a victim in an extremely serious criminal case that's under investigation. Also, it needs to be made clear in her notes that she's not to have any visitors unless the police allow it.'

He and Helena handed over cards with their contact details, and Brynja took them, quickly glanced at them and put them in her pocket.

'OK,' she said.

'And it would be ideal if she could be kept in a private room.'

'That's not an option,' Brynja said. 'Unfortunately.'

'We need to ensure that nothing about her presence here leaves the ward,' Daníel said with heavy emphasis.

'I'll speak to the staff,' Brynja said. 'Although we are all subject to strict confidentiality rules, and we take them seriously.'

Daníel nodded. He had no intention of maligning the woman or the healthcare profession.

'I didn't mean to imply—' he began apologetically before Brynja broke in.

'I assume she doesn't speak any Icelandic, considering she's a foreigner?'

'That's right,' Helena replied. 'She speaks English and French, and maybe other languages.'

'Fine,' Brynja said. 'In that case I can put her in a ward with an old lady from the countryside who only speaks Icelandic and doesn't get any visitors.'

'And that'll be close to the nurses' station?' Helena asked with a friendly smile. 'So you can be sure that nobody goes anywhere near her?'

Brynja sighed, then smiled quickly, indicating agreement.

'The old lady will be happy about that,' she said. 'We'll be even quicker off the mark when she sounds her buzzer, which she does all the time.'

They thanked her for her time, and Brynja marched on clogged feet back towards the ear, nose, throat, burns and arterial surgery ward. But before pushing open the door, she turned and strode back to where Daníel and Helena waited for the lift.

'Can we expect trouble? Gangsters looking for her, or anything like that?'

Daníel turned and looked into her eyes, and saw there a need for some support.

'Hopefully not,' he said, and was about to explain that the case hadn't progressed that far, but they had a lot to go on, and that they would re-examine the case at the end of the day and would decide then whether to place a police presence on the ward ... but Helena spoke first, and was more direct than he would have been.

'As long as nobody knows she's here, then you won't need to worry about any trouble,' she said.

15

It should have been broad daylight by the time Áróra arrived at the coffee house to meet Elín, but it was dim inside, and the gloom outside, which wasn't quite day or night, meant that the light from candles on the tables cast a sinister glow. Áróra would have found straightforward darkness a better option. This endless dusk of the Icelandic winter troubled her, and she frequently found herself with no idea of what the time really was, whether it was daytime or evening. But this really ought to be over by March.

The coffee house looked deserted now, with the morning rush clearly over and the lunchtime trade yet to come. One man sat engrossed in a computer with headphones clamped to his ears, and at the far end she saw a blonde woman, who looked at her expectantly. This could only be Elín.

'You've changed so much!' she said, standing up to kiss Áróra on both cheeks. Áróra looked the woman up and down, but had no recollection of having met her before. 'You get the height from your dad. I don't know how many pictures there are in the photo albums at home of us kids standing next to him to see just how tall he was. He had a massive growth spurt around the time he was confirmed – your grandmother even took him to the doctor.'

Áróra smiled. This was good to hear. After her father's death she had regretted many times that she hadn't asked him about his youth, his relatives and his memories. And Ísafold had felt the same.

It was as if Elín sensed what she was thinking, as her expression turned serious.

'Is there any progress with your sister?' she asked.

Áróra shook her head.

'Unfortunately, no,' she said. 'The police have hit the buffers. They have done their best – especially Daníel – to track her down, but there's been no sign of her anywhere since she disappeared.' Áróra shook off her coat and hung it on the chair. 'Speaking of Daníel,' she said, relieved to turn the conversation in a different direction. 'When did you divorce?'

'Oh, ages ago, darling. He remarried and had two kids, but I haven't been in a serious relationship since. Until now. With Sergei.'

'And that is who you're worried about?'

'Yes. I'm sure it's just me being silly,' Elín said. 'Maybe I'm just delusional. Sergei is a good guy and I'm lucky to have met him.'

Áróra smiled amiably. She wanted to hear the whole story before giving an opinion. It might well be that Elín was being over-suspicious, but Áróra always followed her father's advice and listened attentively. Always – apart from that one time. She would regret for the rest of her life not following her instincts and going straight away to help her sister that last time she called in desperation because Björn had beaten her. That had been the last time that Áróra had bowed to fatigue and her own short temper, instead of responding to the desperate need to protect her sister, a need that had long ago made a nest for itself in her gut. It had been shortly afterwards that her sister had vanished without trace.

But every case was different, and people are as varied as they are many, and she didn't know the woman in front of her now at all. It could well be that she was suffering from a persecution complex.

'Tell me the whole story, from the start,' she said, unwinding her scarf as the sweat started to break out on her neck. She still hadn't got used to how Icelanders cranked the heating right up during the winter months. 'Tell me how you met Sergei.'

The waiter brought them their coffee, and Elín waited until he was gone before starting her narrative.

'I'm a little ashamed to say it, but it was on a dating site. One of those apps,' Elín said.

Áróra shook her head.

'It's nothing to be ashamed of. That's the way things are today. And it's no worse a way to meet people than going to a bar or a club.'

Elín laughed, obviously relieved.

'That's true,' she said. 'I'd had enough of that kind of social life. I found out that guys *my* age who spend their time in bars aren't always one-hundred-percent reliable.'

'So Sergei isn't the same age as you?' Áróra asked, as she had the impression that he was somewhat younger than Elín, who now leaned forward and whispered, as if this was a secret of some sort.

'He's twenty years younger,' she said. 'I'm forty-seven. He's twenty-seven.'

The way she said this came as an uncomfortable surprise to Áróra, and her thoughts went straight to herself and Daníel. There was a fifteen-year gap between them, but she hadn't seen this as an obstacle of any kind. He was the one who'd seen it more as a barrier. But she quickly shook these thoughts off. It wasn't the difference in their ages that had prevented her and Daníel from establishing a relationship. There were all kinds of complications. The main one of which was that he was responsible for the investigation into her sister's disappearance, with all that it entailed.

Áróra carefully took stock of Elín. She was beautiful, shapely and blonde, with pale skin that was smooth and even. She had kindly eyes. They looked maybe a little confused right now, but there was a goodness behind them. She could well understand that Daníel had once loved this woman.

16

Helena and Daníel had just got into the car outside the hospital when his phone rang.

He answered, listened and then said, 'I'm going to put you on speaker, Rannveig. So Helena can hear this as well.'

This meant it had to be the nerd lady from the cybercrime division, who seemed to want to speak to only Daníel because they knew each other 'from way back'. As far as Helena could make out, 'way back' meant around thirty years ago.

'*Hæ*,' Rannveig said, her voice sounding nasal as it filtered through the phone's speaker. 'We've tracked the container. It came from the commercial port and was released by customs to a company number belonging to InExport, which seems to be, as far as I can figure out, some kind of brass-plate business. Our colleagues in economic crime are looking into them right now.'

'Anything more?' Daníel asked, sounding impatient.

'The container was collected by a truck, and the driver had the right documentation with him.'

Rannveig fell silent, as if to irritate Daníel deliberately.

'And?'

'The truck can be seen on the security cameras leaving the port area with the container loaded on the back.'

Rannveig paused again, and Daníel sighed, as if he needed every bit of determination not to shout at her.

'And?'

'We have the number and the name of the owner.'

'Let's hear it,' Daníel said, ready to punch the address into the car's GPS.

'The owner is Lárentínus Ásgeirsson, mid-thirties truck driver, resident in Gufunes.'

Daníel noted down the address, and Helena immediately put the car into gear and drove off – fast.

'There's a patrol car on the way up there with a uniformed squad,' said Rannveig. 'They'll be waiting for you outside.'

'That's great. Thanks, Rannveig.' She made no immediate response, and Daníel waited a moment before adding, 'Thank you for sharing your knowledge with us, Rannveig.'

'Knowledge is power,' Rannveig replied.

Daníel smiled.

'It is indeed,' he said, and Helena heard Rannveig laugh as she ended the call.

'What's that about?' Helena asked. 'That call sounded really weird.'

Daníel grinned.

'It was,' he said. 'It's the remnants of a drunken argument between me and Rannveig about what gives someone a position of advantage in a relationship. It's fair to say that she won that argument and that she likes to remind me of it.'

'Was that a while ago?' Helena asked.

'Yep. Twenty-something years,' Daníel said.

'Jeez,' Helena muttered as she took the turning onto Miklabraut. 'What a weirdo.'

'She never forgets anything,' Daníel laughed.

Helena couldn't help smiling in sympathy. Daníel always appreciated people who were on the odd side.

She swung the car into the middle, and then to the outer lane, and put her foot down. Lárentínus Ásgeirsson's house was just eight minutes away.

17

'What really bothers me is that he's pressing for us to get married, which is understandable, as he needs a residence permit. But when I mention a pre-nup, he either gets angry or dismisses the idea.'

Elín smiled awkwardly as she explained the situation to Áróra, as if she were embarrassed to have got herself into this position.

'It's not pleasant,' Áróra said, encouragingly. 'Do you have significant assets?'

'Not really,' Elín shrugged. 'Not that much anyway. My father paid me my inheritance in advance when he downsized, so my place is debt free, and so is the little apartment downtown that I rent out. That's my main income, as I only sell a painting occasionally now, but I can live on very little, because I don't have debts.'

Áróra nodded.

'Those are actually substantial assets, and certainly far from insignificant for someone like Sergei who has nothing.'

'Of course, that's right,' Elín said. 'But I'm not exactly rich, so it's not as if he wants to marry me for my money. We don't live a life of luxury. Far from it.'

Áróra watched Elín. She seemed to have gone from an almost childish candidness to defensive in a fraction of a second. In a way this was understandable, as these were her personal circumstances under discussion. But it also indicated that she was the sensitive type. She could be easily hurt – and also easily led.

'It could be that Sergei is simply not mature enough to appreciate how important financial security is to you,' Áróra said. 'He's a young guy, and young people are more daring and worry less about the future,' she continued, and saw Elín relax and smile with relief.

'Yes,' she said. 'That's exactly what I was thinking. He doesn't get why my father and I are both concerned that I have enough to live on if things turn out badly. He doesn't want to even consider the possibility that our relationship could fall apart. Refuses to believe it could happen. Which is a young person's outlook, I suppose.'

Áróra smiled back and waited for Elín to get to the point. She had said on the phone that she wanted her to do a job, and that Daníel had recommended getting Áróra to look into things for her.

'Is there anything else about Sergei that bothers you?'

The question hung in the air for a while before Elín shifted in her chair and leaned forward, speaking in a low, confidential voice that was unnecessary in the coffee house, which was deserted apart from the two of them and one other customer, whose ears were covered by his headphones.

'I don't want to sound prejudiced, but it goes without saying that Sergei comes from another culture,' Elín said. 'And I don't know what's usual there when it comes to relationships and stuff ... but there's some woman who calls him at all times of the day and night, and he always goes off somewhere to take the call. He says it's his mother, but I strongly suspect that's not true.'

'And what exactly is it you think I can do for you?' Áróra asked.

Elín laughed awkwardly.

'I don't exactly know. Maybe just use what resources you have to find out what you can?'

Áróra nodded, wondering what resources Elín imagined she would have access to.

'Well, I suppose I can look into his finances, at least, and search for him in the public records,' Áróra said.

Under normal circumstances this wouldn't be the kind of assignment she would agree to. But as it had come through Daniel, she was delighted to take it on.

18

On her way home, Elín felt that it had been a relief to talk to Áróra. Somehow, problems seemed to shrivel up once they had been discussed with someone else. Someone other than her father, at any rate. His tendency was always to inflate a problem; especially one that had anything to do with Sergei.

Elín turned up the car heater, and the mist gradually cleared from the windscreen, so she could see out better. It had been astonishing how like her father Áróra was. So tall and stately, her long hair a dark blonde, with dark-brown eyes; and her bearing and overall appearance were fantastic, as if she were a model. It didn't seem that long ago that Elín had seen her at family gatherings – just as a lanky youngster; so when Áróra had walked into the coffee house it had been a stark reminder of how rapidly time had passed.

Elín decided that she would follow Áróra's advice and delay things concerning Sergei. Holding back for a few days on requesting an appointment with the district commissioner's office to arrange a wedding would give Áróra time to look into his background. She felt a little knot inside her that was more guilt than trepidation. Guilt at being suspicious about the man she loved and bringing in a sort of private detective to spy on him. Maybe that was the whole thing in a nutshell? If she couldn't find it in herself to trust Sergei completely, wouldn't marrying him be the wrong thing to do? On the other hand, marriage was the only way for them to remain together – the only way for him to get a residence permit and stay in Iceland. That was her dilemma. The thought of Sergei having to leave the country for months on end was more than she could bear.

Taking into account everything Áróra had said, she felt it

would be only sensible to ensure she knew as much as possible about her intended – especially if she were to decide against a pre-nuptial agreement, which she was still considering. Her father was pressuring her about one, but Sergei wouldn't hear of it. Perhaps it would be easier to drop the idea if she knew more about Sergei's background. And that would become clearer once Áróra had used the tools at her disposal to check him out. In any case, Elín had given Áróra all the information she had about him, including his passport number and his previous address, and that his mother's name was Galina and that she had heard the name Sofia when he spoke on the phone.

Elín wound down the window as she turned into the street where she lived, so that frost wouldn't form on the inside, and closed it again before switching off the engine on the drive in front of the house. There was a light in the living-room window upstairs, and a warm feeling of wellbeing rushed through her. After living alone for so long, it was lovely to come home to Sergei, with the lights on, the radio playing and hot tea in the pot.

Elín opened the door and as she was about to go up the stairs, she felt a sudden surge of regret. What was she thinking, getting someone to spy on Sergei? Wasn't her suspicion misplaced? She could feel the knot of guilt deep inside her tighten and swell, and in the few moments it took to walk up the steps and push open the door to the apartment, she reached the conclusion that it would be best to tell Sergei everything. She would explain the whole situation.

Those thoughts vanished the instant she was inside. Something was very clearly wrong. Sergei stood in the middle of the living-room floor, yelling in Russian into his phone and trembling from top to toe. But she couldn't make out from his body language or his words whether he was furious or terrified. He slammed the phone down on whoever he had been speaking to and looked at her with staring eyes.

'What's the matter?' Elín asked gently, and went over to him. She placed a hand on his chest, but he jerked away from her touch as if he had been scorched.

'Everything's fucked,' he snapped, and headed for the door, snatching up his jacket and repeating his words with even more desperation in his voice. 'Everything's fucked!'

Then he hurtled down the stairs, and a moment later Elín heard the door bang shut behind him.

19

Lárentínus the truck driver wasn't at home. Uniformed officers had got there ahead of them, and Daníel was about to admonish them for not waiting for him and Helena, when one of them explained that the door had been wide open, so they had looked inside and called out, but there had been no reply.

It was a small, one-storey, detached house in a new estate overlooking the old Gufunes industrial district. It wasn't the most pleasing vista the city had to offer, as the semi-derelict factory had been used for some time as a recycling centre, so the view was of piles of fishing gear and timber, but the houses up here on the slope were neat, and more new houses appeared to be sprouting up, so that it wouldn't be long before this would be a blooming new district.

'Did you go inside?' Daníel asked, and the two officers shook their heads.

Daníel gestured for them to go in, ahead of him and Helena, and they entered, one of them with his hand on the pepper spray at his belt, as if expecting an attack. Daníel had often noticed that police officers who would fearlessly take on tough situations any day of the week became tense in the presence of CID. He wasn't sure if this was because the CID routinely dealt with serious cases, so uniformed officers always expected the worst when detectives were involved, or if it was because they felt that they were under a microscope when the CID was present.

'Nobody here,' one of the two officers said when they had checked every room in the house. 'And the place has been wrecked.'

He was right. The living room looked as if an earthquake had hit it. Smashed glassware and crockery from the sideboard lay scattered across the floor, the sofa had been sliced open so that feathers fluttered around the floor among the shards of glass, and the dining table was broken in two. Daníel glanced into the bedroom and the bathroom, both of which looked normal and untouched.

'This is just a threat,' Daníel said. 'Nobody was looking for anything here, otherwise the bathroom and the other room would have been turned over as well.'

'Unless they found what they were looking for in here,' Helena said, and Daníel nodded. That was a possibility, but his instinct told him that more damage than necessary had been done for this to have been a search for something. There were shards of crockery around the living room, as if someone had been playing at hurling one plate after another at the wall. Anyone searching for something – money, drugs or suchlike – would work systematically, and would be in and out quickly.

Helena appeared from the bathroom.

'There's a woman living here as well,' she said, 'judging by the cosmetics.'

Daníel took out his phone and checked the national registry. That was correct. As well as Lárentínus the truck driver, a twenty-three-year-old woman was also registered at this address. Daníel opened the Book of Icelanders genealogy app, tapped in the woman's name and smiled in satisfaction when he saw the result.

'It seems I'm related to Lárentínus's girlfriend,' he said to Helena as she looked at him enquiringly. 'Going back eight generations.'

'So what? You and I are related eight generations back. We're all related if you go back eight generations.'

'Yep,' Daníel said as they made their way back to the car, waving his phone in triumph. 'But tracing the ancestry like this is useful because it shows me her parents' names. It seems I'm related to her mother, and according to the national registry, she lives in Breiðholt. Let's go.'

20

Elín had told her that Sergei lived in both Britain and France after leaving Russia, so as soon as she was in her car outside the coffee house, Áróra used her phone to register on the GRO database in the UK and to request a username and password for the *état-civil* registry of Département 75, which was Paris. It was as well to drop a hook where a fish would be most likely to bite.

Then she drove to Weights, where she skipped for a while to loosen up, put on her belt and performed four hundred-kilo deadlifts. She stood gasping for breath after the last one, her legs feeling like they had turned to jelly.

'You're fucking amazing,' said one of the regulars, a huge man with a black beard who had been watching from one of the benches.

'Thanks,' Áróra smiled. 'But there are women who can do a 150-kilo deadlift,' she added and sat down next to him.

He hummed to himself and looked her up and down.

'True. But you're too long in the back for that,' he said.

Áróra nodded.

'The height comes from my dad.'

'Your dad was a giant of a man. A fantastic guy.'

Áróra felt an inner warmth. She appreciated how the strongmen of both Scotland and Iceland always spoke well of her father.

'Yep. Bulk that matched his height. But a woman with my height can't even dream of that kind of thing.'

'No. It's the short birds who lift the big weights. But I can get you some testo if you want.'

'Nah. I'm not competing or anything, so I'll give it a miss. I can do without the spots. And the sex drive that comes with it.'

The man laughed and Áróra got to her feet.

'See you.'

The man nodded acknowledgement, and Áróra went out through the big doors, straight to the car. She liked Weights, even though it was basic. It was just a garage with a few lifting benches. It was similar to the places where she had trained with her father since childhood, and the bearded and tattooed musclemen were the types she got on best with and felt most comfortable around. She'd be back tomorrow or the next day to give her arms a workout. Her routine was to train for increased muscle mass for half the year, and to bring herself back down for the other half, simply because this was what she was used to. This was what she and her father had done while he had been alive and competed in weightlifting.

Her phone pinged at the next set of lights, and Áróra quickly checked the screen. It was an email alert – more than one. She managed to open them before the lights changed and saw that she now had access to both GRO and *état civil*.

As soon as she got home, she switched on the coffee machine, and then poured frozen berries, a banana and protein powder into the blender and topped it up with milk. Then she sat down with her shake and opened her computer. She punched Sergei's name and date of birth into GRO, but this didn't return any result. She hadn't expected it to, as this database held only births, marriages and deaths. She opened the *état civil* register with more optimism, as the French state liked to maintain a more detailed register of its citizens, and although it was not as exhaustive as its Icelandic equivalent, it was also divided by region.

If Sergei had ever applied for residency, then this would appear in one of the regional registries, most likely in Paris, where the largest volume of applications and residence permit requests were processed.

Áróra had hoped to come across some evidence of Sergei's stay in France, but she hadn't expected to see what popped up when she typed his name and date of birth into the database.

She peered at the screen and ran the text through an online translator to be sure that she hadn't misunderstood anything. Then she pressed the request button to order the certificates that accompanied the entry: the certificate of marriage of Sergei Konstantinovich Popov and Marie C. Allard, and the permanent Schengen residence certificate issued to him on the grounds of family unification, in this case, marriage to a French citizen. And then there was the death certificate of his wife, Marie C. Allard.

21

Helena was certain that she could see horror in the faces of the girl's parents the moment they opened the door of the imposing detached house in the Hólar district of the city. The woman stood behind her husband, peering over his shoulder as if expecting the worst. Their relief was clear when Daníel introduced himself and Helena as police officers.

'Come inside,' the man said, looking furtively up and down the street, as if he expected someone to be watching the house.

'To be honest, I can't tell you how relieved I am that you're here. Our daughter absolutely wouldn't countenance us calling the police, for fear of reprisals from the thugs who attacked her in her own home.'

'Is she hurt?' Helena asked.

'No. She's unharmed,' the father replied.

'But she's emotionally scarred,' the mother added.

'Yes, they scared her absolutely stiff, those scum,' the father continued. 'I suppose they're drug dealers, or what? What sort of people do this kind of thing? And what did they want with Lárentínus?'

'That's exactly what we're trying to figure out,' Helena said, as she caught Daníel's eye. As usual, his hunch had been correct.

They followed the couple into the living room, where their daughter was huddled under a blanket, her face swollen with tears. From what her parents had just said, she must have been present when Lárentínus's flat was trashed. Helena went over to her, extended a hand and sat by her side, while Daníel took a seat in an armchair facing them.

'How are you feeling?' Helena asked and the girl dissolved into a flood of tears.

'Not good,' she moaned. 'I'm so frightened that those men are going to murder Lalli.'

'Lalli? You mean your boyfriend, Lárentínus?' Daníel said, and the girl nodded, sniffed hard and dabbed at the tears on her cheeks. 'And where is Lárentínus?' Daníel asked.

At this the girl shook her head and her lips clamped shut.

'He said I wasn't to tell anyone.'

Helena heard Daníel give a low murmur of satisfaction. It was so understated that only she heard it. Having been at his side in countless such situations, she knew that he relished teasing information out of people who were determined to keep it to themselves. And he was good at it, certainly. It was a natural talent, coupled with years of practice, and meant that people could hardly keep their mouths shut around him. He leaned back in the chair, as if ready to relax in front of the television, and the girl looked at him in desperation. Helena followed his example, making herself comfortable on the sofa and loosening the scarf around her neck.

The mother stood and watched, and seemed to realise they weren't going anywhere in a hurry.

'Would you like coffee?' she asked.

Daníel looked up at her with a sunny smile.

'That would be lovely, thank you,' he said, and the girl burst into tears once more.

'I don't know anything about any of this,' she gasped, sobbing. 'Just that Lalli was a bag of nerves all night, and in the morning he said I mustn't tell anyone where he is. Nobody at all. He said something about collecting a container for someone. When I went onto Facebook and Insta, it was all there. Everyone posting pictures of a container and cop cars all round it and asking what was going on.'

Helena sighed despondently. Of course, news of the container had hit social media. One photo of the police at work at a crime scene was enough to put the rumour mill into overdrive. There was no longer any point these days in asking the media to keep something back until the right moment, now that everyone had their own media in front of them.

'I didn't understand what was going on,' the girl carried on. 'And then these men came looking for Lalli. They were foreign gangsters, weren't they? And now you're looking for him as well. What's happened with this container?'

'Surely you can see a difference between us and these foreign criminals?' Daníel suggested with a kindly smile.

'We're the police,' Helena added gently. 'Lárentínus has nothing to fear from us.'

The girl shook her head.

'I don't know what this is all about,' she said. 'Lalli said I shouldn't tell anyone. What if he's done something wrong and you're going to arrest him?'

The girl's mother reappeared with a flask of coffee and cups, and the father followed behind with a milk jug and biscuits on a plate.

'Mmm,' Daníel said contentedly, plucking a biscuit from the plate as soon as it was on the table and popping it in his mouth. He accepted a cup of coffee from the mother, added a splash of milk and sipped. 'Excellent coffee,' he said. 'Exceptionally good.'

'We use French roast, but an ordinary percolator,' the woman explained.

'No messing about with espressos here,' the father said, planting himself in an armchair. 'So what's this all about? Why are the police looking for Lárentínus? Has he got himself tangled up in some trouble?'

Helena said nothing, but glanced at Daníel. He had taken the reins and clearly had a strategy to find the truck driver's whereabouts. He finished munching another biscuit and washed it down with a gulp of coffee.

'Unfortunately, I'm not at liberty to tell you a great deal about this, as I'm bound by rules of confidentiality. That's the way we work,' he said, looking at the father, who nodded in understanding. Then Daníel turned to the girl and his gaze was harsher. 'There's a strong likelihood that Lárentínus is involved in a very serious crime.' He fell silent, adding weight to his words. 'Murder.'

The girl buried her face in her hands.

'Good God!' gasped the mother, and the father shot to his feet.

'Shouldn't we get him a lawyer?' he asked – clearly the type who coped best with tension by taking action.

'That would be advisable, yes,' Helena said. 'If you don't have a lawyer, then we can allocate one to him.'

Daníel's eyes were still fixed on the girl, who peered out from between her fingers like a frightened bird in a cage.

'Lalli isn't a killer,' she gasped, her voice oddly small, like that of a little girl.

'Hopefully you're correct,' Daníel said. 'But we need to speak to Lárentínus to get his side of the story. It could be that this is all a misunderstanding that can be put right. But what's vital right now is that we find him before these foreign gangsters do.'

'Tell the police what they need to know, girl,' the father ordered angrily.

She cleared her throat.

'He's in the summer cottage by Elliðavatn.'

'Our old cottage?' the mother asked in surprise, and the girl nodded.

Daníel smiled in satisfaction.

'Thank you so much,' he said to the girl. 'You've done the right thing. Whether Lárentínus has done anything or not, he's safest in our hands.' He looked over at Helena. 'Could you go with the uniformed gentlemen who are waiting outside and fetch

Lárentínus?' he said. 'I'll stay here and get a better description of these foreign gangsters. And I'll finish off this excellent coffee before I have to head out to the airport. Remember?'

He winked at Helena.

She had forgotten that Daníel would have to go to the airport to meet his children, who were coming from Denmark to spend a week with their father. Helena nodded and agreed, and on the way to the door she wondered how Daníel would manage being a dad while this investigation was in progress.

22

When Bisi woke up, she had difficulty working out where she was. It was clear she was still in hospital, as she lay in a snow-white bed, but her surroundings were quite different from those she had seen just before she had fallen into a drugged nightmare. The light that fell through the windows bathed the room in a grey-blue brightness that the fluorescent lights in the ceiling couldn't quite overcome. At her side sat an old woman, who stroked her arm and muttered something unintelligible. This wasn't a nurse, as she wore a shabby pink dressing gown over white hospital attire, and anyway, she seemed too ancient. Bisi often found it difficult to guess the ages of white women, but the deep lines criss-crossing her face left her in no doubt that this person was very old. Bisi tried to lift herself up, but it was difficult with her hands so heavily bandaged. The old woman emitted some kind of cry of delight when she saw that Bisi was awake and rang a bell that hung in a metal triangle above the bed before going back to stroking Bisi's arm.

The door opened and a woman in a white overall entered. There was no doubt this was a nurse or a doctor, as she had a stethoscope hanging around her neck and her breast pocket was full of all kinds of stuff. Bisi tried to peer at the badge that was pinned to her collar, but the name looked very strange. At any rate, the syllables didn't form any kind of a name in Bisi's mind.

'Hello and welcome to Ward A4,' the woman said with a smile. The old woman said something, which the other woman then translated for Bisi: 'She said you were restless in your sleep, so she came to sit by your side.'

Bisi glanced at the old woman and smiled quickly in grati-tude. The old woman smiled back and the wrinkles around her eyes multiplied, and now Bisi couldn't help another, genuine smile. There was something so sweet about the old lady as she sat there with her grey locks, rocking back and forth. But as she smiled, tears appeared in Bisi's eyes and ran down her cheeks. It was such a long time since she had felt like this. It was such a long time since she had smiled. The old woman continued to stroke her arm, and Bisi made an attempt to wipe away the tears, but the bandages were like vast cushions.

'You're suffering a little frostbite on your hands and feet,' the nurse explained. 'You'll be here on the ward while we treat it.'

'Is it true...?' Bisi asked. 'Is it true that I'm in Iceland?'

The nurse looked surprised and nodded.

'Yes,' she said. 'You're in Iceland.' Then she cleared her throat, reached for a small trolley, and picked up a syringe and a sample bottle. 'We need to take a blood sample from you, to check your levels. You had symptoms of hypothermia when you were admitted.'

The nurse put a binding around her arm and looked for a vein. Bisi hardly felt the prick of the needle, but the sight of the red blood that filled the sample bottles that the nurse deftly changed gave her a certain calmness. The flow of blood showed that she was alive, at least. The old woman stood up and watched what the nurse was doing with interest. She said something that made the nurse laugh. Then the old lady laughed as well, apologetically.

'She's surprised that your blood is the same colour as hers, even though you're so much darker.'

The nurse withdrew the needle from Bisi's arm and placed a wad of cotton wool on the entry point.

'I don't think she's ever encountered someone your colour before,' she said cheerfully, winking at Bisi, who looked at the old woman and decided that they must each appear to the other to be thoroughly alien. For a moment they all laughed, and for a fraction of a second the nightmare became something distant, and the container just an obscure memory.

23

Helena didn't feel like running, so she left it to the two uniformed officers to chase Lárentínus the truck driver across the moorland behind the little summer cottage that stood practically by the water's edge, and which didn't look as if it had seen much maintenance for some time. Lárentínus had clearly seen the police car approach, because he had been out of the house and taken to his heels before the car had even come to a halt on the gravel track. One of the two officers pointed towards Lárentínus and asked if this was the guy they had been sent to fetch. Helena had nodded. Lárentínus looked like a chicken as he hopped from one tussock to the next, and the police officers rapidly gained on him. There was nothing easy about running through the heather.

By the cottage stood a neat little van, which was no doubt what Lárentínus had used to get here. It was now blocked in by the police car. Helena looked around inside the cottage, where there was little to be seen; it looked as if the place had been emptied out. She realised that this was one of the places that had been acquired by the water authority as it stood in a protected area and was therefore due for demolition. All the same, Lárentínus appeared to have made himself comfortable, with a mattress on the floor and a little gas heater to keep him warm, and he had clearly needed some consolation, judging by the litter of sweet wrappers and soft-drink cans by the mattress.

'Hey!'

The call came from outside.

Helena hurried out. Lárentínus appeared to have changed his strategy; he'd left the moorland for an overgrown area and was heading for the water.

'Don't do anything stupid, man!' one of the officers yelled at him, but that didn't stop Lárentínus from running out into the water and swimming for it. Helena jogged over to the two officers where they stood on the black sand of the shore and watched him heading away.

'Shall we go after him?' one of them panted.

Helena shook her head.

'No,' she replied. 'There's no point struggling with him in the water. He won't last long in this cold.'

The officer sighed with relief. At this point, he clearly wasn't Lárentínus's greatest admirer.

'I'll call out a rescue squad with a boat, and maybe you can go with them and get him?' Helena suggested. 'That's if he hasn't given up and made for the shore by then.'

'Not a problem. I'm looking forward to cuffing this idiot.'

'Good. Then I don't need to call out the Special Unit. There's so much bureaucracy afterwards when we have to do that.'

She tapped in the control room's number and reflected as she waited for a reply that it would do no harm at all for Lárentínus to have tired himself out before being fished out of the water and arrested.

24

Tumi and Tanja were quiet in the car on the drive from the airport. He tried to chat to them, but as they approached the city he was running out of things to say. He had asked about school, their friends, what they had watched on TV recently, how Tumi was getting on with karate and about Tanja's progress in football, and by the time they were passing the aluminium smelter he had more or less run out of questions, as each one was answered in a monosyllable: yes, no, fine, OK. Getting off to such a difficult start was exactly what he dreaded every time they came to stay with him. Standing at the doors leading from the arrivals hall at the airport, his heart was always full of expectation, and most of all he wanted to rush to meet them, envelop them in his arms and shout out that he loved them. But they would generally slouch out, say a shy 'hi', and there would be a quick hug – more a duty for them than a pleasure.

He watched them in the rear-view mirror and tried to make eye contact, but they each looked silently out of their side windows.

'Do you have much homework to do?' Daníel asked.

'A bit,' Tumi said.

He had grown, and Daníel felt that there was an adolescent feel to him. There was a new bulk to his shoulders and his jaw had broadened. Tanja was still small for her age, and on the plump side, as she always had been. Her mother had sent a long list of what she could and couldn't eat, but Daníel had never managed to keep her to her diet while she stayed with him, so he tried to compensate by keeping them active.

'It's winter holiday,' Tanja said. 'So we don't get homework.'

This was the longest sentence she had uttered the whole way, and Daníel smiled.

'That's nice,' he said, but Tanja said no more. She simply nodded and her attention was again on what was beyond the windows.

As they made their way through Hafnarfjörður, he wondered if he should tell them anything about himself, give them a run-down of his life, but decided he had nothing appropriate to tell children of ten and twelve. He couldn't say anything about the domestic violence and stalking case he had been working on most recently. He couldn't tell them about the container. He felt the bile rise in his throat at the thought of it. He would have to cut down on coffee for a while.

The children leaped – apparently happily – from the car, and in the hall he started the usual lecture: shoes to be neatly placed, coats hung up. And as they did as he asked, he realised how much he had missed them. It was an odd feeling that he missed them as much when they had just arrived as when they had just left.

He took their bags into the bedroom and placed them on their beds. He had asked them at one point if they would prefer to have the room divided into two, as it was easily big enough to be made into two small rooms, but they assured him that they were happy to share a room while they stayed with him. He could understand that. Each was the fixed point in the other's life when they moved between parents – between homes and countries. But that would change as they entered their teens, and judging by how Tumi had shot up, that wouldn't be long.

When Daníel reappeared in the living room, he saw that they had found the packages and stood shyly looking at them, there on the table.

'Help yourselves,' Daníel said.

'Which is mine and which is Tanja's?' Tumi asked.

Daníel shrugged.

'They're the same, so it doesn't matter. You'll just have to choose a cover each so you know which is which.'

'Really?' Tumi's face lit up, and he picked up one of the packets, quickly ripping off the wrapping paper. 'iPhone!' he yelped, and threw himself at Daníel. This time it was a genuine hug, and Daníel held his son tight, kissed the top of his head and breathed in the scent of his hair. He always smelled like clean washing hung outside to dry, and Daníel loved this aroma.

'Thanks, Dad,' Tumi said quietly, and Daníel smiled and loosened his embrace, even though he would he loved to have held on to him for much longer.

Tanja danced in delight around the living room, and Daníel opened his arms wide.

'Doesn't Dad get a hug?'

She rushed into his arms as her brother had done, and Daníel lifted her up and spun around in circles as he had wanted to at the airport.

The children sat at the table and were slotting the SIM cards into place when the door from the garden opened and Lady Gúgúlú came in, this time wearing some kind of a pirate handkerchief on her head and dressed in jeans and a T-shirt.

'Well, well. Bribing the children with consumer baubles to assuage your guilty conscience?'

The children shot to their feet and into Lady's arms, and Daníel felt a twinge of envy. This was the reception he would have wanted at the airport – unbounded delight, warmth, kisses and hugs.

'Can we have a wig competition at your place like we did last time?' Tanja asked in excitement.

'Yes, please!' Tumi said.

Lady bowed smartly.

'At the first available opportunity, little ones. At the first opportunity.'

Daníel smiled, as the joy at seeing each other clearly went both ways.

'It's precisely eight minutes since they walked through the door. Couldn't you wait to see them?' he teased.

'Not a bit of it,' Lady said with a scowl. 'Can't stand kids.'

The children laughed, and there was no mistaking that they found Lady more exciting than their own father, although the phones had certainly earned him a few points. Now he would have to wait for the right moment to let their mother know that he had broken their agreement that iPhones would remain off the list of what was acceptable before they were thirteen. He would have to pick the time and place for that confession.

'Now, then,' he said to Lady. 'Since that's the case, could I ask you to keep an eye on them for a few hours? I have to go back to work.'

'Sure,' Lady agreed without hesitation. 'Shall we order pizza?'

25

Elín still felt numb when Sergei came back home. Under normal circumstances he would have noticed she wasn't right and asked what was troubling her, but everything was strange now; he planted a kiss on her cheek before going into the living room and immediately starting to talk on his phone. He seemed downcast and stressed, but in the light of the information Áróra had given her, she was in no mood to comfort him. She couldn't understand why he hadn't mentioned to her that he had been married before. It wasn't as if that would have been any kind of a deal-breaker – not in this day and age, anyway. And he had lost his wife. Áróra said that her name had been Marie. That wasn't the kind of thing a man should conceal from his lover. Why on earth hadn't he told her?

The questions continued to stack up in her mind, and she didn't know whether to be sad or angry. She would have to speak to him and demand answers. But she would need to find a way to broach the subject and to give him her reasons for asking Áróra to look into his past. She knew he would be angry. She knew him well enough for that; and she could also see that now was not the right moment. He had his phone stuck to his ear and was speaking in frantic Russian. Elín put her head around the living-room door, waved to him and pointed a finger at the floor, indicating that she was going down to the studio. He glanced up, nodded absently and yelled something in Russian into his phone. If only she could understand what he was talking about. Then she would be a step closer to understanding him. What was so completely occupying him at the moment? Was it some family matter? Or was it to do with one of the short-notice jobs he took on? Or what? If she only could understand the language, she would be able to work out what he was saying on the phone, as most other women in a relationship would. There was this language firewall between her and the information any woman had relating to the man she lived with – the man who wanted to marry her.

She had a sudden idea; and before she could feel any pang of guilt or be assailed by doubts, she quickly put it into action. She set her phone to record and left it on the little shelf for keys by the door. It was roughly in the centre of the apartment, so it should pick up Sergei's words whether he was in the kitchen or the living room. As long as he didn't shut any doors, anything he said should be recorded. Then she could find a Russian speaker to translate for her.

The surge of guilt came as soon as she set foot in the studio, and she was on the point of going back upstairs, retrieving her phone and switching it off, but something held her back. Doubt. The doubt that grew and grew inside her as the unanswered questions piled up. The burning one was why Sergei was applying pressure on her to marry him so that he could get a residence permit, when he already had a permit for the Schengen area. There was nothing to prevent him staying in Iceland for as long as he wanted. There was no likelihood of him being deported. And there was nothing that prevented him from working in Iceland. Elín thought of all the times she had lent him money and he had promised to pay her back just as soon as he could start work, and she felt a flush of resentment and shame run through her. She wasn't sure if she was ashamed of being so petty that she regretted sharing money with the man she loved, or if she was ashamed that she'd allowed herself to be fooled.

She pulled out a roll of canvas and laid it on the floor. She had a few frames she had put together, and now she would pour her energies into stretching the canvases and priming them in the hope that this would forestall her tears.

26

The phone had rung just as Bisi had finished packing both suit-cases. She had done all her shopping and run all her errands, and was planning to spend her last three days in Paris sightseeing, going to the theatre and taking long walks along the streets, where she revelled in the atmosphere of sweet melancholy that always took hold of her in European cities. There was something about their beauty, and the past being always so close at hand, that filled her with sorrow at the thought of having to go home again.

Then came the phone call. It was Habiba. She wept into the phone, saying that she was travelling north by bus to her village and wouldn't be returning to Lagos as she was frightened that she would be killed. She said she was terrified that the men who had set fire to their flat would kill her.

'Set fire to the flat?' Bisi repeated. 'What do you mean they set fire to the flat?'

But Habiba suddenly hung up, and although Bisi tried again and again to call her back, she couldn't get through. It was as if Habiba had switched off her phone. So Bisi called her mother.

'You mustn't come home,' her mother whispered into the phone. 'Your father says he's going to kill you. He and your uncle went and burned your apartment and threw Habiba out.'

'What's going on?' Bisi heard the pitch of her own voice rise, her fear becoming obvious.

But she fell silent as her mother hissed back angrily, 'Don't pretend you don't know!'

'I don't know what you're talking about—' Bisi began, but her mother raised her own voice.

'Your brother told us everything, so don't try and deny your shame. We know everything. If you want to live, then keep away.'

Bisi could hear a commotion and then her father's furious voice.

'We worked so hard to educate you and support you, and this is how you reward us?' he said. 'Be ashamed, girl!'

Bisi hung up. She could hear from her father's tone that he wouldn't calm down for some time, and she had no wish to listen to more of the same. This was enough.

She went to the window and leaned her forehead against the glass to cool her face, flushed in anguish after her parents' diatribe and Habiba's heartbreaking farewell. She fought to draw breath and her belly tightened instinctively, in fear at what had just happened.

It was getting dark, and the Eiffel Tower's lights flickered gaily, but the glittering light show did nothing for her right now, rather it underscored her solitude. Now that she had lost her home, this city that she had always longed for and loved had become a terrifying mystery to her. What use were beautiful buildings and famous museums? She had nobody here. Not a single relative. Come to think of it, she no longer had any family anywhere.

27

Lárentínus the truck driver was dressed in a dry track suit, and was slurping hot coffee and munching biscuits, and he seemed to be feeling better. Daníel sat down opposite him at the interview-room table and placed his folder in front of him. The folder was as good as empty, but he had put a few advertising brochures in there to give it a weightier look. It never did any harm to seem to know more than they did.

'The first thing I'd like to know is why you tried to swim for it,' Daníel said with an amiable smile. 'Were you going to swim out to the island and stay there?'

Lárentínus laughed.

'I suppose I wasn't exactly thinking straight,' he said. 'I'll admit that. I haven't been able to do all that much thinking lately.'

'Understood,' Daníel said.

Lárentínus sighed.

'I've just been panicking. Just panic, y'see,' he said.

The door opened and Lárentínus's lawyer came into the room.

'You haven't started, have you?' she said, her voice sharp.

Daníel shook his head.

'No, of course not. We were waiting for you.'

In reality, he had already put out a feeler, and the few words Lárentínus had uttered in reply were enough to give him an idea of how to set the tone of the interview. It was clear that Lárentínus was terrified and completely out of his depth. Providing him with even a slight sense of security meant he would likely be co-operative.

Daníel started the recording, stated clearly the full names of those present and explained the format of the interview.

'My colleague Helena will observe the interview, and she can send me comments and any questions she would like me to ask you through the app on my phone. So if I check my phone, that doesn't mean that I'm not paying attention to what you're saying, but that I have some new information or a question from her.'

Lárentínus looked up at the wall and the dark glass of the window, and clearly imagined Helena behind it. Daníel didn't correct him. In reality, Helena was at her computer in another part of the building. Daníel also didn't mention that numerous others would be watching this conversation through their own computers. The lawyer was aware of this and understood that it could be uncomfortable for Lárentínus to know that all these people were listening in, and that it could break down any trust they might build up.

Daníel opened his folder and took out a printout of a screen-shot, clearly showing the container and the truck's registration.

'This is your vehicle collecting a container that was shipped from Zeebrugge in Belgium, and which was released by customs the day before yesterday. The contents of the container are the reason we are here.'

Lárentínus nodded quickly and eagerly, as if anxious to tell his story.

'Yes,' he said. 'That's me fetching the container.'

'So you confirm that you drove the truck with the container out of the customs zone of the commercial port area?'

'Absolutely. Nobody else drives my truck. I'm a one-man band. The company is me and my truck. I have a smaller vehicle for light jobs. That's just an ordinary van.'

'Did you know what was in the container?'

'No!' Lárentínus cried out his denial in a kind of desperation. 'I didn't have a clue what I was picking up. You have to believe me. I had no idea anything was fishy, or that ... that there were people in the container. That there were dead girls in there. If I'd have known that, I wouldn't have fetched it. I'd never have had anything to do with that job. OK? You have to believe me. I might have done a runner and jumped into the water, and maybe that makes me look guilty, but I had no idea. That's the truth. God's truth!'

'All right,' Daníel said gently, then opened his folder, looked through it, closed it and put it aside on the table.

'I can believe that you didn't know what you were collecting. So let's begin at the beginning. For whom were you collecting this container? Who asked you to do it?'

'Valur.'

'Valur who?'

'I don't know his full name, but I invoice a company called InExport, so he must work there. I've done a few jobs for that guy, mostly small stuff. Delivering this and that, mostly using the van.' At this point the lawyer leaned close to Lárentínus and whispered in his ear. After which he said: 'I had no reason to think there was anything dodgy about this.'

'How did this Valur contact you?'

'He just called me. You can find his number in my phone. He's there as "Valur InExport".'

'The cybercrime division is right now working on drying out your phone after your dip in the water.'

'Ah, OK. Of course. Am I going to jail now?' Lárentínus glanced from the lawyer to Daníel and back. 'I'm asking because I'd really like to be in a cell now – and be there for a few days. Otherwise these men are going to kill me.'

What men? was the question from Helena that appeared on Daníel's phone screen just as he asked the question himself.

'What men are these?'

'Well, Valur and his Russians.'

28

It was on the second day at the Porte de la Chapelle police station that the junkie attacked Bisi. She was a middle-aged woman with light-brown skin, slurring curses in Wolof or creole French, Bisi was too frightened to work out which. The woman had a handbag and used it to batter Bisi repeatedly, squawking that Bisi had taken something of hers. She tried at first to talk to the woman, but quickly saw that this was pointless, instead trying to push her away, yelling at her to back off. She tried both French and English, but the woman wasn't giving up. She was high on something and appeared to not hear a word said to her.

Bisi looked around in desperation, hoping someone in the queue that snaked around the wall of the police station might help her, but the men just laughed, clearly enjoying the show. Finally one of them came over and tried to talk to the woman, but she slapped his face and he backed away, just as she pushed Bisi so hard she fell forward onto all fours. Then the junkie took her place in the queue and crowed with victorious glee. On her knees and scratching grit from her grazed palms, Bisi was close to weeping. She didn't make a habit of breaking down in tears, but now the pressure in her chest felt almost too much to bear. Just two weeks previously, she and Habiba had mixed cocktails, cranked up the music and danced in the living room of their apartment in Lagos. Now the flat was burned out. And Habiba was on her way back to her home village, to live under the shadow of Boko Haram, because of her terror of Bisi's father.

An Arab woman with her hair covered and two small children in tow helped Bisi to her feet and told her she could go to the medical tent, where doctors from Médecins sans Frontières would deal with her injuries and give her painkillers. Bisi shook her head and gasped that she would be fine, that she could look after herself. But the woman caught hold of the sleeve of her jacket and hauled her across the street, past the lunch queue and to the doctors' tent.

'*Merci*,' she said to the woman, her palm on her chest, and the woman smiled and walked away, her children holding tightly to her skirt. One of them turned and looked with wide eyes at Bisi, who did her best to smile. If this were a normal situation it would have been Bisi who tried to help this woman, who was clearly a refugee. Now the tears threatened to return as Bisi realised the misery she faced. She was alone in a foreign city, in a throng of refugees and asylum seekers, hurt, penniless – and homeless as of the following morning, when her stay at the hotel would come to an end, and now she was waiting to be treated, surprised that Médecins sans Frontières worked with refugees even in the heart of Paris.

She had been to summer school in Paris as a young girl, two summers in a row, a month each time. She had learned a little French and to appreciate the cuisine and the culture. But she hadn't got to know any French people. There had been only the other African girls, and she hadn't maintained any contact with them. It would be good now to know someone here, someone who knew their way around who she could go to for advice.

'What happened to you?' asked a white-overalled woman who crouched next to the plastic chair in which Bisi sat.

'I fell,' Bisi said. 'There was a crazy drugged woman who pushed me.'

The woman in white sighed and set to work, cleaning the scratches on Bisi's palms.

'We get so many problems with junkies. The crackheads are nothing but trouble, and they act like this place was set up specially for them. The kitchen has started feeding them first so there aren't any disturbances. Were you in the food queue when you were pushed?'

'No,' Bisi replied. 'The police station. I was told it's the place to register for asylum.'

'Well,' the woman said. 'That queue gets longer by the day. Try to be here early. Do you have anywhere to stay?'

'Only for tonight,' Bisi said, and flinched as the woman applied an iodine-soaked cloth to her palm.

'This is the address of a women's refuge,' the woman in white said, handing her a card. 'You might be able to stay there. But it's the same as here. Be early. Preferably in the afternoon for a chance of getting in for the night.'

Bisi tucked the card away and thanked the woman. Her palms stung less now that they had been treated and dressed. She used what small change she had to buy a Metro ticket back to the hotel, and a distressing thought loomed large as she made her way down into the depths of the underground. Within a few days she would run out of money. Her father had cancelled her credit card. It was linked to his account, so she had no choice in the matter. And her current account was empty. She had spent everything buying presents for the family – and for Habiba.

29

'There were three of them by the gate at the workshop, and when they opened the container, they went crazy, all of them shouting – they even threatened me.'

'Hold on a moment,' Daníel said to Lárentínus, who had gabbled out his account, struggling to hold on to the thread of his tale. He'd gone from apologising and swearing his innocence to talking about the dangerous men who were at his heels, to wanting to be locked up for his own safety. 'Who were these men who met you, along with Valur?'

'I don't know their names, but they're Lithuanians or Russians or something. That's going by the way they talk. To my mind they're all Russians. They all dress the same and talk the same, you know. They have that really weird accent in English.'

This tallied with what his girlfriend had said about the men who had wrecked their house.

'None of them spoke Icelandic?'

'No. Well, yes. Valur, of course. He spoke Icelandic, and the other two English.'

'So you can't be sure that these men were Russians...'

'Oh, well, no, I suppose. Anyway, y'know the sort. Eastern European. Clearly.'

'Do you think you could describe them for us if we get an artist to work with you?' Daníel asked.

Lárentínus glanced at his lawyer, who nodded, and then Lárentínus nodded in turn.

'OK,' Daníel said, and pushed a pen and a sheet of paper across the table. 'Write down the address of this workshop in Kópavogur.' Lárentínus did as he was asked, and Daníel took the paper and read out the address. 'Auðbrekka,' he said. 'And you were instructed to reverse the container up to the gate?'

'That's it. I backed up to the doors, and Valur came round to the cab and told me to wait while they opened the container, so that's what I did. I heard them opening it and messing around, and then there was a thud and a lot of shouting and fuss, and a colossal argument in Russian and English, so I got out and was going to go over to them, when one of the two Russians pushed me back. So I just stood still by the door and waited while they argued it out.'

'Could you make anything out? Any idea what they were arguing about?'

'No. I couldn't understand a word. Those Russians – what I call Russians, you know – were mostly just yelling at each other. And then they banged the container shut and locked it, and one of the Russians came along and took me by the throat, and he shouted something in English about taking the fucking container away. I was scared stiff – they were going crazy and I hadn't a clue what was going on. But Valur got the Russian guy off me and said I should take the container and bury it somewhere.'

'Bury it?'

'Yes. He said I should find someone with a digger and take the container out into the countryside and bury it deep in the ground – and keep my mouth shut for as long as I live. He said he'd pay me and the digger driver half a million each to get the job done right away.'

The lawyer spoke up.

'Didn't you mention earlier, Lárentínus, that Valur said something more to you at this point?'

'Yep. He said that if I fucked it up, he'd skin me alive, slowly, and cut my balls off. So when it was all over social media that a container had been found and the police were investigating it, I reckoned it was best to make myself scarce. You can see why. They came to my place and wrecked it, and I'm sure they would have killed me if I'd been there. That's why I'd really like to be in a cell for the next few days, while these men are on the loose. I really like the sound of solitary confinement.'

'You'll change your mind after a couple of days in custody,' Daníel said.

Lárentínus had little concept of how much of an ordeal solitary confinement could be, but at the moment he clearly saw it as the safest place to be. Which was no surprise. From what Lárentínus had recounted, nobody would want these men on their case.

'Go on,' Daníel said. 'Where did you take the container after that?'

'I went home, up to Gufunes. I was going to leave it outside my place until I could find someone with a digger. But somehow I just felt I couldn't bury it without knowing what was in there. You know, in case it was dangerous or something. I just had to take a look. So I left it on the truck and went—'

Although it went against the grain to stop someone in the middle of their narrative, Daníel held up his hand to interrupt Lárentínus – his account was so muddled, there was no option but to bring him to a halt sometimes.

'What do you mean by dangerous? What did you think could be in the container?'

'Bombs or explosives, or something like that. By now I was wondering if these people were terrorists. At any rate, one of those Russians looked like one.'

'OK, so you thought there could be explosives in the container that could be dangerous for you and the digger driver?'

'Exactly.'

'So you took a look inside?'

'Yeah. And I just...' He fell silent, and Daníel understood

exactly why. He had his own recollections of approaching the container. Lárentínus's voice cracked when he continued, as if he were a teenager and his voice was breaking. 'I just panicked. I ... I don't really know what I did first. I think I rushed to and fro across the street to try and get the smell out of my nose, and then I looked for my phone and was going to call the cops – you, I mean. Then I remembered what Valur had said, so I didn't call the police. Then when I sat down and thought about it, there was no way I was going to get some digger driver involved. I wasn't sure I'd find anyone who could keep his mouth shut for ever, and it wasn't right to have someone else be part of burying five bodies. All for a shitty half a million króna.'

It was clear that Lárentínus had been under the impression that all five women were dead, which indicated that Valur and his accomplices were under the same impression. It was best to let them continue to think that. Bisi would be safe only as long as nobody knew of any survivors.

'So you decided to get rid of the container?'

'Yes. I couldn't leave it outside my place. So I drove around the city for a couple of hours, looking for somewhere there wasn't much traffic, and then I thought of Rauðhólar and dropped it there. I thought that would give me time to think, even though I knew it wasn't a permanent solution. Or, y'know, not what Valur and the Russian guys wanted. But I panicked, and I couldn't think of anything better.'

The lawyer put a hand on his arm and patted it encouragingly, while Lárentínus gave a heavy sigh.

'What happens next?' he asked. 'Are you going to put me in a cell?'

'That seems likely to me,' Daníel replied. 'You'll go before a judge later this evening, along with Oddsteinn, who is the prosecutor's representative, and we, the police, will request that you be remanded in custody for the duration of the investigation.'

'Great,' Lárentínus said. 'Maybe I can relax and get some sleep. Haven't had a wink the whole time. I mean, these guys are seriously heavy. They smashed everything at my place and scared my girlfriend stiff. She's certain they would have killed me. And she's furious that I was doing work for these people, but I couldn't have known it would turn out this way. The time before I just offloaded the container, got paid and left, so how was I to—'

Daníel started, and unconsciously slapped his hand down hard on the tabletop.

'What do you mean, the time before?' he snapped, glaring at Lárentínus, who quailed as he stared back.

'The time before, when I picked up a container for Valur and took it to that workshop place.'

Lárentínus looked at Daníel, who stared at the lawyer, who looked back at him, open-mouthed. It was as if Lárentínus had just realised the truth.

Daníel could no longer sit still. He had to get out of this room, breathe different air and pace the floor to calm himself down. He got to his feet and left.

In the corridor he met Baldvin, who was rushing towards him. His expression left no doubt that he had been listening to the conversation.

'This isn't the first time these men have done this,' he gasped.

Daníel drew a long breath, deep down to his diaphragm, and rubbed his forehead, as if hoping to wipe away the memory of the last few minutes.

'We need to expand the investigation,' Baldvin said. 'We need more manpower.' He fidgeted on the spot, and his deep groan described precisely how Daníel felt. 'Fucking hell...'

THURSDAY

30

Áróra was at Daníel's place before seven in the morning. He had told her that this would be the only time he would have to meet her, as he needed to be at work by eight. There was a tired look to him, but the moment he saw Áróra, his eyes lit up with a smile, and he spread his arms wide and held her tight. They were the same height, so she somehow fitted perfectly into his embrace. She felt the warmth of him through his thin shirt, and for that brief moment she thought she could sense the beating of his heart, and wondered if he was aware of her own rapid heartbeat.

He had made coffee, and the aroma met her as she stepped into the kitchen. He closed the door carefully behind them.

'I hope the children don't wake up right away,' he said. 'It's Dad week, except that this Dad week is ten days, and it came around just as a massive case cropped up at work. Typical.'

'Sorry to disturb you,' Áróra said. An apology was almost an instinctive reaction.

'Not at all, my dear Áróra,' he said with warmth. 'I got you mixed up in this thing with Elín, so I'm the one who should be apologising. I'd been meaning to call you and make a clean breast of things. In case things should turn out...' He paused. 'Ah, well. I'm not saying it'd work out exactly, but more sort of theoretically, because of what you said before ... I mean, if you and I were to be in some sort of a relationship then I'd pass your sister's case to another officer, but I would naturally want to stay involved and support you...'

Daníel fell silent. Taken by surprise, Áróra wondered how to respond as the kitchen door opened and a rangy lad in pyjamas came in.

'Good morning,' Daníel said. 'Tumi, this is Áróra. Tumi's my son.'

'*Hæ*,' Tumi said, without looking at her.

He was somewhere between childhood and adolescence, his physical growth taking off, but his movements were still childishly precise and forceful. He had his father's looks and was a handsome boy. He made straight for the fridge and tucked a carton of milk under one arm, leaving his hands free for cereal, a dish and a spoon, before disappearing through the kitchen door. A moment later, the sound of the TV coming to life carried through from the living room.

Daníel gestured for Áróra to take a seat by the round kitchen table, brought her coffee and asked if she would like toast, but she shook her head. She would have liked some, but thought it would be awkward to talk while she was eating and he wasn't; a crumb-strewn plate showed that he had already had his breakfast.

'Thank you for taking on Elín's case,' he said. 'She's so vulnerable and really needs good advice. I felt it wasn't appropriate for me to be digging into her affairs concerning her new boyfriend. It didn't seem right.'

'It's no problem,' Áróra said. 'It didn't take me long to find something out: this Sergei was previously married – in France, so he already has a Schengen visa.'

'But he's been pressuring her to get married so he can get a residence permit,' Daníel said in surprise.

'Exactly. That's what's so strange about this. I'm wondering what's going on there. And why he hasn't told her that he's a widower.'

'What?' Daníel was startled. 'You mean his previous wife died?'

'Yes, that seems to be the case, according to the French documentation.'

'Hmm.' Daníel looked thoughtful. 'Elín has assets,' he added. 'Maybe nothing spectacular, but she has the house, and I understand there's an apartment she bought with the money she got from her father.'

'That's right,' Áróra confirmed. 'She has a rental income from the little flat and has no debts, so she's financially comfortable. Maybe he's after her property. That's why her father advised her to insist on a pre-nuptial agreement.'

'And Sergei is against that?' Daníel asked.

'Yes, pretty much. Elín says that he changes the subject every time she mentions a pre-nup.'

'I have to say that I find it suspicious that he's pressuring her to get married, considering he doesn't need a residence permit. There's actually no rush to get married – Elín ought to be patient and wait to see how the relationship shapes up.'

'Absolutely,' Áróra said. 'If this is true love, then Sergei wouldn't be worried about waiting a bit longer before making further commitments.'

'True,' Daníel said. 'I'm trying not to be prejudiced against a younger foreign man, and of course Elín is a lovely woman and there's nothing strange about someone falling in love with her. But there's something odd about applying pressure like this, especially if the man already has a valid Schengen visa. She shouldn't give in.'

'I agree entirely,' Áróra said. 'And that's my advice to her. I just hope she listens to it.'

They chatted for a while about Elín and the strange position she was in, but Daníel's words about Elín being a lovely woman echoed through Áróra's thoughts. A memory came to her of Daníel and Didda – as Elín had been called in the old days – playing with a family gathering of children, probably at some barbecue. It had been a delightful and exhilarating day, and Daníel had picked Elín up and run with her until they had tumbled on the grass and everyone laughed. This took Áróra by surprise, as when she had spoken to Elín the day before, this memory of her – young, fair-haired and wearing a loose summer dress – hadn't come to her then.

Was it jealousy, this bizarre emotion that took hold of her as Daníel spoke fondly of his ex? Was it possible to be jealous of something that had happened in the past? And did she have any grounds to be jealous of Daníel? It wasn't as if there was anything concrete between them.

31

'Who's covering the costs?' the doctor asked, looking at Helena over the top of his glasses, which she was sure he wore solely to make him look older. At first glance, she had wondered if he was even of confirmation age. But he'd introduced himself as the duty doctor, and Helena guessed that he must be standing in for the consultant, who was probably playing golf somewhere in the sunshine.

His question was a valid one, and not quickly or easily answered. It was likely that Bisi had neither money nor health insurance, even if it was true that she was a French citizen, which Helena doubted, as Ari Benz hadn't been able to find a woman of this name in any French public registers. If she were, then the bill would go to the French state. But she would have to show them valid French identity documents, and from what forensics had told them, none of the women in the container had identity papers anywhere in their luggage. So Helena gave the only answer that came to mind, so that the hospital could at least issue an invoice.

'The Directorate of Immigration,' she said, deciding that the paperwork would undoubtedly be held up long enough in various levels of bureaucracy for them to find out who should really be paying the bill. The boy doctor seemed satisfied with her answer, so she left him in the corridor and went to Bisi's ward.

Helena found her sitting on her bed, staring out of the window.

'I do wish the poor girl didn't have to have her hands bandaged, so she could occupy herself with some knitting,' said the old woman from the other bed. 'She's so restless, poor thing.'

Helena nodded and smiled at the old lady, who was sitting up, knitting herself.

'She's had a tough time of it. It'll take her a while to recover,' Helena said, and the woman sighed deeply.

'Well, isn't it always the way?' she said, and Helena smiled. She had heard elderly ladies say things like this before.

She took a seat at Bisi's bedside.

'How are you feeling?' Helena asked.

Bisi nodded.

'Better,' she said. 'Except I can't do anything. It's difficult to eat, and I don't know how I will be able to wash.' She raised her hands, both of them wrapped in bandages.

'What have the doctors said about your hands and feet?' Helena asked.

'They're going to check the frostbite today, and they hope that I won't need to have these heavy bandages put back on, just some ointment and that kind of thing.'

'Let's hope for the best,' Helena said. She leaned closer and dropped her voice, even though she knew the old lady didn't understand English. 'The police need your help,' she said. 'We need you to help us find, arrest and charge the criminals who were responsible for putting you in that container.'

Bisi nodded energetically, at the same time looking as if she were holding back tears.

'I want to,' she said. 'I want to help, but I don't think I can. I do not know the names of these people.'

'That doesn't matter,' Helena said. 'We need any information you can possibly give us. What these people look like, what languages you think they speak, exactly how you came to be in the container.'

'But what happens to me?' Bisi asked. 'If I tell you everything, then I won't live long.'

'I'll talk to my superior about exactly what we can offer you, but for the moment we can at least give you a temporary residence permit and police protection.' Bisi nodded and again stared thoughtfully out of the window. 'There's something else, Bisi. Quite apart from whether you come forward as a witness or not, we need your help to identify the other women.' Bisi quickly looked up at her and nodded. 'I'll bring pictures later today and—'

Bisi stiffened and broke in:

'No,' she said. 'No pictures. I want to see them. I need to see *them.*'

32

There was nothing easy about navigating the Paris Metro while dragging two heavy cases. Bisi's back hurt and her arms were numb from lugging her luggage up and down flights of steps and following what seemed to be endless passageways. She had looked up the Metro station she needed for the shelter the doctor had mentioned to her, but it turned out to be closed for refurbishment, and in her panic she managed to miss the next stop and finally lugged her cases out at the following one. Going by the map, it was too far to walk with her luggage, so she took passages and stairs so she could go one stop back along the line, and got out there.

Whether it was this delay or whether she had underestimated how early she needed to be at the shelter to have a chance of spending a night at the refuge, she was too late. She hurried to take her place in the queue behind a woman she guessed to be from Syria. The woman turned, shook her head and smiled her sympathy.

'Looks like we're on the street tonight,' she said.

All the same, they waited until one of the refuge's staff appeared, counted the women in the queue, asked those who had small children with them if they could share a bed with their little ones, and planted a sign in the middle of the queue, calling out that the place was full.

'Je suis désolé.'

The queue behind the sign broke up and the women faded away into the evening, some of them rushing as if they knew of some other place where they might have a chance of a roof over their heads, and others sauntering away, in no hurry. Bisi sat down on a bench. She had no idea of where she could go. At the hotel she had been told that as her credit card had been cancelled, there was no possibility of booking a longer stay; this refuge was full; and she couldn't bring herself to go to the Porte de la Chapelle shanty town among all those men and junkies.

A man sat down next to her on the bench. He had a newspaper that he opened and read for a while. Finally he looked over the top of it at her.

'Are you from Ghana?' he asked.

Bisi shook her head.

'From Nigeria,' she replied.

The man gave her a pleasant smile.

'Ah! We are neighbours. I'm from Côte d'Ivoire.'

Bisi could have guessed that from his accent, the *Nouchi*-French lilt in the man's speech. They shook hands.

'Bisi,' she said courteously.

'Moussa,' he replied amicably.

That was something that not every man would do, introducing himself by his first name, as she had done. In Nigeria she found that many men hung on tight to their titles, wanting to be addressed as Mr this or that, but this one was friendly. All the same, it was a stretch to say that they were neighbours, but being so far from their own homelands and in this foreign environment meant that they were practically relatives.

'I almost thought you were from Congo,' she joked. 'It's the suit, you know...'

The man pretended to be offended, and laughed.

'Do I look like I pull my trousers up to my chest?'

Bisi laughed. It was a West African custom to make fun of the way Congolese people dressed, although Bisi had to admit to herself that she would have nothing against dressing like a Congolese *sapeuse*. The way those magnificent women dressed presented a clear challenge to the patriarchy and showed that those who followed the *Le Sape* tradition of dress and manners were competent women who set their own rules for how they lived their lives. That was exactly what she had always dreamed of. That was what she had already started working towards.

'Were you hoping to stay there?' the man asked, jerking his head in the direction of the refuge. Bisi nodded. She was downcast and felt ashamed of herself in front of this dapper man. Here she sat, well turned out and with two suitcases packed with all kinds of goods, and unable to afford a night in a hotel.

'There has been a quarrel with my family,' she said. 'My father cancelled my credit card. I can't afford a hotel.'

She didn't mention that her flight home had departed that afternoon, that she didn't dare return home.

'Well, now,' the man said, 'that's a terrible thing to hear. And what are you going to do?'

'I don't know,' Bisi said in a small voice. 'To be honest, I have no idea.'

The man looked at her thoughtfully before speaking.

'I know a lady who lives alone in a huge house, and she always has guests,' he said. 'Shall I call her and ask if you could stay with her?'

Bisi's common sense screamed no, howled at her to get away. This was off the scale of any usual helpfulness. They hadn't been talking for more than five minutes before he had made this offer. But going completely against her own instincts, Bisi longed to believe that this was simply help from an honest man who hated to see a sister from Africa in difficulties.

'I have no money,' Bisi said. 'I spent the last few coins I had to get the Metro here.'

The man nodded.

'Don't you have something that you could give her as a token of thanks?' he asked, gesturing to her cases.

Bisi felt immediate relief. If this were an African woman, Bisi would simply open the cases and invite her to make her own choice of something that would equate to her hospitality, or maybe even something more. Then they would both be satisfied and Bisi would know that she had paid her way and would owe nothing more. This sounded like an honest enough proposal.

'Yes,' she said. 'I have some beautiful things that I could give the lady to thank her if she could give me shelter for two or three nights.'

The man nodded, took out his phone and made a call. She heard him explain that he had found a woman in difficulties, practically a neighbour, who seemed to be a delightful person, and he was wondering if she could stay. Then he said 'yes' a couple of times, and ended the call.

'She'll let you stay,' he said. 'But she wants to meet you before she can promise more than one night. 'Understandably.'

'Yes, of course.'

This sounded like a perfectly cautious attitude, and her own common sense finally gave way to hope. As Bisi followed the man, who was gentlemanly enough to take one of her cases and gestured for her to go ahead of him onto a bus, she decided to believe that this was a good plan. In reality, she was out of choices. What other option did she have? To sleep on the street in this huge city? In the cold? She was already shivering even though the sun had barely set, and on the bus she sat with her legs against the warm heater. The man sat at her side, and she wondered whether she should thank him now or later, when she had arrived at the house of the woman who would give her shelter.

33

Daníel could still sense the fragrance of Áróra about him. They had hugged before going their separate ways. He had taken a long breath, pulling in deep the smell of her hair – an aroma of grass and spring – and for a moment he felt a wave of sadness, a longing for sunshine and warmth. But these delicate sentiments had to give way to his concerns for the children. They were supposed to take care of themselves up to midday, when their grandmother, his former mother-in-law, would collect them. He knew they would be fine, that they were mature enough to look after themselves, and seemed to require nothing but cereal and television to get through the earlier part of each day. Of course, Lady was at home, if anything were to come up, but all the same, Daníel felt uneasy. It had been his intention to spend plenty of time with them during this visit, but as so often, work took over, pushing its way to the top of his list of priorities. Now he was in the forensics team's building, staring at the container, which stood in the middle of the open floor. This wretched container.

Jean-Christophe was standing in front of the container, and Daníel apologised as he realised that they had been waiting for him, that everyone stood in a semi-circle like well-behaved schoolchildren. The commissioner and Chief Superintendent Gylfi from CID were there, as were Baldvin, Gutti, Kristján, Oddsteinn from the prosecutor's office and Ari Benz from the national commissioner's international department. Jean-Christophe cleared his throat and began.

'We're recording this,' he said, pointing at a camera. 'You can watch the recording later if there's anything you need to check on.'

Those present nodded their heads, and he began his presentation by pointing out the markings on the door of the container.

'Every shipping container has an international registration number, which identifies the container's owner, even when there are no logos or anything else visible, as is the case with this container. First there is a series of letters that refer to the container's owner, then numbers that are this container's unique identifier, and finally there is a check digit, which is this number in a box. This is used to check whether or not the identification number is genuine, just the same as the check digit in everyone's personal ID number. No container gets to be loaded onto a ship or pass through customs unless it has a valid identification number and the check digit is correct. We traced this container's number to a container rental company in France. Ari Benz at the international department has some information about the company that rented out this container.'

'It looks to be a brass-plate company,' Ari Benz added.

'So we won't get far there,' Gylfi said.

'True. Unless the French police find those who are registered as the company's owners. I'm not optimistic they will though.'

Ari Benz sucked his teeth, an expression of disappointment on his face.

'Well, then,' Jean-Christophe said. 'The customs declaration, which was completed by the shipping company at the request of the importer, InExport, states that the contents were clothing. This is accompanied by an invoice from the same front company that rented out the container. I understand we're checking whether InExport has imported goods in this way before.'

He opened the container and the hinges squealed, until the flat door banged against the side.

'What gives us more leads than anything else is the contents of the container,' he said as everyone moved closer to look inside.

Daníel hesitated though, standing at the back of the group.

He felt the smell of death coming to meet him, and in his mind he could see the bodies of those women lying motionless at the far end of the container, even though he knew that they had been removed. It felt like death was close by, looming over the container like a vulture, and Daníel again felt the rush in his ears and the flicker of lights at the back of his mind, alerting him to the desperation that had so recently filled every cubic centimetre of this steel box.

'The first thing we see are these cardboard boxes, which have been stuck to the floor. They also have glue on their top sides, so our conclusion is that these boxes were intended to form a false front, so if the container were opened, all that would be visible would be a wall of boxes. I assume that the women in the container tore down this wall at some point as a number of flattened boxes were placed under their mattresses and some had also been placed around the walls. I imagine they were trying to use the boxes as insulation against the cold. Next we can see the facilities that had been provided for the women inside the container. There are four single mattresses, four blankets and one duvet, which suggests, perhaps, that initially there were supposed to be four women, and the duvet was added when it was apparent that there would be an additional passenger. There's a travel toilet, of the kind used in caravans, which has been fixed to the wall with bungee cords hooked into lugs. This has been fairly well thought out, but it clearly wasn't good enough, as, either due to the ship's motion or for other reasons, the toilet leaked, which could be why the women tore down the boxes, so they could use them to protect the mattresses. There's also a stack of empty water bottles, empty Coke cans, plastic wrappers from these drinks and boxes that contained chocolate and biscuits. All of these foodstuffs originate in France. It's obvious that all the food and water were consumed on the journey and that the amount needed had been seriously underestimated. There was also heavy weather last week, so all shipping was delayed, presumably making this trip longer than had been expected. On top of that, people need more calories in cold conditions, as the body needs more energy to stay warm.'

Those present went one by one into the container, looking around as the forensics specialist continued his lecture. Then it was Daníel's turn. He took a deep breath before stepping inside, exhaling slowly in the hope that this single lungful would be enough to last, so that he wouldn't have to breathe the air inside. But he had no choice and had to take a breath. He felt that he was breathing in the bottomless misery of those who had been so unfortunate as to find themselves in this dark place. It made no difference whether the women had gone willingly into the container or not; there was no doubt that the journey had been more dreadful than anyone could imagine. Daníel got out quickly. He could check the forensics department's photographs in more detail later. He couldn't stay inside a moment longer.

A number of items had been lined up on a long table on the far side of the room. Jean-Christophe stood behind it, explaining the nature of these items as if he were a chef presenting a buffet in a restaurant. He pointed to some phones.

'There were five cheap phones in the container. All the same make, all with unregistered SIM cards. There were chargers in the women's luggage, but of course there was no power in the container so all the phones have flat batteries. When we switched them on, we found that each one had the same number in its list of contacts, also unregistered, and it had been called repeatedly from every one of these phones. The phone logs are part of the record on the LÖKE system, so you can see that the final calls were made roughly four days before the container was discovered.'

Jean-Christophe moved over to the next set of belongings on the table.

'Suitcases. This is the first of six. All of the cases but one contain cosmetics, so it can be assumed that the women had brought their luggage, expecting to travel. Four have modest cases with clothes, shoes and some personal items, but the largest two cases are stuffed with all kinds of luxury goods. We're talking about expensive watches, high-quality clothing, a couple of pairs of trainers – all designer stuff – and loads of jewellery, perfume and cosmetics. Whoever brought this luggage isn't short of money. But she certainly wasn't prepared for the journey that was ahead of her.'

34

Elín's urge to paint was so powerful that she had already begun sketching on the canvases she had primed the day before, even though they weren't dry. Sergei had put his head around the door the previous evening and muttered that he was going out and would be back late as he needed to help his friend with something. Elín was so absorbed in her work she didn't need to pretend – she barely looked up as he left, and continued to lay out a picture of a woman crouching by a closed door.

Sometime in the middle of the night she had emerged from her creative mode and went to bed, where she slept so deeply that she didn't notice when Sergei came home. But he was there at her side in the morning, and she curled up against his back, her cheek against his hot skin, and closed her eyes again. She didn't manage to get back to sleep, though, and slipped out of bed and down to the studio, picking her phone from the shelf on the way.

She understood nothing of what Sergei said in the recording on her phone. It sounded to her like the usual sounds: *tsja-tsja, sne-sne*. He had clearly made several calls, and at one point the phone rang and Sergei answered. During the first call his voice was calm and he spoke slowly; in the next one he snapped and yelled. Then there was a call during which his voice was gentle and plaintive, before he yelped something and then burst into tears. It pained Elín to hear him weep, and she wanted to go straight upstairs to comfort him, but her heart went suddenly cold when she heard him say, 'Come on, baby. Sofia, baby. Please.' Then the chatter continued in Russian in what sounded like a confidential tone. It wasn't as if she knew what a confidential tone of voice would sound like in Russian, but his frantic, persuasive voice sounded like that to her.

Who on earth was this Sofia? And if this was some Russian word that she had mistaken for a name, why had he responded as he had the day before yesterday when she asked if his mother's name was Sofia? If she had got it wrong, then shouldn't he have laughed and made fun of her? That was what he usually did when she tried to understand or say something in Russian. But that day he had become angry, as if she had touched a nerve. The same thoughts went round and round in Elín's head, as if they were mounted on a roundabout that rolled them through her mind in the same order, again and again, stacking up more and more questions, without her being able to jump off and consider them from a distance.

Why had Sergei said he was speaking to his mother when he had clearly been talking to someone called Sofia? And if it had been an innocent conversation with this Sofia, why not just be open and say so? Could Sergei be in a relationship with another woman as well as with Elín? Did that mean he didn't love Elín? So why did he want to marry her? And why did he keep telling her it was because he needed a residence permit, when that was clearly untrue? Could it be that he was so deeply in love with her – as smitten with her as she was with him – that he wanted to tie her down and was using the residence permit as a pretext for that? Could he be so uncertain of her? And if he loved Elín and wanted to marry her for that reason, who was this Sofia he spoke to on the phone in such a sweet voice?

Elín switched off the recording, but her thoughts continued to spin in circles. The same questions circling around again and again. Circle after circle.

35

The status meeting was unusually short, with Baldvin barking out the key items of information as the group stood and listened. Most of them had cups of coffee or energy drinks in their hands, and they all looked determined to get started on the long day ahead.

'We're still waiting for a conclusion from the forensic pathologist concerning the cause of death of these women,' he said. 'Although we can assume that the way the container was fitted out was in some way the cause.' He looked down at a sheet of paper in his hands. 'Lárentínus Ásgeirsson, the truck driver who collected the container, is remanded in custody for the next four days. He's being co-operative and is willing to tell everything he knows. It seems that he has on two previous occasions delivered similar containers to the same man at the same location, so we can assume that smuggling people to Iceland in containers is not a new venture. The man who booked Lárentínus to fetch the container is called Valur, and according to Lárentínus he works for a company called InExport. That's being checked out right now, and we're also looking into who this Valur actually is. The woman who survived is out of intensive care and is now on a regular ward, where her condition, according to the clinical staff, is good. Helena, you've spoken to her, haven't you?'

Helena cleared her throat and turned to face the group.

'Yes,' she said. 'The woman says her name is Bisi Babalola and that she's a French citizen, but Ari Benz and the international department haven't found anyone of that name in the French records who fits our woman. It might be that she's lying about her nationality, and there could be all sorts of reasons for that. Our suspicion is that she is of Nigerian origin, going by a straightforward Google search which indicates that both the first and family names are fairly common in Nigeria.'

'Has she said anything?' Baldvin asked.

'Not a lot,' Helena replied. 'She says she's ready to help us to find the criminals, but she appears frightened and seems to think that she's in danger from them. So providing her with a feeling of security must be a priority, so that we can get her to talk.'

'Fine,' Baldvin said. 'You and Daníel can see to that.'

Helena nodded. The authoritarian tone that Baldvin adopted whenever he was in a managing role got on her nerves. There was no need to remind everyone that she and Daníel were looking after Bisi. They'd all heard that yesterday. Now Baldvin's chest swelled even further, and a serious expression crossed his face as he held up the sheet of paper.

'We have a court order,' he said. 'This licenses us to search the Auðbrekka address where the container was supposed to have been delivered. We're off in about ten minutes. The Special Unit is going in first. They've been watching the address overnight but haven't seen any activity.'

36

Daníel waited in the car not far from the workshop on Auð-brekka where Lárentínus had delivered the container, watching the Special Unit do their work. They were quick, arriving with tyres squealing, jumping out of their van, black-clad men in bala-clavas, carrying guns and storming through the entrance. A little while later a voice over the comms system announced that the building was deserted and CID could come inside.

Daníel went into the yard and looked around. This was the perfect place to carry out your business if you needed to keep it discreet – the gate was completely out of sight, blocked in by the concrete walls of the neighbouring buildings, and there were no windows anywhere overlooking it. You could do anything here, and nobody would notice a thing; even unload trafficked people from a container. A large pair of garage doors opened onto the unit, as did a normal door, which now stood open. Jean-Christophe stood beside it, handing out gloves and shoe covers to the CID officers.

'Only look,' he said. 'Touch nothing.'

Daníel nodded, took some gloves and shoe covers, and put them on just inside the doorway. He went along a corridor that seemed to lie along the side of the L-shaped unit, leading to a large space that looked to have been fitted out as a car workshop. Baldvin stood in the centre of the open space, making notes on a clipboard.

'It doesn't look like there are any signs of activity,' he said as he glanced around and added to his notes. 'No car lift, no tools, no tool cabinets. There isn't even a slick of oil on the floor.'

The only daylight came from a row of narrow windows just below the roof. These all had panes that could be opened and had clearly been intended to let in air and a little light, without taking up valuable wall space that would be needed for shelves and cabinets. The place had obviously been designed to be a car workshop, but there was no doubt that it had been years since it had been last used as such.

'You need to come and see this,' Helena said from a doorway that had to lead to the office end of the unit. As he hurried over, Daníel wondered how she had been so quick to get inside. She must have sneaked in behind the Special Unit. He was pleased to see that she was keen. This was the drive that sometimes took hold of her when she was on a tough case, pushing her to work without a break until everything had been followed to its end or until they hit a wall and had no choice but to give up. That happened more often than people imagined, and along with it there always came a deep feeling of disappointment, especially when they could see exactly how the land lay but didn't have the evidence to back it up. That would often make it a real struggle to muster enthusiasm for the next case and remain convinced that they could crack it.

Helena stopped by a doorway that appeared to lead to a canteen of some sort. Steel rings were bolted to the door and the wall next to it, and an open padlock hung in one of them. The door itself and its frame were of heavy timber – unnecessarily solid and bulky for the canteen of a garage, where a lightweight door would have served. The canteen, unlike the workshop, showed clear signs of activity.

'Someone's been living here,' Helena said. 'And recently. There are plates and crockery, food in the cupboards and the fridge. The sell-by date on the milk is last week. The vegetables have hardly started to wilt.'

Daníel allowed himself only a cursory look at the space, as he knew that Baldvin was already making detailed notes for the report. There was a microwave, a tabletop stove with two rings, saucepans, spoons, bowls, a sieve hanging on the wall, ladles, chopping boards and ... He hesitated. Where were the knives? Everything needed to prepare food was here, except knives. And knives were the most essential tool besides pots and pans. He cautiously opened two drawers and looked inside without moving anything. The drawers contained nothing more than cutlery and some plastic pots.

'Make a note that there are no knives in the kitchen. No sharp knives, I mean,' he said to Baldvin, who nodded and wrote on his clipboard. 'That padlock and the lack of knives would indicate that people have been kept here against their will. They might have been loaned a knife just to prepare food and then had it taken off them.'

'That's not the only indicator,' Helena said from the far end of the canteen, where a door opened onto a gloomy passage. At the end a small bathroom could be seen, and there were three doors lining the long wall. Helena pushed the first one open, and Daníel shuddered. The room resembled a cell – tiny, dark and windowless. There was a pair of Ikea bunks, each with a mattress, pillow and a blanket, and nothing more. The upper bunk was neat, the pillow smoothed and the blanket folded. The other was a mess, as if someone had just got out of it. The blanket was creased and the pillow showed the round imprint of a head. Daníel backed out of the room, and Helena shut the door, pointing out a thick locking bar on the outside, made from heavy timber.

The other rooms were furnished in exactly the same way, both with locking bars on the doors, installed to hold the people inside prisoner. In one room there were clothes on the floor – a grey hoodie and socks.

'This was what was waiting for our girls in the container,' Daníel said, unsure whether the emotions churning inside him were sorrow or anger.

They stood for a moment and stared at each other; he, Helena and Baldvin.

Baldvin sighed. 'Well, then,' he said. That was an instruction to put on a brave face and get stuck in.

'What's next?' Helena asked.

Baldvin flipped through the papers on his clipboard.

'I want you to work on the girl and create a situation for her that will encourage her to talk. I'm going to meet the owners of this place: the representative of a company called Kuzee ehf.'

Daníel felt the hairs rise on the back of his neck.

'Did you say Kuzee? With a Z? Is the representative a Russian guy called Leonid something or other... ?'

37

Áróra's heart skipped a beat when she saw Daníel's name on the screen of her phone.

'*Hæ*,' she said cheerfully. 'Good to see you this morning, and your son.'

Daníel's thoughts seemed to be elsewhere.

'Sorry?' he said, but then cottoned on. 'Yes, of course. Likewise.'

Áróra felt a pang of disappointment. He clearly wasn't calling to say thanks for dropping by, to put their relationship on a stronger footing or to chat about nothing in particular. He had come across as so sincere and uncomfortable that morning, when he had mentioned that 'theoretically' they could be in a relationship despite his involvement in the investigation into her sister's disappearance. But now his mind appeared to be on something else.

'I need to ask you a few questions,' he said.

Áróra's first thought was that this must be related to Elín and their conversation that morning, so what Daníel said next took her by surprise.

'I need to ask you about the Flosi case.'

'OK,' Áróra replied. The Flosi case was still fresh in her memory: the wife who vanished, the bizarre business practices at the garden hardware company and Flosi's complex personal life.

'I recall that a company called Kuzee ehf, spelled with a Z, came up in connection with that case,' Daníel said. 'Am I correct?'

'Yes,' Áróra replied. 'Kuzee is a property rental company owned by a man called Leonid Kuznetsov. The company owns property all over the city and rents it out at outrageous prices. By which I mean rentals that are way above the market rate. In my view, if someone were interested enough to look through Leonid's accounts, it's more than likely they would discover that Kuzee ehf is a money-laundering operation for the proceeds of organised crime.'

'Ah. OK, thanks,' Daníel said, and it took Áróra a moment to realise that he had hung up.

She felt her heart sink. Had he interpreted her words as being directed at him personally? She and Daníel had worked on the Flosi case together, and during that time she had tried to interest the authorities in Kuzee ehf's director, Leonid Kuznetsov, but without success. That hadn't been Daníel's fault, though, and she hoped now he wouldn't think that she felt it was.

She thought it over from every angle as she cracked a couple of eggs into the blender, added porridge oats, banana and cocoa, and filled it up with milk. Her father had always had a strong belief in eggs as being good for the health, especially when raw. Now sports-energy thinking had gone in new directions, and protein powder had largely taken the place of raw eggs; but she stuck with them for her father's sake. Every time she did something he had taught her, she almost felt that he was standing behind her, nodding his approval, and after moving back to Iceland, this feeling came to her more frequently. Her father would have been happy to know that she was living in Iceland and keeping up her training.

She went into the living room, sat down and drank straight from the blender jug, wondering why Daníel had an interest in Kuzee. This had to be connected to some case he was working on. He had called simply to confirm that his memory had been correct – that this company had been connected to the Flosi case – not to listen to an angry diatribe about the police's failure to investigate properly at the time. What had she been thinking?

It was so strange how she always felt she came across as a fool in her dealings with Daníel.

Her phone pinged, and she saw, with relief, that it was a message from the man himself.

Sorry. Mega-busy. Do you have any docs relating to Kuzee ehf? It's quicker to go to you than the tax office. Haha.

There was a smiley face at the end of the message, and she smirked at the sight of it. He wasn't sulking. He was just busy. She tapped in a reply.

Shall we do a deal? I'll give you the info on Kuzee if you can get the international dept to check on Sergei Popov?

There was a long wait, and Áróra had practically emptied the blender jug when her phone pinged a second time.

We have a deal! Daníel's message read.

38

Bisi wept tears of relief once she was in the neatly made bed in a little room at the home of this good woman on the outskirts of Paris. The woman had offered her bread, cheese and red wine, and told Bisi that she was welcome to stay for a few nights while she got her affairs in order. The house was old and shabby, with paint peeling from the walls and the yard at the back swamped with weeds, but there were beautiful paintings on the walls, and the woman herself was tastefully dressed and very amicable. She had told Bisi to call her Fifi, as that was what her friends called her. Bisi was touched at how open she was – inviting a stranger into her home, especially an African person about whom she knew nothing.

She left Bisi to her own devices, letting her roam the house, saying that she needed to work. Walking around, Bisi glanced in through her door, and saw a room that looked like some kind of library, where the woman was hunched over a computer, absorbed in her work.

It had been a long time since she had last allowed herself to shed tears. This wasn't her style at all. She was a strong person. A strong personality, Habiba always said: when some difficulty came up, she didn't give way, but stood her ground and forced herself to be tough. But now that her troubles seemed to be behind her, at least temporarily, the fear and desperation returned, and she whimpered into the soft pillow.

The linen was clean and smelled as if it had been dried in the sun, and as Bisi closed her eyes, she felt that she was at home in her apartment in Lagos, which she had worked since her teens to be able to own, and of which she was deeply proud. It was a symbol of her independence, of her self-determination. She allowed herself to slip into a daydream about the past.

Most people dreamed of a better future, but at this moment her mind looked back – to how happy she had been, and how free. Now this past was burned to ashes. She had called a neighbour, who confirmed that there was nothing left of her belongings and that the apartment was caked in soot and scorched throughout. It had been pure luck that the fire hadn't spread to other apartments. Then the neighbour had whispered that it wasn't safe for Bisi to return. Many people in the district are angry, she had said. People spat on the door as they passed by.

But after the tension of the last few days, she felt some respite. The red wine and this house – where she could stay in safety for a few days while she tried to find a solution to her problems – meant that she could relax. She felt fatigue envelop her in a way that could not be resisted. And she didn't need to fight this exhaustion. She was safe to rest.

39

Helena had browsed Krónan's cosmetics shelves, dropping into a basket items that she imagined a person with no belongings at all would need in hospital. She had picked up a toothbrush, toothpaste, a pack of disposable razors, but had found herself in difficulties when it came to choosing a hairbrush or a comb. She had no idea what was required for Afro hair. She decided eventually on the comb, and Bisi was pleased when Helena took it out of the bag.

'I can use the wide end,' she said, laughing at Helena's awkwardness. She reached for the comb and picked it up cautiously. The bandages had gone, apart from smaller and neater dressings on a couple of the fingers of her left hand. Helena thought that otherwise her hands seemed remarkably healthy, but she had only the haziest idea of what frostbitten fingers looked like. She knew about as much as she knew about how to handle curly hair.

'I've never had to deal with hair like this before,' she said.

Bisi looked at her thoughtfully for a moment, and Helena realised that her own cropped hair might look odd to Bisi.

'There aren't many black people in Iceland?'

'Not all that many,' Helena said. 'And I'm not close enough to anyone who knows how to look after this kind of hair.'

'The old lady over there looks at me as if I come from another planet.'

Helena glanced at the woman, who lay, apparently half asleep, in her bed by the window.

'She was put in a room with you because she speaks no English and gets no visitors, so there's no likelihood that information about you being here will get out. We still don't know how wide a network these criminals have here,' Helena said.

'And the office people? Isn't there a danger that information could make its way from them to the criminals?'

'Not at all,' Helena said encouragingly. 'Health service staff are bound by confidentiality in every aspect of their work.'

Bisi shook her head impatiently.

'No, I don't mean the hospital staff. I mean the people who came to speak to me earlier, from the Directorate of Immigration.'

Helena felt a cold sweat break out on her back, and she quickly got to her feet, excused herself and left the room.

A young woman sat in the glass-walled office on the far side of the corridor, and Helena marched over there with her warrant card held high.

'Could someone from Immigration have come to visit Bisi today?' she asked.

'To visit who?' the woman asked. 'I've just started my shift.'

'The unnamed foreign national directly opposite.'

Helena heard the sharpness in her own voice, and squeezed out a smile, holding back the urge to yell at the woman to be quick as she peered at the computer, her fingers punching at the keyboard as she called up Bisi's file.

'Yes, someone from there came to speak to her earlier today. It says here that she'll be discharged later to accommodation provided by Immigration,' the woman said with a questioning tone to her voice.

'She's here under the authority of city CID,' Helena snapped. 'And you were given precise instructions not to release any information about her!'

The woman tapped again at the keyboard, leaning closer to the screen as if peering at the small print.

'It says here that the police stated this morning that this woman is under the Directorate of Immigration's authority,' she said in confusion.

Helena longed to bang her head against a wall. This was her own fault. How could she have been so stupid?

'I said that Immigration should be sent the bill, not that she was under Immigration's authority!' she told the woman.

She folded her arms across her chest, leaned back in her chair and glared truculently at Helena.

'From our point of view, that's the same thing,' she said.

Helena had expected it to take days for an invoice to make its way through the system, and even more days for the Directorate of Immigration to work out who Bisi was, by which time the case would be resolved and things would be clearer. But there was no point shouting at hospital staff for her own miscalculation. Now she would have to work fast.

'She's discharged now,' she said. 'She's coming with me.'

'You have to wait for a doctor to discharge her,' the woman said. 'She might need medication or something else.'

Helena forced another smile.

'In that case would you be so good as to call that doctor right away, because we're leaving.'

Without waiting to hear any protest, she turned and marched across to Bisi's room.

'We're leaving right away, Bisi,' she said. 'The Directorate of Immigration wants to put you in a hostel for asylum seekers, which is the first place any criminals would look when it gets out that you're alive. So I'm taking you somewhere else. To a safe place.'

40

'You'll have to decide what part you're playing in this investigation,' Baldvin said ponderously as they drove to Leonid Kuznetsov's home, which was also where Kuzee ehf was registered. 'You can't just jump in and out, doing the stuff you like the look of.'

Baldvin always took his management role seriously, and Daníel knew that he got on the nerves of many CID officers when he started chivvying them around like an anxious parent whenever he was in a position of authority. But it didn't worry Daníel in the least. He had run enough investigations to know that it was an unenviable role.

'I know,' Daníel said. 'Sorry. There's something about this case that's pushing every button I have.'

'First you didn't want to lead the investigation, and then you wanted to be the main contact for the victim, but you dumped that on Helena. And now you want to follow up the accommodation angle.'

This wasn't actually correct. Daníel had never asked to be the lead contact with the victim. He had been allocated that role as he had been the one who found her in the container. His heart missed a beat.

'Hey,' he said. 'I need to make a call to check on the children.'

He found his former mother-in-law's number and hesitated for a moment. Just the sight of her name on the screen was a jolt of discomfort. He bit the bullet and made the call.

'Is there any chance you could have them until after dinner?' he asked after they had exchanged dry-as-dust greetings. That morning he had managed to avoid meeting her, as she had collected the children after he had left for work. This was an advantage of them growing up: they could be left to their own devices for a while, which spared him much of the awkwardness of dealing with his former wife's family, who seemed to have adopted a cold attitude towards him ever since the divorce.

'Of course they can stay with me,' she said. 'I want to make the most of every one of the few moments I have with them.'

This was a jab at him. He knew that, but instead of going on the defensive and snapping back at the woman, he thanked her courteously.

Baldvin had overheard the conversation, and shook his head.

'If there's one thing that's worse than mothers-in-law,' he said, 'it's former mothers-in-law.'

They'd reached their destination in the lower end of the Leirvogstunga district. They got out of the car and walked over to the house. It looked to be almost fully built, but the cladding wasn't finished so that half of the house was concrete grey with the rusty ends of reinforcing rods sticking out of the walls at regular intervals.

'There must be a lovely view from his living room,' Daníel said, looking up at the floor-to-ceiling windows on the main level, facing the sea.

'I wouldn't want to have to wash those,' Baldvin said. 'They must get covered with salt every time the wind blows.'

Daníel hid a smile. Baldvin could see a problem in anything. Daníel followed him up the steps, and Baldvin hammered on the brand-new front door.

It wasn't long before the door opened and Leonid Kuznetsov looked them up and down as they held up their warrant cards. He was of average height, with black hair and the shadow of a beard that he had done his best to shave close to the skin. He wore a snug beige roll-neck tucked neatly into the trousers of a black suit, held up with an expensive, patterned leather belt. He was barefoot, so the impression was that they had caught him either dressing or undressing.

Daníel had expected some kind of resistance or at least a defensive attitude, but instead the man courteously invited them in. They were about to slip off their shoes in the hall when he stopped them.

'No. No, please. Keep your shoes on. It's enough to wipe them on the mat. I've never appreciated this Icelandic affectation of taking off your shoes when you go into any house. You dress up for a party and wear beautiful shoes, but end up walking around in your socks like an idiot. Never liked it.'

Daníel and Baldvin carefully wiped their shoes on the mat and followed Leonid into the living room. Daníel had been right. There was a beautiful view over Leirvogur, and in the distance the city glittered like a pearl necklace as the street lights came on in the afternoon gloom.

'Can I offer you coffee?' Leonid asked, gesturing to a large machine that occupied part of the kitchen worktop at the end of the open living space.

'No, thank you,' Baldvin said.

'Tea?' Leonid offered, and Baldvin shook his head.

'Champagne?' Leonid suggested with a mischievous smile, which vanished as Baldvin again declined.

'No, thanks. We're on duty.'

This third refusal appeared to dash any hope Leonid had that this was some kind of courtesy call, and he turned serious, his face expressionless as he asked in clear English what had brought them.

'Your building on Auðbrekka,' Baldvin said.

Leonid assumed a look of surprise, but it was so artificial it was clearly a pretence.

'Auðbrekka, hmm. You said Auðbrekka?' he muttered. 'I recall that I have a property on Auðbrekka, yes. Yes, of course. I know the building you mean. The garage.'

'Exactly,' Baldvin said. 'What activity takes place there?'

'It's a car-repair place, as far as I'm aware.'

'So you don't know what goes on in the building?' Daníel asked, adding an edge to his voice.

This clearly irritated Leonid, who forced a stiff smile.

'No. I have property here and there in the city that I rent out, and I'm not able to keep tabs on how each tenant makes use of those places. In any case, it's none of my business.'

'Who rents the place on Auðbrekka?' Baldvin asked, his tone dry but still courteous.

'Ah, I don't know offhand,' Leonid said. 'As far as I recall it's a contractor of some sort.'

Daníel gave a loud, impatient sigh. Leonid glanced at him with narrowed eyes, but Daníel said nothing. He continued to gaze at Leonid with an expression that he hoped conveyed some kind of weary derision. It seemed to have the desired effect. Leonid looked offended, although he tried to maintain his composure.

'We're looking for information on the tenant at the Auð-brekka property,' Baldvin said gently.

'I'll email it to you at the earliest opportunity,' Leonid replied.

'We need it right now,' Baldvin said, and Daníel gave a slight shake of his head, as if to demonstrate that as far as he was concerned, Leonid was just one more small-time crook bending the law.

'Right now, as in, immediately?' Leonid asked, and Daníel thought he could see the veins in the man's forehead pulsing. He gave him a thin smile, which appeared to irritate Leonid even further, as while his face was expressionless, his eyes flashed.

As Daníel and Baldvin walked out to the car, having squeezed out of Leonid the information about the company renting the Auðbrekka unit and the person it was registered to, Daníel had the feeling that Leonid was watching them from the window.

He resisted the temptation to turn and see if this was the case until they were in the car. Then he leaned forward, looked up at the large living-room window, and found that he was right. Leonid stood with his arms folded over his chest, glaring down at them.

'This guy is as crooked as hell,' Daníel said, and Baldvin hummed something, as he was already doing two things at once: starting the car and calling the station.

'We have a name for the tenant on Auðbrekka,' he said when someone picked up. 'The company is called InExport ehf and the director is Valur Jón Pálsson. That tallies with what Lárentínus the truck driver stated.'

41

Bisi was welcomed warmly by the woman who ran the refuge, with a promise to help her every day with the dressings on her fingers while the frostbite blisters healed, so Helena left her with a lighter heart than before. Bisi had asked about her luggage, and Helena told her to describe it so they could work out which of the cases in the container belonged to her. When Bisi said that two large suitcases were hers, Helena realised that she meant the last two cases on the video forensics had made of the container, which she had watched that morning.

'Can I ask why you had so many expensive items in your cases?' Helena asked. 'Watches and perfume and that kind of thing?'

'You opened my cases?' Bisi replied, stepping back in offence – almost a physical response to the question. 'If you think I'm a thief, then you're wrong.'

Helena put her hands up, palms out. 'No, not at all,' she said quickly. 'Nothing like that. We're trying to figure out what led up to all this, unpick all the threads to understand how you and the other girls ended up in a shipping container here in Iceland.'

Bisi stared at her for a moment.

'I want my cases,' she said. 'All I have left is what is in those cases.'

Helena nodded encouragingly. 'You can have your luggage back as soon as forensics have finished checking them. Maybe tomorrow. I'll find out for you.'

'OK,' Bisi said, and took a couple of deep breaths, as if making a conscious effort to calm herself down. 'I always have a summer holiday in Europe,' she went on. 'London or Paris or Barcelona. Most often Paris. It's my reward to myself for working hard the whole year.'

Helena nodded. 'That's what most people do,' she said. 'They look forward to taking a break in the summer.'

Bisi gave her a faint smile. 'I love to go to the theatre and concerts and galleries. I always book a ticket for some cultural event before I travel, something that's different to what we have in Nigeria.'

'You're from Nigeria?' Helena asked, and immediately regretted it, as Bisi again stepped back and glared at her angrily.

'Yes! You can see from my skin and my name that I have African origins, but that doesn't mean I don't have French nationality!'

'And do you have a French passport?' Helena asked quietly, hoping to quell the turmoil that appeared to come to the surface for the slightest reason.

'Yes,' Bisi said, and looked away. Most likely because she was lying, Helena thought. 'But it's lost. The people who put me in the container took it.'

Helena nodded. That could well be the case, although Bisi's body language indicated she was not telling the truth. If she genuinely had possessed a French passport, it was more likely that the criminals would have drugged her and put her on a flight, as they had done so many times before, as within the Schengen area checks at airports and immigration were minimal. But that wasn't important now.

'Tell me about your holidays in Europe,' Helena said, and smiled amicably. Building trust was vital here; trust strong enough for Bisi to tell her story and explain the series of events that had led to her being put in a container that ended up in Iceland.

'I always take a shopping list for the whole family, and for friends and acquaintances who know I'm travelling to Europe. There's so much we don't have in Nigeria, so people always take the opportunity to get quality perfumes and things that are difficult to find.'

Helena nodded. 'And people give you money to buy these things for them?'

Bisi looked at her in astonishment. 'You obviously don't know many African people.'

Helena laughed. 'That's true.'

'People think that anyone who can afford to travel to Europe can afford to bring back decent gifts. So all year I save up for the gifts as well, and they often cost more than the trip itself. But it's a status symbol. You know, it gives you all kinds of points on the social scale. Both for me and my parents. My mother loves to have a party when I come home and I hand out presents from my suitcases.'

'And do they pay for some of this? Your parents? Do they give you money to travel?'

Helena couldn't imagine bringing back anything for her own mother after a trip abroad, although she would have been happy to pay up for the occasional box of chocolates or bottle of wine, if she were in any kind of contact with her mother.

'Sometimes a little, but generally not,' Bisi said. 'I don't know how it is here, but in Nigeria we owe a debt to our parents. People who do well for themselves honour their parents by giving them things. My parents made a lot of sacrifices so I could go to college to learn to repair computers, so most of my salary is paid into my father's account, and he puts money by and gives me a reasonable allowance to live on.'

'You must be well paid,' Helena said. 'If you can afford to support your parents, travel and buy expensive gifts.'

Bisi laughed bitterly. 'That's all in the past,' she said. 'I have neither work nor a home in Nigeria any longer. My father stopped my credit card. He could do it, because it was linked to his own account. I'd used up everything I had buying goods for the family, as I have done every year. Except now my family does not want me back.'

'What happened?' Helena asked cautiously.

But it was clear that the conversation was over. Bisi stood up from the sofa in the women's refuge's interview room and went to the door.

'Can the police get me a new French passport to replace the one that was lost?'

42

This place genuinely seemed to be a refuge for women fleeing violence. There were leaflets in various languages in a rack, and the lady who worked here had gone through the house rules with her, which seemed to Bisi to focus on keeping the place clean and being friendly to the other women. Did these house rules and leaflets indicate that the refuge was legitimate? Amicability and hospitality certainly weren't any measure of how much people could be trusted. She'd had her fingers burned that way before.

Bisi had met two women who were staying in the building. One's face was badly bruised, while there was no sign of anything wrong with the other. But they were both old, to her eyes, and although she found it difficult to gauge the ages of white women, grey hair and lined faces told their own story, and one of them was lumpy and dowdy too. At Fifi's place, all the women had been young and pretty, and it hadn't occurred to Bisi until it was too late that a price tag would be attached to Fifi's hospitality.

Marsela had arrived at Fifi's the day after Bisi. She'd tried to talk to her, but she appeared to speak neither French nor English, and laughed apologetically instead of answering Bisi's questions. She was stunningly beautiful – almost unworldly. Her skin was pale and as smooth as ivory, and her hair shone, and was so black that there was almost a blue shade to it when the sun caught it as they sat over the delicious lunch that Moussa had brought to the house. Fifi had filled a plate with food and returned to the computer, where she continued her work, although she mentioned in passing that she was searching for information on the best way to apply for a French residence permit for Bisi. She thanked Fifi courteously, kissing her on both cheeks, and Fifi hugged her, held her hands and looked into her eyes, saying that she shouldn't worry. It would all work out. Everything would be fine.

Bisi could still recall the flavour of the cassoulet and the bread, and the heat of the sun on their faces in the cool of the day in the yard of Fifi's house where they had sat, two lost and hopeless women. Marsela occasionally laughed out loud, for no apparent reason, as if she was crazy. Bisi had believed Fifi's assurances that everything would work out for the best. Or maybe in her desperation she had simply longed to believe that it would all be fine.

Her desperation was less now, as she felt she had already experienced the worst that could happen. But her hopes were also lower. And her faith that everything would turn out well was completely gone.

43

Helena was overcome with sadness at the thought of going home to her little apartment, and the car seemed to drive itself to Sirra's place in Laugardalur. She knew she would be welcome there. She had a key and could let herself in if Sirra wasn't at home. A tacit agreement between them had taken shape. It was something they hadn't exactly talked through, but they had gradually progressed from what she thought of as hook-ups, practically one-night stands, usually arranged at short notice and with zero commitment, into something that Helena still hadn't fully figured out. She wasn't sure if she even wanted to know what it was. She just knew that she didn't want a permanent relationship, as that would demand too much of her time, and she couldn't see how it would fit around the effort she would have to put into climbing the police career ladder. All the same, there was something that continually pulled her to Sirra, and her interest in other women had fizzled out completely.

She suspected that a net was slowly and surely being drawn around her and they would end up in a proper relationship, even though she could pin down nothing Sirra had done to support this suspicion. She was always pleased to see her, and no longer set any rules – such as asking Helena to call in advance or stipulating meetings at particular times. Now she rarely prepared for Helena's appearance with a carefully laid table or by dressing specially, but was to be found reading, cooking or watching TV. Helena was always welcome, she said. No pressure, just be welcome. As a token of this, she had then handed Helena a key. Helena had wanted to run for it, as she knew that this was how cohabitation started, and living with Sirra wasn't something she wanted to tell anyone about. The fact that Sirra was subject to court proceedings and awaiting a verdict in a case that Helena had worked on made things awkward, and it would only feed the rumour mill if it were to get out. The whole Flosi case and Sirra's role in it had made the headlines. But despite all this, Helena had accepted the key and was increasingly tempted to make use of it.

When she entered the living room, Sirra was on the sofa with her laptop on her knees.

'Are you working?' Helena asked.

Sirra shook her head before stretching upward for a kiss. 'No. Just looking around online and checking the news,' she replied. She closed the laptop and put it on the table, and Helena sat down at her side. 'What's new with you? How are you feeling?' she asked, to Helena's surprise – not so much at the question but her tone of voice.

'What do you mean?'

'I imagine you're working on this latest barrel of fun?'

'What? Is it in the news?' Helena sat down and reached for her phone and opened the state broadcaster's web page. It was only a matter of time before the news broke officially – rumours had begun to circulate almost immediately on social media.

'Yes,' Sirra said. 'It's shocking. You'll all need counselling after being involved in a case like that.'

Sirra laid an arm across Helena's shoulders and pulled her close. Helena closed her eyes and enjoyed the scent of Sirra's hair. She had recently cut it to shoulder length and had also begun to use some hair products with a herbal aroma that Helena loved to breathe in deep. Perhaps this case was having more of an effect on her than others did. She was tired, and Sirra's presence didn't fill her senses with the same churning passion as it had so often before. Now she longed just to curl up in her warm embrace and go to sleep.

'That poor thing who survived,' Sirra said.

Helena smartly sat up straight. 'Fuck. Is that in the news as well?' She could feel her heart beat rapidly in her chest. This was bad. This was something she had hoped wouldn't leak out.

'Yes,' Sirra said. 'I hope she doesn't feel too awful.'

Helena was on her feet. It was only to be expected. Everything leaked sooner or later, especially with such a large team of investigators, and with the hospital, the Directorate of Immigration and others all involved. But it was a setback she had hoped wouldn't crop up right away.

'Excuse me a moment. I need to call the station and request a police guard for the women's refuge.'

44

It was evening by the time Áróra looked up from the computer. The only light in her living room was the pale-blue glow from the screen. She had been too absorbed in her work to get up and switch on a light. Dusk came early these days, and she often found that she had no idea what the time was. The depths of winter seemed to switch off her sense of time. It was getting on for dinner, but she was still full after the egg shake earlier in the day, and decided a snack later would do if she needed it.

She had the information Daníel had asked for, and more. It appeared that the scam she had discovered connected to Flosi's company was no longer operational. In itself, that was no surprise, because both Leonid and his henchmen had discovered that she was digging into their affairs, so had no doubt made efforts to cover their tracks, in addition to which, Flosi's company was in receivership following the tragedy that had engulfed the family.

Kuzee ehf appeared to be solely a property outfit of some kind. Although it hadn't been defined as such, according to the documents, the company received rents from twenty-three properties dotted around the capital region, most of which looked to be commercial premises of some sort or another. A little digging into the details had given Áróra an overview of how the company worked: Kuzee ehf bought commercial buildings in poor states of repair here and there around the city and immediately rented them out. She had found sales documents relating to two of these properties on the website of the estate agent that had handled them recently and that hadn't yet taken down the details. Judging by the information available, these were both such lousy buildings that nobody with an ounce of common sense would have looked twice at them. But Kuzee had. Now it seemed that the company had rented out both immediately, and was receiving sky-high rents for them.

Áróra had tied her hair up in bun and put her coat and shoes on before she had even taken a conscious decision. She had to check this out. The first of the two properties was in Kópavogur's Smiðja district. There was little traffic at dinnertime, and with the frosty, dry streets allowing her to enjoy her Tesla's sharp handling, she was there within ten minutes. This was a commercial unit, a narrow slice of a building sandwiched between two others, both of which were car workshops. The doors of one were open, and she saw two people still at work. Áróra got out of the car and went over to speak to one of them.

'We're closed, sweetheart,' he said.

'I was just wondering if you know anything about the place next door,' she said, pointing at the narrow frontage.

'What, that?' The man shook his head as he stepped out onto the forecourt and gazed at the frontage. 'You'd need your head examined if you're thinking of buying that. It's a complete wreck. It's been empty for years, and as far as I know the roof leaks, there's no power and the windows ... Well, you can see what they're like.' Áróra nodded and looked at the windows. The frames seemed rotten and the glass of one was broken. 'Not that I'd get in the way of someone who wanted to do the place up. It does us no good to be next door to that, but anyone buying it would have to know exactly what they're letting themselves in for.'

'Actually, it's been sold,' Áróra said. 'Have you met the new owner?'

This was clearly news to the man, who stared at her in astonishment.

'You don't say,' he said. 'I hadn't heard anything about that. I haven't seen a soul around here.'

'That's just it,' Áróra said. 'You don't know the company that bought it? It's called Kuzee ehf. With a Z.'

The man shook his head.

'Kuz... what? What sort of name is that?'

Áróra shrugged and seeing the man was on the point of asking why she was so interested in the place, she hurried back to the car, raising a hand in farewell. She called a word of thanks to him as she got in the car, waving to him again as he watched the Tesla speed away.

She left the Smiðja district behind and headed northward onto Sæbraut. The other property Kuzee ehf had acquired was on Barkarvogur, and she was already sure that there would be no activity to be seen there either. She switched on the radio to listen to the evening news, and received such a surprise, she swerved off the road and pulled into a bus stop.

The news reported that a container found at Rauðhólar contained the bodies of four dead women, and one woman still alive. According to a statement by the chief inspector, there was suspicion that the discovery was linked to organised crime. Áróra snatched up her phone, and her fingers shook as she punched in a message to Daníel:

Heard the news. I guess this is connected to what you asked about? Sorry to mess you around. No hurry checking out Sergei. Good luck with this. I'll send you the Kuzee info shortly.

She was about to pull away when a reply from Daníel pinged on her phone:

THANKS! it read. *Tough case. Checking Sergei out now.*

Áróra felt a stab of guilt for having made a deal for the information she had searched out, even though she had asked jokingly and this was clearly an informal arrangement. Now Daníel would have to take time out from a hugely serious operation to put in a request for information about Sergei, which would probably yield nothing and was no doubt unnecessary.

She tried to shake off this uncomfortable feeling, reminding herself that Daníel was the one who had asked her to get involved in Elín's and Sergei's affairs. She put her foot down and growled from between clenched teeth to put the awkwardness behind her. 'A predator growl', her father had called it, recommending that she should always use it whenever she doubted herself. It reset your thoughts to the right wavelength, he said. But it didn't do the trick right away, and as always when she felt bad, her sister Ísafold came to mind, bringing with her the usual nagging guilt Áróra felt about giving up on her not long before her disappearance.

Áróra braked at a red light, checked the phone screen and found her conscience assuaged. The uncomfortable feeling that she had acted foolishly suddenly vanished. She couldn't tell if it was the predator growl that had made this happen, or the shiny red heart GIF that shone out from Daníel's message.

45

Daníel was hurrying across the road to the commissioner's office when he received Áróra's message. She'd obviously heard the news and seemed upset at having suggested exchanging information. Not that this bothered Daníel. It went without saying that he would obtain the information she needed – which they both needed. He had been the one who had asked her to help Elín by looking into Sergei's background.

He took the flight of steps in three strides and tapped on the glass of Ari Benz's office. He stood up to let him in, and in the same movement swept his jacket from the back of the chair and put it on.

'Are you going home?' Daníel asked.

Ari looked at him in shock.

'It's the match, man!' he said, and when Daníel still failed to understand, said: 'It's an international.'

'International what?' Daníel asked in confusion. He hadn't seen any news other than reports relating to the container.

'Iceland-Croatia!' Ari almost shouted.

'OK. I haven't been keeping up with the football over the last few days—' Daníel said, but got no further as Ari interrupted him, his voice an eighth higher in disbelief.

'Handball! What's the matter with you? There's an international starting in half an hour and getting to the world championship is riding on this match. You're not firing on all cylinders, are you?' he said.

Daníel laughed.

'Definitely not,' he said, hands in the air. He offered Ari a paper bag. 'A burger from the better kiosk at Hlemmur.'

Ari took the bag, peeked inside and sighed.

'OK. Considering you've brought me a bite to eat and that

saves me time on the way home, you get ten minutes. What are you after?'

Ari sat in his chair and switched on the computer.

'Sergei Konstantinovich Popov,' Daníel said. 'He's a Russian national. I'd appreciate it if you could check on him with the authorities in France. He was married to a French citizen by the name of Marie C. Allard and was issued a Schengen area residence permit on the basis of this marriage. It would be useful to know if the name turns up anywhere with the French police or with Europol.'

'Russians. Russians everywhere,' Ari Benz muttered, tapping rapidly at his keyboard.

Daníel coughed and Ari looked up with an enquiring expression on his face.

'Before you finish that, I ought to let you know this isn't to do with the container case. This is something personal.'

'OK,' Ari said, and continued to tap at the computer. 'None of my business.' He stood up, switched off the computer screen and glanced at his watch. 'Eighteen minutes to the match. I aim to be sitting on the sofa with a beer and a burger when the whistle goes.'

Daníel followed him along the corridor and down the steps.

'I've not had anything from other countries relating to the container case. So, nothing new,' Ari said as they left the building, heading for the car park on the Skúlagata side.

He stopped and looked at Daníel with an expression on his face so serious, Daniel thought he must be about to say something else about the handball match.

'I detest people who put other people in shipping containers,' he said instead.

Daníel felt something approaching a sob of emotion take shape in his throat, so he replied in a voice so low it was almost a whisper.

'Me too,' he said and their eyes met.

Ari laid a hand on his shoulder.

'Fifteen minutes to the whistle. I'll thump you if you don't watch it.'

Daníel laughed and walked towards Hverfisgata, while Ari opened the door of a glistening, dark-blue Mercedes-Benz sports car.

Daníel stopped and called over to him.

'Is it a coincidence that you bought a car to match your name?' he asked.

Ari laughed.

'Just the opposite,' he said. 'I was so pleased with the car that I decided to name myself after it.'

He sat behind the wheel, shut the door and wound down a window so he could stylishly rest an elbow there, as he put his foot down and screeched away in a cloud of burning rubber, a look of deep joy on his face.

Daníel watched him leave, and went over to the station. He was going to borrow a patrol car to collect the children. They always enjoyed a ride in a police car, and it was a bonus that parking it with the blue lights flashing outside her smart detached home in Garðabær would irritate his mother-in-law.

46

Elín rested her head against Sergei's muscular chest and listened, luxuriating in the depth of his breathing. His fingertips gently brushed her shoulder, and she felt a wave of contentment. They had spent a pleasant evening together and Sergei had been more relaxed, and he was being so gentle and sweet to her that she wondered why she had ever been suspicious about him. Her doubts had been so strong, she had brought in a cop and a private detective, no less. Tomorrow she would tell both Áróra and Daníel that she had made a mistake and there was no need to dig into Sergei's background. People had a right to some privacy, even within a relationship.

Sergei planted a kiss on her forehead, and she murmured quietly. She purred like a cat being stroked and could feel her heart swelling with love. She kept taking herself by surprise. She hadn't imagined that there could be any love stronger than hers for Sergei, but every time their relationship hit a bump in the road it was as if her heart grew a little afterwards, making room for even more love. This evening her heart had grown a lot larger. After all the suspicion and bad feelings, and Sergei's inattention and anxieties, it was such a delight when he came home relaxed, with a bag full of food that they cooked together and a bottle of wine that they finished in bed. She had enjoyed his undivided attention, and they had laughed and made love, neither of them sparing the kisses and sweet words. *I love you, babe*, he had whispered again and again, and she had reciprocated. *I love you, Sergei – ég elska þig.*

There was one thing, though, that had to be dealt with, that had to be clear, and she hadn't decided quite how to approach it. When she did it came out as a white lie.

'I was in touch with the district commissioner's office today,' she said, amazed at how convincing her own lie sounded. But there was no way she could tell him that she had had him investigated. 'And they said that you have a Schengen area residence permit and that you're married to a French woman.'

Sergei slid his arm from under her head and moved to the edge of the bed. He sat there, hanging his head and staring into his hands.

'What else did they say?' he asked, his voice low and oddly tight.

'They said you're a widower. That your French wife died.' She reached out, running her fingers down his back. 'Why on earth didn't you tell me?'

'Marie,' he said. 'Her name was Marie.' Elín continued to stroke his back and could sense his breathing become halting, as if he were holding back a sob. 'It's too painful to talk about it. I've been wondering for a long time how to tell you.'

Elín sat up and moved close to Sergei, pressing herself against him.

'You can tell me everything,' she said, planting a row of little kisses on his neck.

'She was depressed,' he said. 'So depressed that she no longer wanted to live. I thought that I had cured her, that love had cured her. But soon after we were married, it turned out that it wasn't like that at all. There's no cure for such an illness.'

'What happened?' Elín whispered.

'She jumped from a cliff onto a rocky beach and ended her own life.'

FRIDAY

47

Daníel always found it a challenge to start the day at the mortuary, but today this feeling was worse than ever. There were four corpses on the steel tables. This was all that remained of four women who had until recently been living souls with hopes and dreams. Their dreams had become a nightmare, so terrible that it could hardly be imagined.

Jóna the pathologist was a straight-backed, commanding presence, the bun knotted on the top of her head like a grey bird's nest. Her expression was generally somewhere between anger and sadness, and today Daníel felt that it was particularly appropriate.

'These woman are all young, around twenty,' she said in her own particular, instructive tone that often reminded Daníel of a computer game avatar. 'Two are Caucasian, one of them with typical Eastern European dentistry, one of Asian origin, probably Chinese, and one is black. My best guess is that she's of West African origin.'

Jóna stopped at the table closest to the wall, where the black girl's body lay on the table, rigid and covered by a white sheet that almost reached her shoulders, so that the top of the Y-incision could just be seen.

'She's the only one who has taken me by surprise,' she said. 'The other women died of hypothermia. I mean, that's what I consider the most likely cause of death, although there is no single factor that supports this conclusion. I found indications of frostbite on their extremities, brown colouration of the digestive tracts and contusions that certainly indicate it, and considering the circumstances in which they were found, it's the most likely explanation.'

'And what's different about her?' Daníel asked, inspecting the face of the girl, which had once been dark brown but had now taken on a greyish hue.

'Taking rigor mortis into account, I estimate that she was the last to die. But it's difficult to use rigidity as an indicator when the bodies have been in a cold environment. My report has been uploaded to LÖKE,' Jóna said. 'You can read all my findings there. But there's one thing I thought you would want to see for yourself.'

She took the block from beneath the body's head and turned the girl onto her side. The stiff body seemed unwilling to accept the laws of gravity and her arm remained rigid beside her. But Daníel's attention was drawn to the back of the girl's head. There was a patch where Jóna had clearly shaved away some hair, and in the middle of this area, in the back of the skull, were two deep depressions.

'Her skull has been cracked, and there has been a bleed into the brain. Pretty serious, going by the X-rays. She received at least two heavy blows to the head, and for some reason there is no open wound, the skin is unbroken and as she has all this thick hair, this wasn't apparent during the initial examination.'

Daníel stared at the black curls. What had happened inside the dark, cold container? How had this girl's death occurred?

'Could she have fallen against something inside the container?' he asked. 'If there were heavy seas, perhaps?'

Jóna shrugged.

'It's possible,' she said. 'I've been in touch with Jean-Christophe, and forensics are looking out for anything that could explain these injuries. But as there is no loss of blood, the only possibility would be to find hairs on whatever she could have fallen against. Otherwise, we're looking at an inconclusive cause of death.'

'Hmm.' No detective liked to hear the word 'inconclusive' when it came to pinning down a cause of death – especially under circumstances such as these. 'Are there pictures of this? Of the injuries?' he asked, and Jóna replied instantly.

'It's all filed on LÖKE: photographs, X-rays, diagrams. Now we're just waiting for results from the drug and DNA analysis.'

Daníel nodded. The DNA results would probably tell them little in this instance, other than a rough idea of where these women had come from.

'Of course, you can see what I and everyone else can see...?' Jóna said, her avatar delivery giving way to a questioning tone.

'What's that?' Daníel asked.

'All of these women, or rather, girls – as two of them don't yet have their wisdom teeth – are unusually beautiful. Attractive figures, pretty faces.'

Daníel's eyes went to the next table, and the next. Jóna was right. Despite the strangely colourless, mottled complexions, it was obvious that all of the girls were beautiful. Each had her own characteristics, but Daníel could see that with a little make-up, the right clothes and their hair dressed in a way that was something more than the basic washing and combing the pathology department provided, they would all be fabulous. If they were alive.

'It looks likely to me,' he said to Jóna. 'That it was their beauty that took them to their deaths.'

48

Áróra had woken up raring to go, ready to make the most of the day ahead, starting with a five-minute plank and a hundred deep knee-bends before coffee, eggs and a cold shower. But now, facing Elín in the studio on the downstairs floor of her house, it felt as if all the energy had been sucked out of her and that she was in exactly the same situation as she had so often experienced with her sister, Ísafold. Elín appeared to have completely changed her mind concerning this Russian boyfriend of hers, convinced that he was an angel in human form, and that she had been completely misguided in asking Áróra and Daníel to look into his past.

'What about the calls you mentioned?' Áróra asked. 'With this woman Sofia, which he always leaves the room to answer?'

'He explained that,' Elín said. 'This Sofia is a friend of his former wife. They often talk about her – about Marie. It's painful for Sergei to talk about the past, so he shuts himself away, says he doesn't want to ruin our happiness with these painful memories.'

Áróra sighed.

'And what about his lies about having a residence permit? Using that to apply pressure on you to get married right away. Don't you think that's strange?'

It was as if Áróra had hurled steaming hot coffee in her face. Elín backed away sharply and her tone changed.

'It's because he loves me,' she said with a passion. 'Maybe it's difficult for people to understand a relationship with an age difference, but anyone seeing us together would know right away that we're in love.'

Áróra raised her hands.

'I wasn't saying there's anything wrong with being in a relationship with someone older or younger,' she said quickly, hoping she hadn't offended Elín.

'So what exactly are you saying?' Elín asked, now wearing the stubborn, defensive expression that Áróra had so often seen on her sister's face when she had tried to protect her from Björn's violence.

'I'm simply pointing out that it could be worth your while getting independent advice, because you could be in a toxic relationship. Sergei could be manipulating you and could be telling you untruths concerning his circumstances—' Áróra was interrupted as the studio door behind her opened.

'Are you talking about me?' a man's voice demanded. 'I heard my name. What are you saying?'

Áróra turned, and it was hard to say which of them was taken more by surprise. He wore a track suit and large white shoes. A heavy gold chain hung around his muscular neck, and his angry eyes glared at her. She had encountered this man before. And that hadn't been a pleasant experience.

49

Baldwin chaired that morning's case meeting with the energy he always displayed when he was in charge of an investigation. The chief superintendent watched wordlessly from the sidelines, and by the look on his face he seemed satisfied with the progress Baldwin reported, as he had clearly studied all the case notes that had been added to the files.

'The cause of death of three of the women appears to be hypothermia, while the fourth died as the result of a bleed on the brain following a heavy blow to the head. It's now vital that we get the survivor to give us her account of what happened.'

Baldwin gave Helena a sharp glance, and she wanted to remind him that Daníel was the one who had been given the role of communicating with the victim. He had pulled her along with him, so it wasn't her problem alone that there was so far no statement from her. She would tackle this today. It was time to apply some pressure to Bisi to get her to open up. Helena made no reply other than a nod of acknowledgement, and Baldwin moved on to the next item on the day's agenda.

'I know all your phones are buzzing all day long right now, but I would like to remind you that only the chief superintendent replies to enquiries from the media or from anyone else who's curious about how things are going. For the moment we won't put our energies into finding out how the information leaked out, but it's now public knowledge that one of the women survived, and we can expect that there will be attempts to locate her. That makes it even more important that we keep tight control of what information about the case is released and when. If you refer enquiries to the chief superintendent and he can't be reached, then I'm your next option. All right?'

Everyone present nodded, almost as one.

'Today we're having Lárentínus the truck driver work with an artist to produce likenesses of the men who took delivery of the container. Gutti and Palli are on that. Daniel's with the international department with Ari Benz, to check the Europol and Interpol lists of women who have disappeared to try and match them against the pathologist's descriptions of the victims' ages and characteristics. You guys all have work to do, so...' He paused and corrected himself. 'You all have work to do, so let's get on with it and do the best we can.'

Helena gave Baldvin a lighthearted wink, and he returned a faint smile. Although he was old-fashioned and set in his ways, Baldvin did his best to remember that the investigation team wasn't exclusively male. She was often told that women could also be 'guys', but Helena had a standard response to this, which usually raised a laugh: 'When you refer to your wife as "my guy", then I'll accept that women can also be guys.'

The meeting was over in ten minutes, and she and Daniel parted in the yard behind the station, promising to try and meet for lunch, although they both knew the chances of that were slim. Daniel walked to the gate so he could jog over to the police commissioner's office, where the international department was located. Helena took a seat in a patrol car with a uniformed officer who would take her to the women's refuge.

50

Bisi recalled being disturbed when Clara joined the group. There was something strange about all three of Fifi's guests being women who had found themselves cast adrift, and who all needed European residence permits. When she mentioned what an odd coincidence this was, Fifi replied that she had told Moussa to keep his eyes open for women in need of help, on his way to and from work. She was helping one to find the best way to obtain a residence permit, so she could easily help others do the same.

Moussa confirmed what Fifi had said, telling Bisi that he worked right next to Porte de la Chapelle, that it pained him to see all the people in the queue, and that his heart went out especially to lone women. They weren't safe there among all those Arabs. Moussa came across as sincere, and Clara, who also came from Côte d'Ivoire, assured her that he was a good man. It wasn't as if Bisi could argue with that. There seemed no end to the help and hospitality that Fifi and Moussa offered. On the evening Clara arrived, Fifi cooked for them, and they all drank too much, laughing with, and at, Marsela, who needed little encouragement to howl with laughter.

Bisi was delighted to meet Clara, and they both felt they had a bond that crossed borders and colonial languages, as they were both of Yoruba extraction. When she looked at Clara, Bisi felt like this was one of her cousins standing before her. She had a broad face and high cheekbones, just like Bisi, and her nose was narrow and straight, like those of Europeans. Clara maintained that she could speak Yoruba, but it was so littered with French words that Bisi protested and told her she was talking crap. This elicited a burst of laughter, and while they continued to try to converse in Yoruba, they switched regularly to a mixture of French and English.

Clara had a slim waist, with broad hips, and heavy breasts that looked ready to burst out of her dress, which was the only garment she had. She aired it every evening, pegging it to a clothes hanger and letting it flap in the breeze in the window of the room next to Marsela's, which Fifi had allocated to her. Bisi tried to give Clara a top and a skirt, but both were too small for her, so the day after Clara's arrival they all went with Fifi to a second-hand clothes market, where Clara picked out the most colourful things she could find that would fit, and Fifi paid, saying that Clara could pay her back later.

Marsela wandered through the market, rummaging through the piles of used clothes, laughing out loud without replying when Fifi tried to ask if she needed anything.

'Hey, the strange one,' Clara whispered to Bisi, pointing at Marsela as she giggled and hunted through the heaped-up clothes, and Bisi wasn't sure whether she meant there was something not right in Marsela's head, or that she might be possessed by an evil spirit. But that didn't really matter; Bisi understood that Clara meant Marsela wasn't like most people.

When they were back at the house, Fifi said that she would find a town or a city in some other part of France where it would be easier to get access to a police station for the three of them to apply for asylum. Bisi wondered how Fifi could know that Marsela wanted asylum in France when she couldn't even get her to say whether she needed clothes. Although they had spent some days together, Bisi still hadn't been able to find out where Marsela came from, or how she had managed to end up in Fifi's house in Paris.

51

'I just don't know what went on between Sergei and Áróra this morning,' Elín said as they set off in Daníel's car.

He'd decided to ask her out for a drive around town. *Just like in the old days,* he said when he'd called ahead and Elín had reluctantly agreed.

'It was something very strange,' Elín continued. 'It was as if they knew each other, but neither of them gave me any explanation. Sergei just showed her the door. She's been trying to phone me ever since, but I don't trust myself to take a call from her. I think I've got myself into a mess by asking you to check on Sergei. And it was definitely a mistake to involve Áróra.'

'Elín,' Daníel said, trying to speak to her, but Elín was clearly in no mood for listening.

'I simply don't know why I was so distrustful of Sergei. He's a decent man, and we've been really great together. I'm sure I was just stressed or something, and I think Dad's distrust of him must have triggered my doubts. Dad's very prejudiced when it comes to foreigners.'

'Elín,' Daníel said gently.

She glanced at him, but carried on talking.

'And although I don't have any prejudice against foreigners, I think I must have allowed the language barrier to get on my nerves. It's not easy, being so clueless about what he's saying on the phone, and somehow it always sounds threatening, but now I feel ashamed of thinking like that.'

Daníel pulled up at Aktu-Taktu and rolled down the window.

'Two small cones,' he said to the man who leaned out of the drive-in kiosk's window.

'Which dips?'

'None,' Daníel said. This was an old habit that he and Elín had shared, an ice cream while they drove and chatted. There was something comforting about eating ice cream while cruising the city streets or parking somewhere and looking out over the sea. Their conversations were always easier when they were both looking out through the windscreen and not at each other.

The two ice creams were handed down from the kiosk window. Daníel took them, passing one over to Elín. He drove around the kiosk, onto the eastbound lane on Sæbraut, made a completely illegal U-turn and headed west.

'I'd forgotten about our ice-cream outings,' Elín said. 'Until you called and asked me out for a drive.'

Daníel smiled, bit off the tip of his ice cream and winced at its chill against his teeth. Elín laughed, and for a moment he felt he had gone back in time, to old habits, old feelings and an old love.

He slid the car into a space by the Sun Voyager sculpture overlooking the bay and switched off the engine. Then he turned and gazed gravely at Elín. She stared back, and he could see from her expression that she was on the defensive.

'If you're going to say something unpleasant about Sergei, then I don't want to hear it,' she said. 'I've worked out that this was all just me getting things round the wrong way. I honestly don't know what came over me.'

'Elín,' Daníel said, this time with a sharper note to his voice.

'What?'

'You must listen to what I have to say.' Elín looked at him with an enquiring look on her face and her ice cream lolled to one side. Daníel reached out, put his hand gently on hers and moved it to straighten her ice cream. 'I've been with my colleague in the international department and got some information from him, about Sergei—'

Elín cut him off.

'I know all about him being married before and how he lost his wife. Áróra told me that, and Sergei and I have talked this over and we're completely open with each other.'

She turned away and stared out of the passenger window, as if she wanted to check on how the thick cloud cover darkened Esja's slopes. Daníel was familiar with this response, the way she turned away and the expression that said she had made up her mind. This meant that she was not inclined to listen. But now it was important for her to pay attention – vitally important.

'Elín,' he said. 'Did Sergei mention at all that he had been suspected of his wife's murder?'

52

When they reached her house, Elín was still dabbing at the dribble of ice cream on the front of her coat with the thin Aktu-Taktu serviettes. Daníel stopped the car and placed a hand on her arm.

'You can call me whenever, night or day,' he said, and she nodded in response. She felt too numb to say anything – unable to form coherent enough thoughts to put into words.

Daníel got out of the car and walked around it to open the passenger door for her, and when she got out, he wrapped his arms around her and held her tight. 'Anytime,' he whispered in her ear. 'For whatever reason.'

She nodded again, smiled quickly and went towards the house.

She felt that her head was about to burst. No, not just that it was about to burst, but that it was ready to split in two, leaving a different Elín on each side. One was the Elín who was deeply in love and who believed Sergei's explanations. The Elín who wanted to surrender to love and to see where it took her; the Elín who wanted to take chances, open her mind and soul to the delights that life offered, to tell caution to go to hell. This Elín wanted to snuggle up tight against Sergei at night, kiss, make love and laugh. She wanted to drink his tea in the mornings with candles on the table, wash his clothes and fold them with love, watch TV with his head resting in her lap.

On the other side was the suspicious Elín. This Elín had asked Daníel and Áróra to find information about Sergei. This was the frightened Elín.

If she looked at the whole thing with ice-cold clarity, then maybe she had good reason to be frightened. She turned and watched as Daníel drove away, and for a moment she wanted to run after him, call out to him to stop and take her with him, away from the mess she had got herself into. Daníel had information from this Ari in the international department, who had been in touch with the police in France. They'd said that Sergei's wife Marie had tumbled many metres to her death on a stony shoreline, and there had been no witness other than Sergei, who said that she had jumped. The French police found it suspicious that this had happened only a week after Sergei had been issued with French residency. On top of that, he was the sole beneficiary of her will and his wife's assets were significant. This had triggered speculation that Sergei had been in a relationship with another woman, although he denied this and the police had no evidence to back up the claim.

Elín took out her keys and opened the door to her studio. She couldn't bring herself to go upstairs. She couldn't trust herself to look Sergei in the eye right away. She needed to muster her courage, to get control of the two Elíns battling it out inside her head.

But it was obvious as soon as she went into the studio that there would be no opportunity to think things over. Sergei stood there in the middle of the room. His face was red and puffed up, as if inside him there was a boiler, and the pressure was building up steam, to the point of being ready to blow.

'What did he want?' he snarled from between clenched teeth.

'Nothing. He just wanted to chat,' she said. There was no doubt – this wasn't the moment to bring up his dead wife.

'Did he say anything about the container?' Sergei demanded, coming close and gripping her upper arms tightly.

The frightened Elín almost expected him to shake her, while the other inner Elín wanted to accept it and to have those strong arms hold her even tighter, to hold her and offer her a warm, safe place in his embrace.

But suddenly she was more confused than ever. What on earth was he talking about?

'Container? What container?'

The fog in her mind grew thicker and the pain stretched all the way to the back of her head, so that all she wanted to do was run a hand over it to see if there was a split in her skull, a gap through which all the misleading, crazy thoughts would escape in a burst of smoke. But with Sergei holding her tight, she couldn't move a muscle.

'The container,' he shouted. 'Did he say anything about the container?'

Elín slowly twisted her head to one side, as the stinging pain would not allow her to shake it.

'I don't understand what you're talking about...' she gasped, but when Sergei replied, it wasn't just her head that she seemed cloven in two, but her heart as well.

'This ex of yours is one of the cops who's investigating the container that was in the news,' Sergei hissed, shaking her. 'The container with the dead girls.'

53

Áróra sat in her car, watching a gentlemanly Daníel walk around his own vehicle to open the door for Elín. Áróra switched off the lunchtime news bulletin. They hugged. It was such a long, tender embrace that Áróra felt a strange pang. She reproached herself for being silly as she watched Daníel drive away. Any feelings between Daníel and his former wife were no concern of hers, but at the same time she wanted to know which of them had ended their relationship. She reached into the glove compartment, took out a packet of chewing gum and put two pieces in her mouth, but she'd barely begun chewing when her phone rang. She felt a surge of contentment to see Daníel's name appear. It made her happy to know that he had called her immediately after dropping Elín off. That meant that she was in his thoughts. She took out the chunk of chewing gum and put it on the dashboard.

'Hello?'

'Are you all right?' was the first thing Daníel said. 'I heard that you had a confrontation with Sergei this morning.'

'I'm fine,' Áróra said. 'But I'm concerned about Elín. I've encountered this Sergei before, a few months ago. Him and his mates stood and watched as one of them put me in a headlock and made all kinds of threats.'

'What?'

'Yep. Too long a story for any details, but in a nutshell, I had the idea of selling the tax authorities information relating to a money laundering operation. Sergei and his pals didn't take kindly to that, and they convinced me it wasn't a great idea.'

'Good grief, Áróra.' Daníel sounded horrified. 'Why didn't you come to the police? To me?'

'Like I said, they convinced me that would be a bad idea.'

'I'm in shock hearing this,' Daníel said.

'It goes with the territory,' Áróra said. 'There can be all kinds of comebacks when you search for ill-gotten gains.'

'*Jahérnahér*,' Daníel said, and Áróra smiled. This was something her father had sometimes said when something took him by surprise. *Jahérnahér*. 'You haven't considered a different line of work?' Daníel added, and Áróra laughed out loud.

'No,' she replied. 'Let's just say that my salary includes a decent danger premium.'

Daníel laughed as well. Then he was silent for a while and Áróra wondered if he was still on the line, so she cleared her throat. That was enough to spur him back into speaking.

'I have some bad news about Sergei,' he said. 'The French police suspect him of pushing his wife off a cliff. She lost her life.'

'That's quite something.'

Áróra had long ago put Sergei down as a small-time thug, so this was much bigger than she would have expected.

'And now I'm very concerned about Elín, who appears to be confused and completely at a loss.'

'I can understand the position she's in,' Áróra said. 'She's in a relationship with a man she loves, but knows deep down that it isn't healthy, and could be downright dangerous. I had years of talking to a woman in this position – my sister.'

Just the thought of Ísafold sent a jolt of pain through her. Sorrow could be remarkably painful.

'I know, Áróra,' Daníel said, his voice warm and fond. 'But now it's time for you to take a step back. I'll make regular checks on Elín today and I'll have a patrol car from the station park outside their place for a few hours, to let Sergei know that he's being watched. I'd never have got you involved in this if I had thought that Sergei was a dangerous man.'

'Too late,' Áróra said, starting the car. 'I'm outside their place right now and Sergei has just come out of the door.' Her eyes followed him as he went over to a little Yaris and got in. 'And I'm going to tail him today.'

54

Bisi sat in the back of the people carrier with Clara, while the middle seats were occupied by Marsela and Nadiya, a new girl who had so far not said a word to anyone. Dozing as night fell, Bisi felt herself sent to sleep by the monotony of the darkness on the motorway, the soothing music and the murmured conversation between Fifi and Moussa in the front seats.

A sharp elbow jab from Clara woke her as the car came to a halt.

They appeared to be in what Bisi guessed to be a deserted car park. A pink glow shone into the night on the far side of the woods surrounding them, and she guessed they must be on the outskirts of some city.

At the other end of the car park stood a flatbed truck loaded with a container. She and Clara peered out of the window, while Marsela and Nadiya got out, folding forward the middle row of seats so that Bisi and Clara could follow. They all stood in a knot, shivering in the evening chill, and Bisi wondered what Fifi was saying to the driver of the truck, who stood and smoked beside the container.

'I know you're not going to like this,' Fifi said as she returned to the group. 'But this is the only way I've found to help you. We need to get you across the border into Belgium, as it's a lot easier to apply for asylum there. There are no queues, and applications are handled quite quickly. And while the application is under consideration, you get accommodation and money every day.'

'I still have some time left on my tourist visa,' Bisi said. 'I can show it if I get stopped at the border, so I can walk or drive across.'

'I can't,' Clara whispered sadly. 'No visa. I'm illegal.'

'It's best for you all to stay together. That way you can support each other,' Fifi said, like a stern teacher ruling on a playground dispute.

'And we have found a man who is prepared to take you across the border into Belgium,' Moussa added, pointing to the truck driver, who stood hunched beside his vehicle.

Moussa and Fifi set off towards him, and the four of them followed like obedient children.

It wasn't until it dawned on them that they weren't going in the cab with the driver, but in the container that rested on the truck's flatbed that fear set in. Bisi clutched Clara's arm as her friend protested that she didn't want to go in there, as if the foreboding they silently shared was the only thing that was keeping her in touch with reality.

'It's just two hours,' Fifi said. 'Two hours, max. It's best if you don't have anything on you that makes it possible to trace who you are. I have untraceable phones for you so we can keep in touch over the next couple of hours.' She held up one of the phones. 'If you're stopped at a border, say you're from Iraq or Eritrea. Refugees always get asylum.'

Fifi handed each of them one of the new phones, then held out her hand, indicating that she expected them to give her their own phones. Clara protested at handing hers over, but after a moment's resistance she followed Bisi in giving up her phone, her link to the rest of the world, taking the replacement and tucking it away.

'I've pre-loaded my number into each phone,' Fifi continued. 'And we'll be in close contact the whole time.'

Bisi looked with terror at the open door of the container in front of them, and was on the verge of weeping openly, like Clara, who clearly didn't want to set foot inside the steel box, while Marsela walked in circles around the car park, tapping her head as if knocking at a door and hoping that someone with more sense than she had would answer it.

It was Nadiya who was the first to make a move. She hurled away a half-smoked cigarette, handed her passport and phone to Fifi and climbed into the container. Bisi felt numb with uncertainty but was relieved that Clara seemed to be calming down. Her tears had stopped by the time a small car drove into the car park and pulled to a halt. A girl who looked like a film star stepped out.

'This is Jia Li,' Moussa said, as he extended a gentlemanly hand to help her climb unhesitatingly into the container.

Bisi felt a surge of confusion. This girl showed no concern, as if she saw this mode of transport as nothing out of the ordinary. Did she know something the others didn't?

Fifi gestured Bisi and Clara to the open container.

'Like I already told you, it's better if you don't have your passports or anything traceable on you, in case the truck is stopped at the border. I'll drive across with your passports and phones and will meet you on the other side. If everything works out as planned, then it should only take an hour and forty-five minutes.'

Looking back later, it felt to Bisi that she and Clara arrived at the same decision at the same moment, sometime between Moussa pointing his flashlight skyward and saying that Belgium lay over there, and Fifi telling them that they were welcome to come with her back to Paris and to try the queues at Porte de la Chapelle again, if that was what they preferred. It was their own decision. That made their fear seem such a childish, ungrateful thing, and Bisi had felt a pang of regret at being ungrateful to Fifi and Moussa for all the efforts they had made to help them.

Marsela followed them in, and they sat close together on the floor while Moussa and the man who had brought Jia Li arranged a wall of cardboard boxes at the end of the container so that it would look full if anyone were to open it at the border. Then the flat door slammed shut and they sat in complete darkness, until Nadiya switched on a torch, and they saw the cartons of food and the shrink-wrapped packs of water bottles, and realised that these were their rations – and that this journey was going to be much longer than just a couple of hours.

55

Daníel had made Áróra promise that she wouldn't leave her car, that she would keep the doors locked and wouldn't hesitate to drive away if Sergei became aware of her presence. She faithfully promised all this, and immediately broke her promise when she saw Sergei get out of his car at the coach terminal. He disappeared through the doors, and Áróra couldn't resist the temptation to follow him. She wrapped her scarf tightly around her neck, covering half of her face, and set off in pursuit.

The terminal was packed with people. The crowds flowed from the arriving coaches, and tourists returning from sightseeing tours and travellers arriving from around the country mixed together in one milling throng. Sergei was sitting on a bench in the middle of the waiting area, fiddling with his phone. He was clearly waiting for someone. Áróra went to the café and took a seat that had a view of the waiting area, but where she was partly hidden behind a hoarding advertising glacier trips and a large potted plant, which was remarkably green, considering it had to sustain the blasts of cold air that blew in every time the glass doors slid open.

Áróra hung her coat on the back of her chair, then went to the counter and surveyed the dishes on offer, presented in large, brightly-lit photographs on the wall. Hamburgers. Meat balls. Hot dogs. Seared sheep's head. Chips. She could do with a bite to eat – not the sheep's head, though – but there was no time now, so she asked for sparkling water, glancing over to the waiting area, where Sergei sat and waited patiently.

She took her seat again, sipping her sparkling water, and hadn't got far into the bottle before Sergei stood up and headed for the sliding doors with his arms spread wide. A dark-haired woman ran the last few steps into his arms, and he lifted her up, spinning her around in a circle. Then their lips met in a long kiss that made it clear that she was something more than just a friend. And she certainly wasn't his mother.

Áróra raised her phone and held the sports-mode button down, capturing every moment, every movement and every expression on their faces in a series of shots. Sergei took the woman's case and they left pressed together, his arm around her shoulders.

Áróra followed, but hesitated inside the door until they had stowed the woman's case and taken their seats in the Yaris. Then she jogged to her own car, got in and put her foot down in pursuit as they headed for the city centre. It wasn't a long journey. The Yaris came to a halt on Ingólfstorg, and Áróra watched the couple go hand in hand into the Center Hotel.

56

Daníel's stomach twisted into a knot at the sight of his former mother-in-law's Range Rover, parked in the space outside his house. What had brought her here? The stress of leaving the children to themselves for yet another day was bad enough, without her making things worse. She certainly didn't spare her efforts in that direction. After the divorce, she had transformed from Daníel's number-one admirer into a vindictive witch, so that any dealings with her relating to the children were fraught with frustration.

'You forgot Tumi's orthodontist appointment,' she hissed as soon as Daníel opened the door. He and his former wife had jointly decided that the process of straightening Tumi's teeth would be continued in Iceland, where it had begun, as there was no orthodontist near his ex-wife's new home in Denmark, which was further complicated by her determination to live a carless lifestyle. The upshot was the decision to continue the appointments in Iceland, and the lad didn't have far to go now to achieve the perfect Colgate smile that his mother desired.

'I'm here to collect him for just that,' Daníel said. 'The appointment's two-thirty.'

'It *was* two-thirty, but it was changed,' his mother-in-law retorted. 'My daughter knew you'd forget, so she asked me to make sure. And it turns out she was right. We've just come back.'

'They've been tightened up,' Tumi said, pulling back his lips to show his braces. 'Can we have ice cream for dinner? It really hurts to chew when they've been tensioned.'

'Of course, my love,' Daníel said, agreeing to the request mainly because his mother-in-law was listening. It had the intended effect as she snorted in disgust.

'Some things never change,' she muttered to herself on her way to the hall. 'Bye, my darlings,' she called out to the children. 'See you tomorrow.' She turned to Daníel and her tone turned colder. 'I imagine it's best they come to me, as I don't suppose you've taken any time off even though your children have come to stay?'

The comment cut deep, and he was angry with himself for letting her get to him.

'No. It would be ideal if they could be with you tomorrow,' he said, holding back the caustic retort that came to mind. 'I'm up to my eyes in a multiple-murder case.'

'Oh, well,' his mother-in-law mumbled as she disappeared through the door.

Daníel felt the room temperature jump by at least a degree with her departure. Now he could breathe more easily. He went over to Tanja, who was absorbed in something by the living-room window. She had removed some of the soil from his large palm tree and was shovelling it into small yogurt pots.

'What are you up to, sweetheart?' he asked, running a hand fondly over the top of her head.

'I'm planting chickens,' she said. He squatted down next to her and saw that she had some dried chick peas in a plastic bag.

'Chick peas?'

'Yes. I'll water them and after a few days the chickens will start to grow.'

'A chick-pea plant? Is that what you mean?'

'No,' Tanja said. 'A chick, a little chicken.'

Daníel looked at her in surprise.

'You can't grow a living animal from a seed,' he said.

Tanja glanced at him with a forbidding look.

'Lady said so,' she replied, and the stubborn streak she had so often manifested as a small child made a reappearance in her expression.

Daniel sighed. For her age, Tanja seemed a little too apt to believe everything she was told. He'd have to speak to her mother. He'd also have to speak to Lady about telling the children outlandish tales.

'Are you sure that Lady was telling you truth?' he asked cautiously.

'Yes!' Tanja replied, offended at the suggestion. She handed him a chick pea. 'Look. If you look at it carefully, you can see the little chicken's face.'

57

Elín was more subdued and humbled than she had been that morning. In fact, her expression was so crushed it gave Áróra a stab of pain, it reminded her so much of her sister. Ísafold had been through a never-ending carousel of denial and crisis, depending on whether Björn had beaten her or was at his most penitent, with gifts and romance. While Elín said that Sergei had never laid a finger on her, Áróra was sure that she could see a similar pattern of emotions as those her sister experienced.

'I don't know what to think,' Elín said. 'I'm just completely shattered.'

Áróra sat down in an old wine-red armchair that occupied the centre of the studio space and cast her eyes over Elín's paintings, which were scattered here and there at varying stages of completion.

Elín pulled a picture from the back of a stack that leaned against one wall.

'This is a typical picture from before I got to know Sergei,' she said. It showed a mostly dark, gloomy background, with grey and black storm clouds in the sky, and a little human figure in a corner, tiny and alone. 'And see what I've been doing more recently.'

She gestured at what was around her, and Áróra saw clearly what she meant. Her more recent works were all lighter and brighter, many of them showing hands touching and holding each other, fingers entwined, the intimacy clear.

'I know it's wonderful to be in love,' Áróra said. 'But if you look objectively at your relationship, Sergei knows everything about you, and you know as good as nothing about him.'

'So what's knowing and not knowing?' Elín said. 'Maybe

people have a right to keep some things to themselves, to have a few secrets. I can easily understand that it wouldn't be pleasant to explain that you've been suspected of murder.'

Áróra could see that Elín was clutching at straws. She knew exactly how this worked: these straws would gradually twist themselves together in her thoughts to form a cord, which would be a strong strand of hope by the time Sergei came home and provided her with an emotion-laden explanation of just why he had kept his mouth shut about something so important. Áróra decided it was time to put her cards on the table.

'I've met Sergei before,' she said. 'He and a few of his friends broke into my home, and one of them assaulted me, choking me while the others made threats. And Sergei watched without a care in the world.' Elín stared, open-mouthed, clearly too astonished to say anything, so Áróra continued. 'It was because I was working on a case centred around a money-laundering operation. Their visit was a way of discouraging me from investigating further.'

Áróra decided not to say that she had intended to sell the information she obtained. That aspect had nothing to do with Elín and could lead her to invent excuses for Sergei's behaviour.

'In short, Sergei is involved with people who are active in laundering money, and they don't hesitate to resort to violence.'

'God,' Elín gasped, and looked around the studio in desperate confusion, as if searching for something; a lost thread that she could draw towards her and pull, so that all this new information about her lover would suddenly make sense.

Áróra took out her phone.

'I was concerned when I saw Sergei here this morning and recognised him, so I hung about outside and followed him when he left,' Áróra said and handed her the phone, with the photo of Sergei and the dark-haired woman in a deep clinch at the coach terminal. 'He went to fetch this woman as she got off the FlyBus.'

Elín stared at the picture, using two fingers to enlarge the faces of Sergei and the woman, and scrolled to the subsequent pictures, examining them carefully. Finally, she got to her feet and handed Áróra the phone.

'Well, that's not his mother,' she said drily, and Áróra shook her head. Elín went to a cupboard at the far end of the studio and took out a phone. 'I'm sending you a recording,' she said. 'It's Sergei having a conversation in Russian. It would be good if you could get this translated and make notes of what's being said.'

Áróra felt her phone shiver in her hand as it took delivery of the file, and she nodded.

Elín went to the door and opened it.

'I need to be alone for a while now,' she murmured.

58

Daníel blinked a couple of times, looked away from the computer screen and out of the window, and then back at the screen. He had the LÖKE database open in front of him, showing the likeness produced by the artist working with Lárentínus the truck driver of one of the men who had been present when Lárentínus had delivered the container to the place on Auðbrekka. Daníel had scrolled quickly past the other two images, which were supposed to be Valur and one of the Russians. This second Russian looked familiar.

He reached for his phone and found the screenshot from Ari Benz of the French police report about Elín's lover, Sergei Popov. There was no mistake. The two images were very alike. Daníel placed his hand over the computer screen, covering the man's forehead, and then did the same with the image on his phone to ensure that it wasn't just the man's close-cropped hair that made them look so similar. It could be that the picture drawn up from Lárentínus's descriptions was some stereotype of what an Eastern European criminal would look like – a broad face, shaved head and a gold chain around his neck – and that's what made Daníel feel that there was a similarity. But the facial features were alike. The nose was broad, his lips thick and his eyes were set deep in his head, making them look small and dark. The face was egg-shaped, but the jaw structure was strong, and the neck swathed in gold chains was bull-like.

Was he imagining things, or getting two cases mixed up? Was the mental load getting too much for him? Daníel caught hold of Baldvin's sleeve as he passed his desk. Someone else's opinion was always useful when you started to doubt your own judgement.

'Do these two guys look alike?' he asked.

Baldvin put on the reading glasses that hung on a cord around his neck, leaned forward and peered from the screen to the phone and back again a few times.

'Definitely the same man,' he said with decision. 'Where did you get the photo?'

'From Ari Benz,' Daníel replied. 'But connected to another, more minor case.'

He had no desire to explain Elín's affairs to Baldvin, and risk a reprimand for using police resources for a personal matter.

Baldvin studied the two pictures for a little longer, and then stood up straight, looking at Daníel over the top of his glasses.

'You'd better follow this up,' he said.

Daníel nodded his agreement. He logged out of the system, pulled his jacket from the back of the chair and dropped his phone in his pocket.

'Would you call the Hólmsheiði prison for me?' he said to Baldvin as he set off. 'Let them know that I'm on the way and need to get Lárentínus to identify a picture.'

59

Elín was in Áróra's thoughts all the way to the translation agency, where she had an appointment with a Russian language interpreter. She felt uncomfortable about leaving her alone at home, knowing that Sergei could return at any moment, with Elín inevitably demanding answers. But the police car parked outside, and the police officer sitting in it as he watched the house from the driver's seat, would no doubt discourage Sergei from doing anything rash. Elín had said that he had never been violent, but Áróra was in no doubt that Sergei could be. She recalled vividly the crushing headlock, her struggle to breathe and the tears that flowed when she had been threatened. Those tears had done nothing to wipe the smirk from Sergei's face as he looked on.

It wasn't far from Elín's place up to Mjódd, where Áróra spent some time choosing a space for the Tesla. She avoided tight spaces where there was a chance that the next car's door could dent its glistening paintwork. There were few things as annoying as a dent in a new car. She finally found a suitable spot further up, and jogged up the steps to the agency.

The interpreter introduced himself and the hourly rate, and they went to a small side room with three armchairs and a little coffee table. He was a diminutive, delicate man, swarthy and with greying sideburns. He smiled shyly as he gestured to Áróra to take one of the armchairs.

'I imagine it's best if you have the phone so you can pause it when you need to,' Áróra said, and placed the phone with the audio file on the table between them. He nodded and tapped the play button. He listened to no more than a few moments before pausing it and looking at Áróra.

'You're aware that this is a private conversation, probably recorded without the knowledge of the person who is speaking?'

This was a question Áróra had expected.

'Yes, I know,' she said. 'As I told you on the phone, this is on behalf of a desperate woman who doesn't completely understand what her partner is doing. It would be a great help to her if she could be sure whether or not he is in a relationship with another woman, as he's pressuring her to marry him. She has assets, you see.' She looked imploringly at the interpreter, who gazed back thoughtfully. 'In this instance the language is a hindrance. In a normal relationship people can make out some of what their partner is saying on the phone. But in her case she has no idea.'

This did the trick. The interpreter nodded and set the recording to play again.

'Fur and feathers,' he said. 'To hell with it.' He paused the recording. 'It's an idiom, or an expression. Something that's said when people are embarking on a big job. It's something hunters used to say before they went hunting. It's like when theatre people say "break a leg".'

Áróra nodded and kept her impatience in check. She hoped that there wouldn't be a cultural lesson accompanying every sentence. He re-started the recording. There had been a pause, as if the hunting expressions were the final words of one part of the conversation. Then Sergei could be heard speaking again and the interpreter translated.

'He says hi, and then asks if everyone in the chain or the process will keep their mouths shut because the container...'

The interpreter fell silent and listened, and Áróra saw the shy diffidence vanish from his expression, replaced by a new look. He snatched the phone from the table, stopped the replay and handed it to Áróra as he got to his feet.

'I'm not getting involved with this,' he said, his voice shaking. 'Please leave. I want nothing to do with this.'

He rushed from the room, and as far as Áróra could see, the man was terrified.

60

Daníel asked one of the warders at Hólmsheiði to print out the picture of Sergei, as he had forgotten that he couldn't take his phone into the interview room. Now he was sitting opposite Lárentínus, who had confirmed that Sergei was one of the men who had threatened him when he had arrived at the unit on Auðbrekka to deliver the container. Now though, he was begging Daníel not to leave right away. He felt sick at the prospect of returning to his cell.

'I told you,' Daníel said. 'Being in solitary confinement is no joke.'

'No, I know. I know,' Lárentínus said. 'I just hadn't realised that when you're isolated from everyone and everything, your sense of time changes. It passes so slowly while your head's spinning with thoughts.'

This wasn't the first time that Daníel had heard such complaints; far from the first time. People generally became increasingly co-operative during an investigation's progress, the longer they spent in isolation. Not that this applied to Lárentínus. He had co-operated from the moment he had been hauled, soaking wet, from Elliðavatn. And they had only requested a short custody period.

'They split your days up, don't they?'

'That's it,' Lárentínus said. 'Two half-hour spells out of the cell every day. That's apart from time spent talking to the police. So I wouldn't object to talking a bit longer.'

'You only have another day in isolation,' Daniel said. He swallowed his impatience and took a deep breath. An extra few minutes wouldn't make much of a difference to the investigation.

'Is there anything in particular you want to tell me?' Daníel said, looking at him enquiringly. It seemed to him that Lárentí-nus was about to burst into tears.

'No, not at all. I just feel so guilty. I suppose that's normal, considering someone died in my truck. It's just preying on my mind. And I can't think of anything else when I'm alone in the cell.'

'It's perfectly normal to feel bad after getting caught up in a case like this,' Daníel said. 'You could ask to speak to a priest.'

Lárentínus nodded.

'Yes,' he said. 'Maybe I'll do that.'

'Well, I have to go.' Daníel got to his feet and pressed the buzzer. 'Try and do exercises in your cell,' he told Lárentínus. 'And ask for some books.'

'I'm not in the habit of reading much,' Lárentínus said.

'You're also not in the habit of being in custody,' Daníel replied. 'Give it a try. It helps the time pass.'

Lárentínus left the room accompanied by a warder. As Daníel watched him go, he felt sorry for the lad. He would end up with a conviction for obstructing an investigation, but he hoped that his helpful, co-operative attitude would be taken into consider-ation.

As Daníel opened the locker in reception to fetch his belong-ings, he heard his phone vibrate. He looked at the screen and saw two messages from Áróra. The first was an audio file attach-ment and the second was a short message:

This is a recording of Sergei making a phone call in Russian. I suspect that he's connected to the container business.

Daníel felt goose pimples rise all over his whole body, and he realised this was one of those occasions when all the pieces of the puzzle started forming a picture. It was a picture with plenty of gaps, and the pieces were coming from different directions, but they were starting to fall into place.

61

Bisi had flatly refused to identify the girls from the photographs taken in the mortuary. She said that she needed to see the bodies, to meet them and speak to them. Now she was doing exactly that. Jóna the pathologist stood silently in one corner with a notepad and a pen, while Helena accompanied Bisi with a recorder.

Stopping by the first one, a girl with a broad face and black, shoulder-length hair, Bisi leaned forward and kissed her forehead. Helena shot a questioning glance at Jóna, who nodded to acknowledge that it was all right to touch the bodies. It seemed that she had taken from them all of the samples that would be needed.

'She is so blue,' Bisi said. 'She is so blue – such a strange colour now. In life she had pure-white skin. Thick white skin that you couldn't see through, like you can with some white people.' She touched the girl's ice-cold cheek and looked up at Helena. 'Her name is Marsela,' she said. 'And I think she came from Albania. It's difficult to tell, because she was so crazy.'

'Crazy?'

'Yes. She just laughed and laughed. As if she had lost her mind. She understood no French and no English. Maybe she was not very clever. But she seemed to be happy. Always light-hearted. Until we were in the container. Then she started crying instead of laughing.' Bisi stooped over the girl, whispered something to her and kissed her forehead again. Then she stood up straight and went directly to the next one.

'This is Jia Li and she's from China,' Bisi said, taking hold of the girl's hand. 'She came directly to the container and the rest of us had not seen her before. She thought she was going to

London to learn nail cosmetics. She was going to learn how to do acrylic nails and all sorts of stuff, work in the west for a few years and then go back to China to open a nail bar there.'

Bisi stroked her hand and inspected her nails, which were carefully manicured and lacquered red, except for the nail of her index finger, which was broken off short.

'She died first. Then Marsela.'

Jóna made notes, and Helena swallowed. Bisi seemed so calm and controlled as she whispered words of farewell to the Chinese girl's body. Helena paused the recording for a moment, as these were clearly words not intended for anyone else.

These moments in the mortuary were a strange blend of a statement and a farewell. Helena was suddenly aware of the cold, blue fluorescent light in the room. This was a brightness that was suitable for the work that was done in this place, but which was exceptionally cold for such an emotional moment of goodbye. It would have been more fitting to have had something to make this gentler – flowers, or the softer light of candles, soothing music.

Bisi bent over the third and kissed her forehead.

'Nadiya,' she said. 'From Ukraine. She came to Fifi's house the same day that we left to go to the container. She was brought up on a smallholding by her grandmother. They had four cows, pigs and chickens. But while Nadiya was studying in Kiev she met a man who forced her to travel to Russia, then Germany and then all over Europe. He said that if she didn't, he would kill her grandmother. He promised her a painful death if Nadiya didn't do everything the men who bought her from him told her to.'

62

By the time the rolling started, a whole day had passed since the last phone's battery had died. They were clearly the cheapest phones available and the chargers that came with them were of little use in the container. The last they had heard from Fifi was that there had been a slight delay and that they would be collected at any moment. By then they had experienced crashes and engine noises, felt themselves being swung through the air, then more bangs and vibration. Bisi had managed to keep herself calm the whole time, comforting Clara, who wept, certain that they were doomed. And Bisi had tried to get Marsela to sit down while the container was moving so that she wouldn't fall and injure herself. But when she sat down, Marsela also wept. It was as if her thought processes went into action as soon as her body stopped moving, and her fears set in.

Nadiya was the one who spoke the best sense: 'Someone's paid for a container, and even provided food, water and a toilet, so they clearly mean for us to reach a destination in one piece.'

This calmed Clara, but she started to weep again when Nadiya added, 'The thing is to accept what's expected of us at the other end.'

She told them that they were all to become prostitutes, that they would have to allow many men to fuck them every single day, and all they would get in return would be food. She said that some of the men were revolting, stinking, with infections and bad breath, and some of them were sadists who would hurt them. She told them that there was nothing helpful about Fifi and Moussa, and instead of being their friends, these people were traffickers. Jia Li shook her head and repeated again and again that she was going to learn nail tech in London and she was going to be a beautician, while Bisi struggled to breathe and Marsela again scuttled around the container, hammering at its walls.

'Why didn't you tell us?' Clara yelled. 'Why didn't you say so right away back at that house? When we still had a chance to escape?'

'That would have been bad for my grandmother,' Nadiya said, and their thoughts went from the container to Ukraine and the old woman who peeled potatoes, sitting on a little stool in front of her house, throwing the peel to the chickens that pecked around her feet in the sunshine. The tales of Nadiya's grandmother stilled some of their fears and they all felt an intimacy with her, and they forgave Nadiya as the journey continued and there were more stories of her grandmother. Of them all, she was in the worst position, as she was the only one of them with any family to worry about.

63

Clara lay on the steel table along with the others, and by the time they reached her, Bisi was overcome. Her strength and self-control were exhausted, the tears flowed unchecked down her cheeks and she felt that she was about to choke.

'Clara, from Côte d'Ivoire,' she whispered to Helena, who was hesitatingly following her from one table to the next. 'My friend.'

She asked for a chair because she felt that she was about to collapse. The woman in the white doctor's coat who stood in the corner rolled the office chair that had been at the desk over to her. Bisi sat and held Clara's arm with her bandaged hand. She could not leave her yet. She knew full well that Clara was no longer there in her body, but souls had a habit of hovering close by for a long time, while they worked out that their time on earth was over.

That was what she and Clara had talked about. When Jia Li died, they had pledged to each other that whichever of them survived longer would continue to talk to the other, to explain matters for her, to wish her success in a new dimension. To say farewell. And that was what she had done, although now she would still have to say farewell to Clara. She had been too weak to speak when Clara died in the container; too weak and too frightened.

'Clara, *ore mi*,' she whispered to the cold corpse. 'You're dead now, in this cold and distant country. You mustn't hover here over this body of yours. It's better for you to fly away. Free yourself from your body, search for those who murdered you and wreak revenge on them. Come to them in their dreams and torture them as they deserve. Turn your sorrow into anger, my sweet Clara. Be strong.'

She stroked the grey arm, took the tissue that Helena handed her and dried her eyes. Then she rose to her feet and looked into her eyes. Her strength had returned.

'Well, what do you want to know about them?' she asked.

Helena gazed back at her gravely.

'Everything,' she replied. 'I want to know everything you know about them. Any information you can give us helps to identify them so that we can find their families, and so that we can bring those who did this to justice.'

Bisi nodded. There was a lot she could tell the police, but she would have to be sensible. She would have to stay calm and get a feeling for what she could safely tell and what to keep to herself.

She would have to be cautious when choosing her friends, and when deciding what information she would divulge to them, and she would have to be clear about what she would get in return. She had handed her fate to others before, without conditions, and she'd had her fingers burned.

64

The interpreter sat in an interview room and translated the recording as Baldvin played it for him in sections. Daníel sat at Baldvin's side, and next to the interpreter sat Gutti, who noted down key points as they came up. The whole thing was recorded, and Daníel was aware that the chief superintendent was watching the activity from his office computer, with Oddsteinn, the prosecutor, at his side, and no doubt others from the investigation team who were still at work.

The interpreter listened for a moment, nodded, and Baldvin paused the recording while the interpreter relayed in Icelandic what Sergei had said in Russian on the phone.

"'We're fucked,'" the interpreter repeated after Sergei. "'The idiot truck driver dumped the container by the road and the cops are already on it.'"

Baldvin and Daníel each caught the other's eye. This in itself was enough, but Baldvin set the recording to play again. They would have the whole thing translated. Sergei's voice could be heard, sounding slurred, as if he were drunk, but Daníel realised that he was in tears.

"'The cops don't normally interfere with us, but everything will go crazy if they find a body. Let alone five bodies!'"

The recording had clearly been made before the news had leaked out that one of the women had survived.

"'You have to come, Sofia,'" the interpreter said, translating Sergei's words. "'You'll have to come and help out. Everything's fucked. I can't deal with this on my own.'"

Daníel played the next section and for a long time nothing was said, as Sergei wept and sniffled, muttering something at which the interpreter shook his head, as this was too confused for words to be made out.

Glancing at his phone, Daníel saw that he had two messages from the chief superintendent and one private message. Hell! He had forgotten about the children. By now they must have finished watching the movie he had let them rent after dinner. He hadn't had it in him to ask his former mother-in-law to take them, so he quickly tapped in a message to Lady Gúgúlú and there was an almost instant reply:

They're already in my arms, darling.

That was a relief. Lady would see to it that the children had a pleasant evening. At any rate, they'd have more fun than they would with their dad.

Daníel opened the messages from the chief superintendent, and his thoughts were again clear and focused, deep in the case:

That's sufficient. Green light from Oddsteinn to arrest SP, the first message read.

Who is Sofia? was the second.

Daníel got to his feet and left the room. He stood for a moment in the corridor and leaned against the wall. He could feel his heart beating heavily, and the coldness of the wall through his shirt was calming. He selected Áróra's number, and when she answered, he felt an overwhelming longing to see her, to look at her, to sense the smell of her, to be close to her. But right now there were more urgent things to attend to.

'Was she staying at the Center Hotel, the woman you saw Sergei meeting?' he asked.

'Yes. In any case, I saw them go in there with her luggage,' she replied. 'What's happening?'

'We have a warrant to arrest her and Sergei,' Daníel said.

65

Bisi seemed dazed after the visit to the mortuary, and Helena couldn't bring herself to drive her straight back to the refuge and leave her alone there with her thoughts and memories. As they walked over to the car, she fished her phone from her pocket and called Sirra.

'I'm so sorry, Sirra. I know you've prepared something special,' she said, speaking fast. 'But I've just come from taking a trafficking victim to identify bodies and I don't have it in me to leave her alone right now.'

This was too much information, but she had to explain to Sirra why she was pulling out of their dinner at the last moment. Especially as Sirra had gone out of her way to invite her, instead of just saying that she could come if she felt like it. It was obvious she had made an effort.

'I'll take her for a meal somewhere so she has company this evening.'

'Come here,' Sirra said. 'And bring her with you. No problem to put another plate on the table.'

Helena hesitated and ran through her mind every possible scenario under which this could affect the case, but couldn't think of any.

'I'm not sure it's exactly professional—' she began, but Sirra interrupted.

'Being a decent person is never unprofessional, and regardless of anything else, I imagine you both need to eat.'

Helena thought she should let Bisi decide.

'My good friend has invited us for dinner,' she said, switching to English. 'Would you like that?'

Bisi looked at her quickly, and Helena thought she could see the suspicious look return to her eyes.

'Do I have to stay the night there?'

'No, not at all,' she said firmly. She hadn't realised that an invitation to someone's home could appear suspect to Bisi. 'We'll go there and have a meal, and then I'll drive you back to the refuge. Only if you want to. We can also go to a restaurant to get something to eat if you prefer.'

Bisi looked at her enquiringly for a moment, and then nodded.

'I would like to go to your friend's house,' she said.

They drove in silence to Sirra's place, where Bisi's and Helena's doubts vanished, as a smiling Sirra opened the door and welcomed them in, and they were met by the enticing smell of lamb roasting in the oven.

66

While in the container, Bisi had managed to stay calm by re-assuring the others. Even Nadiya, who seemed to have been confident for much of the time, had eventually appeared to despair. So Bisi had moved up a gear. She became a mother figure to the others. She was the one who opened her arms, and the other girls crawled to her in the shelter of the sanctuary she had pulled together from the mattresses. When they huddled together they were able to keep themselves warm, and the movement and the noise no longer seemed so overwhelming when she could concentrate on the sound of the other girls' breathing.

Bisi made sure they all had chocolate and drank water when they were too seasick to eat. By making sure that she took care of the others, her thoughts spent less time dwelling on what would happen once the journey was over. Nadiya's accounts of the revolting men she had been forced to service, of the beatings and humiliations, had initially terrified her, but eventually what was waiting for them at the other end no longer mattered, as all her thoughts and energies were focused on surviving the journey. She would have to take one step at a time. She would face each ordeal in turn. It was as if she and Clara had made a silent agreement that they would look after the girls together. They developed a set of house rules: nobody was to stand up. They should only crawl about the container so that they wouldn't fall, as the movements came like hammer blows, as what they realised could only be a ship carrying them plunged then hauled itself back up again from each trough. The rule was just one mouthful of water at a time to avoid seasickness. Bisi tried not to think about how long the water would last, but allowed herself to be

comforted by Nadiya's assurances that they were valuable mer-
chandise and everyone had an interest in them arriving alive and
well at their destination. How else were they supposed to service
all those vile men who would be queuing up to fuck them? So
there had to be enough water, and the same applied to the chocolate and the biscuits. Her main concern was that Jia Li kept
nothing down and seemed to be losing strength faster than the
others.

Jia Li had vomited all over the travel toilet and wept con-
stantly. Bisi and Clara crawled to her, trying to comfort her and
get her to lie down with the rest of them in the nest of mattresses
so they could keep each other warm, as the temperature inside
the container had dropped sharply. When she had nothing more
to vomit and simply retched, Jia Li gave up and lay down with
them. Bisi stroked her hair and whispered to her about how
much she was looking forward to visiting her nail bar in London
to get a set of the coolest acrylics for her toes and fingers, and
about how they'd go for a stroll along Oxford Street and stop
somewhere for a cocktail, taking care to sip daintily through a
straw so as not to spoil their fabulous nails or the fresh lipstick
they'd just treated themselves to – tales she knew herself were
nothing but lies.

A day later it became obvious that Jia Li was never going to
become a beautician. Bisi woke up to see that she had stood up
from the nest and torn off all her clothes, and was shouting out
loud that she was hot. A little later she was unconscious, and although they dressed her in her clothes again and sandwiched
her between them to warm her, she was soon as cold as ice and
they couldn't wake her.

67

Elín sat on the floor in the little darkroom that was part of her studio, and which she had fitted out back when she had been working mostly with photography. The snug, soft darkness enveloped her like a blanket, and she was calm even when she heard Sergei's footsteps on the stairs. When she had heard the car outside, she had decided to hide in here. It wasn't so much that she was frightened of Sergei, but that she was confused and hurt, and didn't trust herself to speak to him. More than likely she would burst into tears without being able to say a word, and after seeing the pictures of him with that woman, she didn't want him to try to console her.

She had heard him calling her upstairs in the flat, and now he was on his way down the stairs. She heard the studio door open.

'Elín?' She heard him take a few steps into the studio before calling again. 'Elín!'

She held her breath. She needed more time to think, to calm herself down. She had heard things today about Sergei that didn't add up, and other things that added up perfectly with what she had suspected. Such as the woman at the coach terminal. That was no kiss between friends. It was not the kind of kiss you give your mother. Nobody sticks their tongue down their mother's throat. The kiss had confirmed all the painful suspicions that had preyed on her mind more and more as the phone calls became more frequent and he took pains to avoid talking about them. What was hardest to believe was that Sergei was a violent man. Of course he looked tough and was proud of it, saying that his was the normal street fashion in Russia. His look was simply what was cool. But she found it inconceivable that he could have stood by while someone else choked a woman. He was such a gentleman. He was quick to help old ladies in the shops, carrying their bags, opening doors, gesturing for women to go ahead of him in queues. She couldn't imagine him grinning and looking on while someone else abused a woman, as Áróra had assured her he had done in her house. And the idea that he could have murdered his former wife was completely ridiculous. He had never been charged, only suspected.

The studio door banged shut and she heard his footsteps going upstairs, and then her phone rang. She frantically fumbled for it, frightened that Sergei would hear it from upstairs. He clearly had his phone to his ear as it was his name on the screen. She muted the ringtone and let it ring out. She couldn't talk to him now. Just couldn't bring herself to do it. She had no clue what to say.

Hello was too bland for the emotions churning inside her. *Go to hell* would be closer to the mark. And then there was the pain in her heart that she wanted to let out in a wail. She longed to whisper *my love*, and to hear him respond with sweet words of his own.

The phone stopped ringing, and Elín was about to get to her feet and slip out into the studio when there was a loud banging at the front door.

'Police! Open up!' a voice called.

Elín sat in indecision for a moment. Should she wait and let Sergei open it, or go to the door herself? What did the police want? Was this just Daníel here to check up on her? She rose from the darkroom floor, went through the studio to the front door and opened it. Two uniformed police officers stepped past her and hurried up the stairs, and another went into the studio to look around. Daníel followed behind them, holding up a sheet of paper.

'We are here to arrest Sergei K. Popov on the grounds of suspicion of involvement in human trafficking,' he said.

Elín felt faint. Trafficking? What was going on?

'Daníel, what are you doing here?' she demanded. 'Are you pinning something on Sergei to protect me?'

She instantly regretted her words the moment they left her mouth. She knew Daníel better than that.

'My darling Elín,' he said, his eyes serious and dark, as they always were when he was sorrowful. 'It's much more serious than that. We are arresting Sergei and a woman called Sofia, with whom he has a connection, on suspicion of their involvement with the deaths of the four women in the container.' Elín opened her mouth to speak, but found herself unable to say a word. 'The recording you passed to Áróra provides the evidence. He outright admits having been behind this – and more.'

The two officers came down the stairs with Sergei in handcuffs. He was docile, and Elín wanted to tell them that as he wasn't resisting, there was no need for the man to be restrained, but she was stunned into silence and stared at Sergei as the officers led him away between them.

'Get me a lawyer, Elín. I need a lawyer!'

'There's no need for that,' Daníel said to her in a low voice. 'We'll make sure he's allocated a lawyer.'

Elín followed them out onto the pavement, where she watched the officers put Sergei in the back of a car and drive away.

'Is there anyone you'd like me to call for you, Elín?' Daníel asked. 'Shall I give you a lift to your dad's place?'

But Elín didn't reply. All she could think of was that she had been right all along. Her suspicions had been completely correct. The woman's name was Sofia.

68

Áróra was standing on her hands against the wall when the doorbell rang. She was sweaty and dishevelled after a twenty-minute session of forty rapid press-ups alternated with forty fast knee-bends, followed by balance exercises that finished up with some careful handstands. She was waiting on a parcel from her mother, containing 'a few odds and ends', so she was expecting to see a postman outside, but instead Daníel stood there, one hand on the door frame, leaning towards the door so that she almost expected him to fall inside when she opened it. He had a paper bag from a burger joint in his hand.

'May I come in?' he asked, and she instantly stepped to one side, hoping he wouldn't smell the sweat. 'I bring dinner. I'm on the way home, so I thought I'd drop in and give you an update.'

'How did it go?' Áróra asked.

Daníel sighed.

'Good. Sergei Popov and Sofia Ivanova are both locked up in cells and will be questioned tomorrow when lawyers have been appointed for them.'

He slipped off his shoes and went into the living room.

'That sounds good,' Áróra said, taking a bottle of red wine from the sideboard and showing it to Daníel. 'Would you…?'

'Yes. Please,' he said, taking a seat on the sofa. 'Maybe one glass.'

She handed him one and took hers with her to the bathroom.

'I'm just going to take a quick shower,' she said. 'I was doing exercises when you arrived. I won't be a moment. Just take it easy.'

Daníel nodded and sipped his wine. Áróra hurriedly stripped off her training gear and stood under the torrent of hot water.

She washed her hair, using the shampoo as shaving foam to scrape smooth her armpits and legs. Getting out of the shower, she checked her toes. It was a while since she had last had a pedicure. She considered quickly painting her nails, but decided against it and went instead for the hair dryer. When her hair was dry, she rubbed moisturiser onto her legs, applied a little powder to her face and added a touch of lip gloss. She finished with a quick squirt of perfume behind her ears, under her throat, on each wrist and on her crotch.

She wrapped herself in the dressing gown and tied it around her waist, and stood still for a moment as she opened the door, wondering whether to go to the bedroom and get dressed, or go into the living room in just the robe. This wasn't exactly a sexy dressing gown, although there was nothing wrong with it – turquoise silk decorated with fire-breathing dragons. She inspected herself in the mirror and was satisfied with what she saw. She looked fresh and her newly blow-dried hair didn't look bad. She decided to go for it, and if Daníel found it uncomfortable, then he would leave.

But Daníel's preferences weren't put to the test, as when Áróra appeared in the living room, he was stretched out on the sofa, fast asleep. Áróra looked down at him, and didn't have the heart to wake him. He looked lovely so relaxed, with a day's worth of stubble on his cheeks. She took the woollen blanket that she usually curled up under to watch TV, and covered him with it. Then she switched off the living-room light and took the wine with her to the bedroom.

69

'Can I apply for asylum here in Iceland?' Bisi asked when they were in the car, having left Sirra with kisses on both cheeks, in the French manner, and a heartfelt hug. Sirra had been quite right that it was much more pleasant to have a meal in a home than in a restaurant, and Helena was pleased that she had agreed to bring Bisi with her to dinner.

'Yes,' Helena replied. 'As you're a victim of human trafficking, you have the right to a six-month stay in Iceland. But then you would have to work with us – I mean the police – to get to the bottom of who brought you here in that container, and you would have to be prepared to testify against them.'

'And if I testify, could I stay?'

'At least for six months,' Helena said.

'And what happens after six months? Would I have to return home?'

'After six months you could apply for a further six, which is plenty of time to work on an application for a long-term residence permit.'

Bisi didn't reply, and there was silence in the car for a while. They were sitting at traffic lights when Bisi took a deep breath and sighed heavily. When she spoke again, her voice was clear and direct.

'I want to testify against them all,' she said. 'I can tell you the whole story from the beginning. There are names, and I can identify pictures, and I have addresses. But only if I get to stay. I want a written paper with a promise, and a lawyer who will confirm that the promise is valid.'

'You'll get a lawyer who will look after your interests,' Helena said, and felt her heart leap and beat fast in anticipation. This was a huge step. Few victims of trafficking could or would testify. The families of some were often threatened, while others were simply too frightened for their own lives to bear witness.

'OK,' Bisi said. 'I will testify. I cannot, under any circumstances, return home to Nigeria.'

'So you are Nigerian?'

'Yes,' Bisi said. 'But I can't be any longer. Because I am like you.'

'Like me?' Helena asked, and wondered if she had lost the thread of the conversation. 'What do you mean?'

'Like you and Sirra,' Bisi said. She caught Helena's eye, and laughed. 'Did you think I believed it when you said she was just your good friend? I can see in her eyes that she loves you. And your feet touched under the table.' Helena gasped in surprise. It hadn't occurred to her that Bisi would realise the true nature of her relationship with Sirra. 'And because I am like you, I cannot go home,' Bisi said. 'I was found out, and my father set fire to my apartment and threw Habiba out. I fear he would kill me if I return home.'

Helena pulled the car over to the side of the road and brought it to a halt. This was the reason why Bisi had not wanted to admit that she was from Nigeria. She was terrified of being sent back there. And presumably this was also the reason why she had fallen into the hands of traffickers, and why she had ended up in the container. Helena leaned over to Bisi and hugged her tight.

'I'll do everything I can to help you,' she whispered. 'Everything I possibly can.'

70

Habiba was a wonderful cook, and Bisi never failed to be consumed with anticipation when she came home to the aroma of bean stew and fresh akara that would lead her from the street to the yard, where Habiba would be sitting on a lemonade crate in front of the three-legged pot, deep-frying the spicy fritters. It had been food that brought them together, as Bisi had called every day at the food stall where Habiba worked to buy rice or fried fish and grilled maize balls. Habiba had joked that she was like one of those single guys who always bought take-away meals on the way home from work. Bisi had stressed that she was a *professional woman*, someone with a career ahead of her, and her job at the computer workshop was the most important thing in her life. Her parents had paid to put her through technical college, and now she was being a dutiful daughter by being successful.

Habiba had told her about her life in the north of the country, where everything was paralysed by the endless conflict between Boko Haram and government forces. The same week that Habiba had been supposed to become betrothed to the old man with a beard her father had chosen for her, Boko Haram attacked the village, and Habiba had used the turmoil as an opportunity to run away. She had travelled to Lagos with a foreign journalist, and was practically starving by the time the owner of the food stall gave her something to eat and then allowed her to work for food.

Their daily chats around dinnertime sometimes stretched out long past the food stall's closing time, and they made a habit of walking home together, occasionally stopping at a bar for a drink. It was after one such time that Habiba kissed Bisi goodbye before getting on the bus to go home to the room she rented. Bisi had been startled, as she had expected no more than the usual peck on her cheek – not for Habiba's lips to rest for so long against hers so that Bisi could sense the alcohol on her breath and the sweet food smells that enveloped her like a cloud after her day's work. The forecourt of the Oshodi bus station was so busy that nobody seemed to notice this long, deep kiss, or Bisi's reaction. The bustle of the bus station, all the little cars coming and going, and people on their way with bundles, children tagging along behind them, continued as if nothing had happened, but for Bisi everything had changed. The beer she had drunk churned in her stomach so that she wanted to be sick, but her heart lifted with a joyful anticipation she had never before experienced.

The next day she invited Habiba home for a drink, and it wasn't long before Habiba quit her job and became Bisi's housekeeper. The housekeeper title was just a pretext, as there was an agreement between them that they would be a couple of a sort – Bisi being the breadwinner and Habiba the housewife, looking after clothes and food and the household.

Habiba was a Muslim and prayed daily, but the day before she moved in, she took off her hijab, saying that she wouldn't wear it any longer. Bisi was never able to find out whether she felt it wasn't appropriate in this district, or that she thought her sinful new lifestyle was an affront to the faith she had grown up in.

Even though Habiba was quiet and said very little, Bisi was completely certain that she was as happy as Bisi herself was, as she glowed with pleasure whenever Bisi came home and they sat in the yard with a drink and a meal, with pleasant music playing on the radio and the smell of charcoal in the air. The week before her trip to Paris, they sat in the cool of the evening with cocktails in their hands, and she looked at Habiba, dressed in a cheap print dress, and smiled.

'In Paris I'll buy you such beautiful clothes, Habiba,' she said, and squeezed her thigh. 'You'll be so pleased when I come home with suitcases stuffed full.'

Áróra felt slightly foolish, slipping back to the bathroom and quietly into the shower to again shave the legs she had shaved the night before, in case bristles had appeared. She soaped herself all over, rinsed herself off under a blast of cold water and dried herself rapidly, then brushed her teeth and applied skin cream. Thinking about it, this was decidedly odd behaviour, not least in light of how the previous evening had turned out, and considering Daníel no doubt needed to be at work at eight o'clock. But she wasn't about to let him encounter her with morning breath and bed hair.

She wondered whether to just wear the dressing gown, but decided against it, stealthily opening the bathroom door and tiptoeing to the bedroom to pull on a top and jeans. The fitted jeans were snug, and the top was cut low enough that she hoped it was sexy, but everyday enough not to look out of place this early in the morning. This was nothing so smart that she could be considered to be dressing up.

There was no sound from the other room, so Daníel had to still be sleeping, as it wasn't yet seven o'clock. In the kitchen she filled the coffee machine and allowed water to gush for longer than necessary into the sink to allow Daníel an opportunity to wake up. When there was still no movement, she went to the living room and peered over the back of the sofa.

She felt even more foolish when she saw that Daníel was gone. The sofa was deserted, the blanket folded and the cushions neatly lined up. There was a little note on the coffee table, in Daníel's handwriting.

Thank you, and sorry. I have to relieve the babysitter.

Babysitter? So his children were still staying with him. Áróra wasn't sure whether to be happy or sad that he had come to her instead of going home to his children.

To prevent herself from brooding, she sat at the computer and decided it was time to get back to what she had meant to do a long time ago – to find out more about Leonid Kuznetsov.

She opened a folder of the information she had on him, hoping to stumble across something that would give her an opening or some new angle. That would give her a pretext for calling Daníel, and then she could ask him about his children, and even invite him to call around again. Or was that pushing things too far? It irritated Áróra – who usually considered herself confident, not one to hesitate when seeking out what she wanted – that she should always become a shrinking violet around this man.

72

Daniel woke to the sound of voices from the kitchen, and he scrambled to his feet, pulling on a T-shirt. He found Tumi and Tanja sitting at the kitchen table in their pyjamas, engrossed in their phones while they munched cereal from bowls. Lady Gúgúlú marched through the room holding a carton of milk, for all the world like an old-school provincial housewife.

'To what do we owe the honour of being graced by your presence?' Lady asked, her voice dripping with sarcasm.

'I didn't want to wake you when I came home,' Daniel said. 'You were sleeping so soundly on the sofa in front of *Ru Paul's Drag Race*. I thought you might be doing some kind of unconscious therapy by sleeping in front of your rival.'

'Lady's way cooler than Ru Paul,' Tumi said through a mouthful of cereal and without looking up from his phone.

Daniel looked in astonishment at his son. It would never have occurred to him that Tumi would have even heard of Ru Paul, let alone that he had ever seen one of the shows.

'Thanks, darling,' Lady said, blowing Tumi a kiss and fetching a mug from the kitchen cupboard, filling it with coffee and handing it to Daniel.

He took the mug gratefully, sat at the table between the children and patted Tanja's hair.

'What's new, my darlings,' he said. 'Have a good time yesterday?'

'Just fine,' Tumi said.

'Loads of fun,' Tanja added. 'Lady was the best of all of them in the show.'

'You took them to a drag show?' His voice had a sharper edge than he had intended, and Lady stiffened and turned.

'Well, what was I supposed to do?' she spluttered. 'I got your message just before I was supposed to be on stage.'

'I didn't know you were working. I'd have found someone else if I'd have known. A night club isn't the ideal place for youngsters.'

'Hey, what?' Lady said. 'I was really strict with them, and only let them have two beers each. Not a drop more.'

The children sniggered into their bowls and Daníel sighed.

'I'm sorry,' he said. 'I didn't mean to be unpleasant. Yesterday was just a dreadful, long day at work. Sorry I was so late getting home.'

He felt guilt gnawing at him about going to meet Áróra after work in the hope of finding a little comfort instead of coming straight home to his children.

'It's all right,' Lady said, making the sign of the cross in the air in front of Daníel's face. 'Sins absolved.'

Daníel smiled and bowed his head in mock humility. The children sniggered again. Tanja looked at Daníel with what looked to be complete sincerity in her eyes.

'Is Lady our step-mother or step-father?' she asked.

'Neither,' Daníel said in astonishment. 'We aren't—'

'Step-mother!' Lady said. 'Mother, darlings. I've always dreamed of being a mother.' She kissed the two of them on the tops of their heads and made for the kitchen door. 'Now, I'm off to my humble abode. Please don't think of knocking before midday. Mother needs her beauty sleep.'

'We're just friends,' Daníel told the children, unsure whether or not they were taking on board what he was saying, as they were immersed in their phones, which he now cursed himself for giving them. Their mother would also give him the sharp side of her tongue when they came home to Denmark with new bad habits. His own phone prevented him from starting what would be a difficult conversation about screen time. He stood up and went into the living room to take Áróra's call.

'*Hæ*,' he said. 'I'm really sorry I nodded off on your sofa. It's just so relaxing being around you.'

Áróra laughed.

'That's maybe not the effect I would like to have,' she said.

Daníel's heart beat faster. How should he answer this? He hunted through his mind for some suitably clever reply, but the moment was gone and Áróra laughed again.

'Just kidding,' she said, and quickly continued. 'I have some information for you about Leonid Kuznetsov.'

'Ah. And?'

'Yes, he has close links to the Russian mafia. From information I've been able to gather from other countries, he seems to have been mostly a gofer for much more powerful people. He's no big fish, even though that's the image he likes to project here in Iceland.'

This was interesting.

'Would you send me the information you have?'

Áróra agreed, and Daníel said goodbye and ended the call before he was tempted to retrace his steps, back to their initial words about the effect Áróra had on him. But going by what she just said, it seemed she was open to knowing something about how strong his attraction for her was. Maybe she was giving some thought to the idea of them being in a relationship of some sort.

73

'I have some background on Leonid Kuznetsov that could help us crank up the pressure on him,' Daníel said to Baldvin as they went up the steps at the station. 'I have a strong suspicion that he's involved in all this, but we need more we can pin on him than just being the landlord.'

'We'll go and talk to him today,' Baldvin said. 'Just an informal chat.'

Daníel nodded and followed Baldvin into the meeting room, where the investigation team was waiting for the morning meeting to start.

Baldvin started the meeting by announcing that he was going to give them three things to be happy about.

'The first piece of good news is that the woman who survived the ordeal in the container, Bisi Babalola, is prepared to testify and to participate in identifying suspects. So, that gives us a strong basis on which to prepare a case, even though we still have a lot of ground to cover.' Baldvin nodded to Helena in tacit ac-knowledgement, and she nodded back.

Baldvin wasn't at all bad, even though taking the lead some-times went to his head. He had taken Daníel and Helena by surprise by offering to handle all the work involved in applying for a six-month residence permit as a victim of human trafficking – producing reports, filling in forms and amassing certification. Daníel knew that Helena was not only delighted at being able to hand all this over, but was also pleased that Baldvin was showing real leadership by offering to lighten the workload of his team.

'I presume the witness has been allocated a legal represen-tative?' Oddsteinn asked from his corner of the room.

'Yes,' Helena replied. 'That's been done, and the legal representative is in a meeting with Bisi now.'

Oddsteinn nodded, satisfied, and Baldvin returned to where he had left off.

'The other piece of news is that the owner of InExport, Valur Jón Pálsson, has neither gone up in smoke nor left this earthly existence. The bad news is that he's left the country. It seems that he was on the first flight after the container hit the headlines.'

'He's on Europol and Interpol wanted lists,' Ari Benz said. 'We know he flew to London, and from there to Paris, but we still don't know if he travelled any further.'

Baldvin fidgeted for a moment, and an expression that looked almost like triumph appeared on his face, although he didn't go so far as to allow himself a smile.

'The best news of all is that last night two individuals were arrested, suspected of involvement in this case.'

There was a moment's silence in the room, and then everyone nodded and mumbled. This was as much jubilation as it was possible to allow themselves, as while arrests were always a major step forward in any investigation, they knew better than anyone that all kinds of unexpected twists could still change the course of their work, right up to the very last moment.

'Their names are Sergei Popov and Sofia Ivanova,' Baldvin continued. 'He is a Russian citizen and holds a Schengen residence permit. She is a French citizen of Russian origin. They're being held at Hólmsheiði and are waiting to be brought here for questioning.'

74

For Sofía's interrogation Daníel would have preferred to have Helena at his side. They had developed a way of practically being able to read each other's thoughts that made the whole process easier when they worked together. Baldvin had initially wanted them to question Sergei, until Daníel had reminded him of his indirect connection that could prejudice the process.

So Baldvin had put Helena and Kristján in one interview room facing Sergei and his lawyer, while Daníel was teamed up with the young, ambitious Gutti. Knowing he was keen to learn, Daníel was confident that Gutti would follow his lead in the interrogation.

The moment he entered the room, Daníel saw that Sofia Ivanova was not going to be co-operative. She sat, arms folded over her chest, and was leaning so far back in the chair that she was almost lying down – a pose she no doubt hoped would demonstrate her lack of concern. But Daníel had seen this kind of body language often enough to know it only indicated arrogance. Those who thought they were smarter than the police or who felt they were in some kind of superior position often sat like this as it meant that making eye contact with their questioners involved literally looking down their nose at them.

He didn't recall having met Sofía's lawyer before, and the man appeared to be ill-prepared, still going through the papers in front of him and repeatedly pushing back into place the glasses that had slipped down his nose.

'What precisely is Sofia suspected of?' he said in Icelandic. Sofia jabbed him with an elbow, and he repeated the question in English.

'Involvement in human trafficking,' Daníel replied. 'Illegal coercion, deprivation of freedom, reckless conduct, endangering life, manslaughter and possibly murder. All of these come under the Icelandic penal code, and although the case is yet to be fully clarified, it's more or less certain that most of these will be on the prosecution's list of charges.'

The lawyer nodded, and continued to flip through the paperwork. Daníel could see pearls of sweat appear on his forehead.

'In other words, we believe her to be behind the trafficking of five women in an uninsulated shipping container across the North Atlantic in the middle of winter, resulting in the deaths of at least three of the women by hypothermia. In addition, we believe the way the container was outfitted contributed to the death of the fourth, probably in a fall, and that the fifth was in serious danger of losing her life.'

Daníel saw the lawyer glance quickly at Sofia, as if checking that this was the same woman as he had spoken to in the preparatory interview just now. There was no doubt that Sofia had fed him a very different story. He pushed his glasses up his nose again and cleared his throat.

'Sofia has no comment to make and reserves the right of a person suspected of a crime, as laid down in law, to decline to answer questions.'

Daníel looked at Sofia for a while and was sure that she smirked back at him. For a moment he considered going in strong, letting Gutti loose with a torrent of questions, while he sat and stared back at her with a grin on his face, but he wasn't sure that the thick hide this woman had grown would be penetrated so easily. He got to his feet and tapped Gutti's shoulder, and he followed his example, looking surprised.

'Well,' Daníel said. 'We'll leave it there.'

Then they left the room.

75

Kristján read out the names for the recording of all those present at the interview, stating the charges as they were listed on the warrant. Sergei glanced briefly at them, but otherwise didn't look up from the table. On the other hand, his lawyer was cheerful – from his demeanour, anyone would imagine that this was one of the best days of his life.

'Well, Sergei,' the lawyer said. 'I must stress that according to the law you have a duty to tell the truth, but you also have the right to decline to answer questions and you can decline to discuss matters that could implicate you further.'

'I will not be saying anything,' Sergei said. 'I'm saying nothing. I have nothing to say because I don't know what you are trying to pin on me. I think this is just Daníel's personal jealousy because I am with his wife.'

Sergei muttered his words into his chest without looking up.

'In fact, she is his former wife.' Helena felt herself bound to correct him. 'As far as I'm aware, it's fifteen years since they divorced. As you are well aware.'

'You have a colourful past, Sergei,' Kristján said, consulting the paperwork in front of him. 'At least, that's what the French police tell us.'

Now Sergei looked up.

'She threw herself off that cliff,' he said, peering at Kristján through narrowed eyes. 'And nobody can prove otherwise. Proof, y'see. You need proof, don't you?'

The lawyer's eyes switched in confusion from Sergei to Kristján and back again.

'What exactly are we talking about?' he said. Kristján handed him the documents Ari Benz had obtained concerning the death of Sergei's wife in France. The lawyer looked through them, and shoved them firmly back. 'Let's stick to what Sergei is suspected of here in Iceland. Not dig up some old case from France.'

'Of course,' Kristján replied. 'It's just interesting, as it indicates the character of the man.'

'I don't give a fuck what you think of my character,' Sergei snarled. 'Show me the evidence, if you have any, otherwise my lawyer can get me out of here. I'm not going to sit in a cell if you don't have anything.'

Helena took out the picture the artist had produced under Lárentínus's guidance, and placed it on the table.

'This likeness has been drawn on the basis of a witness's recollections of one of the Russian men who took delivery of a container in a yard on Auðbrekka last Monday. In the container were the bodies of four girls, and one woman who was close to death. This looks remarkably like you, Sergei.'

'I don't think so,' Sergei said. 'That could be anyone.'

Helena smiled.

'We also have a recording of you speaking in a telephone conversation, to Sofia, about the shipment of these women and their deaths.' Now Sergei was taken aback. He shifted in his chair and glanced questioningly at his lawyer.

'We need to hear this recording,' the lawyer said.

'Of course,' Helena replied, and started the recording. Sergei's overwrought voice could be heard speaking in Russian. She let it play for a moment, before switching it off. She handed the lawyer a folder.

'This is a translation completed by a court-appointed translator, word for word.'

The lawyer took the papers, but Sergei leaned back in his chair and grinned.

'Did the police record this?' he asked. 'With a warrant?'

'No,' Helena said. 'Elín, the woman you live with, recorded this on her phone.'

'Then this recording isn't acceptable as evidence,' Sergei said. 'Not if it was obtained illegally. I didn't know I was being recorded and never gave my consent for it. And I don't suppose Elín had a court warrant allowing her to record me. If that's everything, then you don't have anything on me.'

Helena smiled as she stood up, and Kristján did the same.

'Your knowledge of Icelandic law is letting you down, Sergei,' she said. 'Your legal representative will be able to inform you that in this country things are different. Here we are able to present this kind of recording as evidence, and whether or not it's accepted in court is at the judge's discretion. Now, I think you should have a conversation with your lawyer about whether you're better off continuing to pretend you're innocent, or if it might be more advisable to come clean and tell us the whole story.'

76

Helena and Kristján appeared in the corridor just after Daníel and Gutti had left their interview room. Their expressions showed that they hadn't got far with Sergei.

'How did you get on?' Helena asked.

'Nothing at all,' Daníel he said. 'We'll try again tomorrow. When they realise we mean business, they'll be more talkative.'

'Were you watching?' Helena asked as Baldvin and Oddsteinn emerged from the room where they had been following both sessions via video links.

'Yes,' Baldvin nodded. 'But that wasn't much of a start. What sort of tactics were those, Daníel, winding the session up so quickly?'

'I could see right away that she wasn't going to say anything. She's not the type to open up. And she seems confident that we don't have anything solid on her.'

Oddsteinn sighed.

'That's just it. We don't have anything concrete to pin on her,' he said. 'We know from this recording that Sergei appears to be talking to her, because he addresses her several times by name, and from what he says to her we can assume that she was aware the women were being shipped here in a container. But that's all. There's nothing in the recording that confirms she's a participant in this. The only hint we have is what he says right at the end – that he can't deal with this on his own and she'll have to come to Iceland.'

'I'm certain she's involved,' Helena said. 'We'll have Bisi's testimony today, and I'm sure Sofia's name will come into it somewhere. I can feel it.'

'Feelings aren't enough, Helena,' Baldvin said in an avuncular tone that Daníel immediately saw irritated Helena. 'The bastard in there is correct when he says that we need bullet-proof evidence. And I don't expect to get her custody extended,' he added. 'I'd say that you're fortunate to have her for three days, and you'll have to make the most of the time you have.'

'Agreed,' Daníel said. He knew that Oddsteinn was right too. 'We'll question her again tomorrow and then we'll crank up the pressure. People tend to be more co-operative the longer they're held in solitary confinement. I'll let her know that she's being taken back to Hólmsheiði now.'

'Hold on!' Ari Benz called out as he hurried along the corridor towards them just as Daníel opened the interview-room door.

77

Sofia sat bolt upright in her chair as the door closed behind Daniel, and she stared at him with wide eyes. The smirk was gone from her face, replaced by a serious expression.

'We have to stop the recording,' Ari Benz said, following Daniel into the interview room, where the app had already started the video and audio recordings.

Daniel hesitated.

'It's standard practice that all conversations are recorded and a lawyer has to be present,' he said, standing motionless by the door.

'Yes,' Ari Benz said, and switched to English. 'But these are special circumstances.'

Sofia looked at Daniel and smiled. The arrogance was gone and there was something sincere about her smile now. Daniel looked from her to Ari, and he sensed that they both knew something he didn't.

'OK,' Daniel agreed. 'We're stopping the recording at 12:15 due to special circumstances. Those present in the room, in addition to the suspect, are Daniel Hansson of the city police CID and Ari Benz from the national commissioner's international department.'

He lifted a finger as an indication that they should wait and say nothing until the app delivered a confirmation that the recording had been stopped. Then he took a seat at the table facing Sofia, who seemed dubious that the recording had genuinely been suspended, as when she leaned forward, she whispered so that Daniel could barely hear her.

'I'm a cop,' she said. 'I'm from a department of French CID that investigates organised crime. I'm here as an infiltrator. Interpol is aware of who I am.'

Daníel was too surprised to say anything, and glanced questioningly at Ari, who nodded to confirm that she was telling the truth.

'Why didn't we know about this earlier?' Daníel asked, looking at Ari. 'Overseas officers aren't cleared to pursue an investigation here unless the national commissioner's office has been informed.'

Ari shrugged.

'The information just came through,' he said. 'It's unusual for it to be sent *after* an infiltrator has already arrived on the scene, but there appear to be special circumstances relating to this case.'

'Could we speak in private?' Daníel said to Ari Benz as he stood up to leave the room.

Ari followed him out into the corridor, where Baldvin and Helena were waiting, their at excitement at a new development obvious. Daníel stalked past them, seeing their surprised looks as he went into an empty interview room, with Ari following close behind him.

'Isn't this all very odd?' Daníel asked. He had met police officers from other countries before when they had been working on assignments in Iceland, but the Icelandic police had always been informed in advance. If they were arrested, this was generally a tactic or for show, and the request for their arrest would come from the international department.

'Well, not strange, exactly, but they are certainly unusually late in informing us of her presence,' Ari said. 'I'll inform the chief superintendent. The commissioner has already been informed, but there's no need for this to become common knowledge among the rest of the team.'

'Does Sofia have a handler here?'

'Yes, her supervisor is present in Iceland and is supposed to escort her back tomorrow. I've been sent all his details.'

'She's leaving? We don't get to question her?'

'No. She's not suspected of any crime in Iceland. Or in France, for that matter. She's been undercover as this Sergei's girlfriend as a way of infiltrating the organisation behind this human trafficking. The French police want her released right away. They say we can have a copy of the report when their part of the investigation is complete.' Ari sighed heavily. 'Welcome to the world of international policing.'

78

Elín sipped the tea she had made with a cheap teabag dug out from the furthest reaches of the kitchen cupboard and realised now that Sergei's caravan tea was a thousand times better, as he had never tired of assuring her. This was in a way symbolic – nobody appreciates what they have until it's gone.

She had barely slept for most of the night, stretched out in the bed that now seemed much too large, weeping for Sergei. But she was also angry. Now that she was up and sipping tea she felt the rage burning in her breast like a flame. It wasn't just that Sergei had concealed so much of his past from her, he had also openly lied to her. Now it seemed that he had been in a relationship with another woman the whole time they had been living together. This stung, and made her furious, all at the same time. Then there was the humiliation: looking into other people's eyes and knowing that they knew. And she would have to tell her father the whole story. She would never be able to conceal such a shock from him. He could always sense how she felt. No doubt the day would come when he would remind her that he had warned her, that he had known better and that she was just a silly girl who had let a Russian gangster lead her by the nose.

A knock on the door downstairs interrupted her thoughts. She wrapped the dressing gown closer around her and tied the belt tighter as she went down the stairs. Judging by the hard, fast knock, this had to be the police. That was just how they had banged on the door when they came to get Sergei yesterday.

Elín turned the lock and the door swung inward. The first man pushed her hard against the wall so the other two could get past her and up the stairs. They ran up as if they were in a hurry, while the one who had pushed her aside stayed there with her.

She was about to take to her heels out of the door, but he put a hand on her chest, just below her throat.

'No,' he said.

Elín felt the anger that had been burning inside her slide down into her belly where it became a hard knot that sucked all the energy from her. She knew one of the pair who had gone upstairs. This was a friend of Sergei's, who had come round a couple of times for a beer. He had been courteous and pleasant to her. She had brought them a tray of cheese and biscuits, and he had politely thanked her and took the time to chat to her about this and that. There was none of that courtesy now as he came down the stairs and marched past with her laptop and phone in his hands.

'Is this his computer?' demanded the one who held her by the throat.

She shook her head.

'No. It's mine,' she gasped. 'The police took Sergei's.'

'And his phone too?'

She nodded, and the man released his grip and followed the other two out to a car that had its engine running at the kerb in front of the house. Her instinct was to call Daníel, but then she realised that they had taken the only phone in the house as she had got rid of the landline long ago. She thought about knocking on the neighbours' door and asking if she could use their phone, but what was she supposed to say?

She'd had enough of Sergei and the police, and everything else. It was time to regain her bearings. Time to think. Time to mourn. Time to paint.

79

The half-clad house in Leirvogstunga looked to be weeping blood – the damp sleet made rivulets of rust seep from the exposed ends of the concrete's reinforcing rods. Daníel's eyes instinctively went to the big living-room window from which Leonid had watched them drive away two days ago. His heart beat faster as his eyes met Leonid's, standing in the same place as before, as if time had stood still and he and Baldvin were turning back moments after they had last departed.

As Leonid opened the door and welcomed them in as courteously as before, Daníel saw that he was dressed differently this time. Now he wore a shirt with a green silk tie knotted high at his throat. He was still barefoot, and as Daníel slipped off his shoes, despite Leonid's protestations that this was unnecessary, he understood why. The floor was as warm as a radiator beneath his feet, and Daníel, who rarely envied anyone anything, felt a sudden longing for underfloor heating of his own.

'Well, gentlemen,' Leonid said as he escorted them into the living room. 'May I offer you refreshments?'

They both shook their heads, and Leonid clearly decided against offering them a seat instead, and took a position with his back to the window, arms folded across his chest as he waited.

'We need to ask about your connections to certain people,' Baldvin said, and Daníel handed Leonid the list that Áróra had sent him that morning.

Leonid quickly scanned it. Then his chin jutted forward and he smirked.

'I have heard of some of these people,' he said.

'Heard of them?' Baldvin repeated. 'Is that all? You were in prison in Russia with two of them and were convicted of a crime with one of them.'

'That was principally a misunderstanding,' Leonid said and the smirk disappeared, replaced by the same blank expression they had seen last time, which settled like a shadow on his face. 'Why are you digging up my past?'

'Mainly to see if it connects to your present,' Baldvin said.

'Once a villain, always a villain,' Daníel added, watching the veins on Leonid's neck swell and pulse.

He hooked a finger under his collar to loosen it.

'I came to Iceland to escape from the past,' Leonid said, and Daníel felt that his English had become unusually clear. 'In Iceland I am engaged only in honest business.'

'You're sure you haven't been making up for your past by moving to Iceland?' Daníel suggested. 'Turning yourself into a big fish in a small pond, instead of the small fish in a big pond you were before?'

'I don't see what you mean by big fish and small fish. I don't understand,' Leonid said, squeezing out an unwilling smile.

'You had a lot of income flowing into your bank accounts for several years,' Baldvin said. 'Then that stopped. Maybe you fell out of favour with some of those big guys in other countries you were – how shall I put it ... cleaning up for?'

'If you're accusing me of laundering money, then go ahead and do so, and provide evidence,' Leonid said, his smile again vanishing into a blank expression. 'But Daníel's friend ruined some excellent business I was engaged in earlier in the year and since then my cash flow hasn't been the same.'

'What?' Baldvin asked, glancing questioningly at Daníel.

80

Áróra had completed two five-minute super-planks and was psyching herself up for a third when Daníel called. Her hand was so damp with sweat that the phone slipped from her grasp, and she had to wipe her palm on her trousers before picking it up from the floor. She had clumsily managed to hit the green button as she dropped it, so as she put it to her sweaty ear, she dropped straight into the middle of what Daníel was saying, and he didn't sound happy with her.

'Sorry,' she said. 'Could you start from the beginning? I missed what you said to start with.'

'Are you kidding?' he asked, and seemed to be genuinely annoyed.

'Uh, no. I picked the phone up and dropped it.' He was silent and Áróra wondered if he had hung up on her. 'Hello?' she said, and heard Daníel sigh.

'I heard that you tried to pull a fast one on the Russian mafia,' he said. 'To be honest, I can't imagine what you thought you were doing. You must have been out of your mind.'

'I don't see why that comes as a surprise,' Áróra said. 'I already told you about it.'

'What?'

'Yes, I told you that Sergei and his pals came to my place and one of them had me in a headlock while they convinced me it wasn't a great idea to sell information about them to the tax authorities.'

'Hold on...' Daníel hesitated. 'Was one of these pals Leonid Kuznetsov?'

'Yes,' Áróra said. Daníel was silent for a moment, and then Áróra heard a sound that seemed to be a growl.

'It would have been useful to have known that,' he snapped. 'In future don't bother giving me information if you're only giving me half the story. This puts me in a difficult position, to say the least.'

Áróra completed three more five-minute super-planks after the call, and the sweat coursed from her in rivulets. The bloody cheek of the man. How was she supposed to know exactly what Daníel wanted to hear, and when, and what not to tell him? She'd just as happily do without getting half the story from him as well. How was she to know what connections he was making as his investigation progressed? She was relieved that she had hung up without a word instead of yelling back at him. It was always better to remain outwardly calm. That was what her father had taught her:

No matter how much you want to shout and find an outlet for your anger, you'll always feel better later on for having kept your mouth shut.

81

Daníel regretted having been so sharp with Áróra as soon as the conversation was over; to be accurate, as soon as she hung up on him, as he wasn't sure she had heard everything he had said before she ended the call. He knew he would have to call her to apologise, and the sooner he could do this, the better, as otherwise it would weigh on his mind, only making him increasingly anxious.

But it wasn't just to assuage his own conscience that he needed to speak to her. He realised that Áróra was in a key position, and there was every chance they would need to call on her during the investigation. She was the one who could link Leonid to Sergei. That alone meant that Leonid's involvement in the case was more than just as the landlord of the property that had been the container's destination. Áróra had seen them together, and her formal testimony to that effect would be enough to justify calling Leonid to the station to make a statement. Daníel would enjoy every moment as he watched the arrogant smirk slip from Leonid's face as he sweated it out it a stifling interview room.

Baldvin parked the car in a space in the yard behind the police station, and they got out. It was snowing again. A white layer of flakes was settling on the cars, as light as a feather – the slightest breeze would have blown them away.

'Do you want me to call this woman, Áróra, and get her to come in to make a formal statement about having seen Sergei and Leonid together?' Baldvin asked. During the drive back from Mosfellsbær to the station, Daníel had explained the situation to Baldvin, who in turn felt that Daníel was being over-sensitive about having raised his voice a little, as he put it.

And Daníel was not inclined to explain to Baldvin that Áróra was someone especially dear to him – that there had long been a romantic spark between them.

'No, it's all right,' he said quickly. 'I'll do it—' But he was interrupted by his phone ringing. He paused outside the door and waved to Baldvin to go on inside.

Ari Benz was on the line.

'There's something we ought to look into before we release Sofia,' he said.

Daníel felt his heart skip a beat.

'Too late,' he said. 'She's already been released. What do you have in mind?'

'I was looking through the case files the French police sent me concerning Sergei,' Ari said, and Daníel could hear the click of the mouse on the desk in front of him. 'What strikes me as odd is that Sofia Ivanova seems to have been part of the police investigation into the death of Sergei's wife.'

'What?' Daníel stepped back out into the yard, where flakes of snow fell on his face, the extent of what Ari had told him gradually taking shape in his mind.

'Yes, very strange,' Ari said. 'I don't see how she can be an undercover infiltrator when Sergei, and presumably all the other crims, know she's a cop.'

82

Gurrí, the shift manager at the refuge, was deeply upset when she opened the door for Helena, but did her best to stay calm and not disturb the residents. The sounds of children playing somewhere in the house could be heard, and a radio sounded from one of the rooms. The aroma of toast carried along the corridor. Anyone would think that this was just a normal home on a normal day, alive with happiness.

'Thanks for coming so quickly,' Gurrí said.

'No problem,' Helena said. 'I was coming anyway to collect Bisi so she can make a statement at the station. Tell me again what you said on the phone.'

'I don't know if there are some crossed wires, but a woman from the police already came to collect her. A French police woman.'

Helena immediately felt a cold sweat break out down her back. There was only one French woman Helena could think of who could have come for Bisi. She fumbled for her phone, called up Sofia's mug shot from the LÖKE file, and held it up for Gurrí.

'Is this the woman who fetched her?'

'Yes...'

'Fuck,' Helena said. 'Where was the police guard? The officer who was supposed to be looking after her?'

'He checked the woman's ID and some sort of international warrant stating that she was there to fetch Bisi, and he said Bisi would have to go with her. Bisi was terrified when she saw the woman and found out that she was being taken away. She cried and said she didn't want to leave, and she called out and shouted and held on tight to me. It was just awful. It ended up with the policeman lending the French woman his handcuffs. She handcuffed Bisi. The policeman said that everything appeared to be in order, and he just left, but the woman dragged Bisi out and forced her to get into a car. She howled in terror. I'll never forget it. There's something really strange about all this.'

Helena searched with trembling fingers for Daníel's number, while Gurrí seemed to be in shock.

'I didn't know what to think. Nobody from the police had been in touch with us to let us know she was supposed to be going away. But when Bisi hugged me as the woman was taking her, she whispered to me to call you and ask you to help.'

Daníel picked up.

'Could Sofia have escaped?' Helena could hear how taut her voice sounded. 'Is she going around town with a police ID in her pocket?'

'Yes,' Daníel said. 'It seems she's some sort of undercover officer from the French police, working on human trafficking. We had a request from the French police to release her immediately, so we did. But now I have some other information that's confusing, to say the least. Why do you ask?'

'I'm at the refuge. Sofia has been here and taken Bisi away.'

There was a silence on the line, and when he spoke again, Daníel's voice was dark and heavy.

'Hell. We can't afford to lose our witness.'

'I know,' Helena said. She could hear Daníel's breath coming fast, along with a rhythmic clatter that she reckoned had to be him running up the stairs at the station.

'Check the refuge's CCTV,' he panted. 'We need a description of the car she's driving. I'll get an alert out right away.'

'What the hell's going on, Daníel? Is this Sofia a cop or not?' She could hear him stop to catch his breath.

'She's a cop,' he said. 'But it looks like she's a bent one.'

Helena closed her eyes for a moment. She could see the whole case collapsing in front of her eyes. Without Bisi they wouldn't have enough evidence. She should have taken a formal statement from her earlier. She should have applied some pressure on her long before now. Helena had the urge to go outside, onto the steps, and scream with all the power in her heart and soul.

But instead she sighed and muttered from between clenched teeth.

'Fuck, fuck, fuck.'

83

Helena set a speed record on her way to the airport, using the lights and siren to get priority, and pushing the car to its limits. Right now she would have liked something with a better turn of speed. Many of the cars the police used were showing their age, and the traffic division tended to get the newest and fastest ones. It wasn't often that CID needed to move quite this fast. Once they had checked the CCTV and found the car Sofia had driven to the refuge, Daníel had alerted the airport police. A picture and a description had been circulated immediately, and there had been a report practically right away that the car had been seen on its way through Hafnarfjörður, heading towards the south-west region.

It turned out to be a rental car that Sofia had picked up before she had been arrested, and the airport police had found it in the short-term car park outside the terminal, but hadn't been able to locate Sofia or Bisi inside the terminal building itself.

While she drove, Helena listened to the conversations through her police radio, which was linked to Daníel's.

'They went through security about twenty minutes ago,' the airport police's contact reported. 'But they're nowhere to be seen right now. There's quite a crowd today so it's not easy to check CCTV. We have customs working on it with us as well to search the terminal.'

Helena leaned to counteract the centrifugal force as she hurtled up the final bend. She brought the car to a halt on the pavement outside departures, leaving it with the lights flashing as she raced into the terminal.

'Get them to let me through!' she snapped into her radio as she ran towards the entrance to the departures area, and felt as if a whole medley of Christmas tunes jangled through her head, all playing at the same time, while all she could make out was *jingle bells, jingle bells*, the familiar stress trigger making itself felt. 'Get them to let me through!'

There could be all kinds of obstacles stopping police officers getting into the departure lounge of the terminal itself, the domain of the airport's own force, and as Helena reached the top of the stairs, she found that her suspicions were correct. The security guard adopted a pose reminiscent of a stone wall. He stood directly in front of her, arms folded across his chest, glaring stubbornly back at her. *Jingle fucking bells*.

'I've no authority to let you in,' he said, acting as if the ID she waved in front of him wasn't there.

'The airport force knows I'm here,' Helena said. 'We're after two people who mustn't be allowed to leave the country.'

'Hmm,' he murmured, continuing to glare at her, without moving. Helena found Daníel in her phone and was waiting for him to pick up when, to her relief, she saw a young police officer running towards her from inside the terminal.

'Helena?' he asked.

She raised her ID, and they ran together through the security check area, into the staff passage and out into the broad corridor that led to the departure gates.

84

'We've checked the whole terminal, all the way to the outer gates,' the young airport police officer said as they hurried down the long corridor, scanning the crowds on their way. 'One's tall and black, and the other one's short and white?'

'That's about it,' Helena said. 'There should be pictures of them on your system. Their names are Sofia and Bisi.'

'Every gate has been alerted, so there's no chance of them leaving the country,' he said. 'Nobody's being let onto any aircraft as long as the search is in progress.'

'OK, that's good,' Helena said. 'But we're concerned that one of them, who's a suspect, could harm the other, because she's a key witness.'

'Yes, OK,' he replied and continued to check the faces of everyone they met.

Now they were at the D-gates for departures to destinations outside the Schengen free travel area. Uniformed police and customs officers seemed to be everywhere, watching people streaming into the terminal from arriving flights, and heading in the other direction towards the gates. Helena looked around. If the two of them had come here and seen all the uniforms, Sofia would no doubt have been alarmed. She might even have retraced her steps back into the building. But then they would presumably have been seen. Her gaze came to a halt on a door at the corner of the D-gates area and the corridor.

'Have the toilets been checked?' she asked.

'Yes, the girls from customs checked all the female toilets.'

'And the men's?'

'The men's toilets?' A look of surprise appeared on his face. 'Yes, I think so...'

Helena didn't wait for him to finish speaking, but raced towards the door.

'Go and get two big guys!' she called out as she ran, not bothering to make sure he had heard her.

She stopped at the door, cautiously pushed it open and peered inside. The room was empty apart from one man who stood at one of the basins, washing his hands. Helena held up her police ID and put a finger to her lips. Then she gestured for him to leave the room. The man didn't bother with the dryer, but picked up his bag with wet hands and hurried out, a look of fright on his face.

Helena padded towards the two inner cubicles. Both doors were shut, although the locks showed green. She stepped slowly, heel first before transferring her weight to her toes so that the sound of her footsteps wouldn't be heard. At the first cubicle she gingerly pushed the door and it swung slowly open. Nobody was in there. She took a step to one side and pressed just as gently at the other door. There was some resistance. She pushed harder and it still didn't move. She stood motionless for a moment, wondering whether or not to put her shoulder to it or to wait for reinforcements.

But she didn't get as far as making a decision. The door flew open and Sofia's uppercut to the jaw sent Helena tumbling off balance, catching the back of her head against a urinal as she fell. Then everything went black.

A moment later she came to. She sat up, although she didn't remember having sat down, and the little room was full of people. A woman in a customs sweater was holding a cold towel to the back of her head, and close by stood Sofia, in handcuffs, as she argued with the police officer holding her.

'I am a police officer,' she said again and again. 'French police. You have no authority to arrest me.'

The officer held two passports, one wine-red and the other green.

'She had both their passports,' he said to Helena as she scrambled to her feet. She had to support herself with one hand against the wall. 'This one's French and the other is Nigerian.'

Bisi was nowhere to be seen. The young police officer pointed to the shut cubicle door, which now showed its red bar, indicating that it was locked.

'She won't come out,' he said. 'She's sitting in there and crying. She seems to be drugged.'

Helena took a deep breath and blew hard, to dispel the dizziness she felt. Then she knocked on the door.

'Bisi,' she called in a low voice. 'It's Helena. Please come out. Everything will be fine now.'

The door opened a crack and Bisi's terrified face appeared in the gap. She opened the door when she saw Helena, stepping unsteadily forward. Then she caught sight of Sofia with her hands cuffed, and threw her arms around Helena. They struggled to stay upright, each of them supporting the other.

'Please don't let Fifi take me away,' she whispered in Helena's ear. 'She's the one who put us in the container.'

85

'I woke up, freezing cold, and some men were shouting,' Bisi said.

She had agreed to make her statement as soon as the medical checks had been carried out. A female police officer from Keflavík had driven her and Helena back to town after a call at the clinic for a check-up, where she had been given an antidote inhaler to counteract the sedative Sofia had forced on her. The doctor agreed that she was fine to be interviewed, and Daníel had arranged everything, calling Oddsteinn from the prosecutor's office back in, along with Elva, Bisi's legal representative.

Now they had a two-hour narrative of how Bisi's confusion and loss of direction in Paris had resulted in her becoming easy meat for Sofia and her fellow traffickers, how the women had been tricked into getting into the container, and a description of the horrific time spent in it. It was clear from Bisi's account that the pathologist's conclusion had been correct: three of the women, Jia Li, Marsela and Nadiya, had died of hypothermia. But the fate of the fourth, Clara, was still unclear.

'Do you think that Clara was still alive when the container was opened?' Daníel asked.

Bisi nodded.

'I don't think so,' she said. 'I know so.'

'How can you be sure?' Daníel asked cautiously, but his tone was not mild enough.

'Why do you not believe me?' she snapped, and shot to her feet and marched back and forth. 'Why can't you just listen and believe what I am telling you? You were the one who found us in the container, weren't you? You saw for yourself what it was like!'

Daníel raised his hands to signify he gave up.

'I believe you, Bisi,' he said, his voice gentle. 'I believe you.' This was the third time during the statement that she had been on her feet. 'And, yes. I was the first of the investigation team on the scene. I discovered that you were alive, and I saw the conditions. I saw the women dead and you lying there among them, and for a moment the horror of it all changed to hope when I discovered that you were alive.'

Bisi stopped her pacing and folded her arms where she stood, glaring at him in suspicion.

'PTSD,' he muttered almost inaudibly and Helena gave him a faint nod of acknowledgement, knowing that people suffering serious trauma can often respond aggressively to the slightest doubt.

Helena had been quiet throughout the statement session, and he had asked her before they started if she wouldn't prefer to rest. The doctor who had checked her over in Keflavík had said that she had a touch of concussion. But she had insisted on being present, and Daníel had decided that now was not the time to mention the blow to her head to either the chief superintendent or to Baldvin. He knew well how important it was when you had put everything into an investigation to see it come to a conclusion. There was no way of sitting at home and waiting for news.

'The reason Daníel is asking,' Helena said quietly, 'is that we must record everything absolutely precisely so that the case against the criminals is completely watertight. Nothing must be left in the slightest doubt.'

Elva pulled Bisi's chair back to the table and gestured for her to take a seat.

'We have to finish this, Bisi,' she said. 'I understand that this is a very difficult part of your account, but Daníel and Helena must hear your story, precisely as you gave it to me this morning.'

Bisi sat down and took a deep breath.

'Clara lifted herself up when the door of the container opened,' she said. 'It could just as easily have been me who tried to get up to ask for water. But it was Clara. She sat up and began to call out for water and help. The man who had shouted the most went out, and then two of them came back in, still shouting, and one of them hit Clara on the head with what looked like a metal bar. Twice. Hard. So hard that I heard her skull crack.' Bisi closed her eyes and her head jerked, twice, as she relived the horror of it. 'And I did nothing,' she whispered. 'They murdered my friend, and I did nothing. I didn't dare move. I lay still and pretended to be dead so they wouldn't kill me as well.'

86

Bisi pored over the pictures of the men – photos of Sergei, the yet-to-be-found Valur, and Leonid Kuznetsov, mixed up with mugshots of a few regular offenders and one or two police officers. Elva sat at Bisi's side and whispered to her to take all the time she needed, to be sure, while Helena and Daníel sat opposite her at the table, restraining their inner longing to urge her on. Helena could feel a faint vibration from Daníel as he sat at her side, one leg pumping up and down, as if this was his safety valve, venting excess pressure. She felt the same, except that her own pressure valve was, as usual, a Christmas tune that had jangled ceaselessly through her head since they had been at the airport. 'Jingle Bells'. For whatever reason, a few lines of doggerel fitting the tune had formed in her mind, about a cat hunting mice. *It is so fun, it is so fun, to chase the mice, in the palace of the Queen*, ran through Helena's head again and again, while Daníel's leg continued to quiver.

Bisi finally put a finger to a picture.

'This man was there,' she said, pointing to the picture of Valur. 'And this one,' she added, indicating Sergei.

Helena sighed with relief, and the Christmas song playing through her head dropped a little in volume. It would have been a disaster if Bisi hadn't got a proper look at the men, or hadn't remembered their faces well enough to recognise them. It would have been even worse if she had pointed out one of the police officers. That kind of thing had happened before in cases they had been sure were totally bullet-proof. People's memories were unreliable, and staring at a picture for long enough could make you think you knew the person.

'Do you see any others you recognise?' Daníel asked, and Helena knew he was hoping she would recognise Leonid.

But Bisi shook her head.

'Only these two,' she said, placing the pictures of Valur and Sergei to one side. 'This one opened the container,' she said, one finger on the photo of Valur. 'And this one shouted and shouted,' she added, pointing to Sergei.

'Did either of these men strike Clara on the head?' Helena asked, finding it somehow appropriate that she had a thumping headache of her own.

'No,' Bisi said.

'I'm asking again, as we must confirm this,' Daníel said. 'You are certain that neither of these men struck Clara?'

'I am certain,' Bisi said. 'There is no photo of that man.' She picked up the picture of Sergei and inspected his face before handing it to Helena. 'This is the man who yelled when Clara sat up, and he went out of the container. Then he came back with another man and kept shouting until the other man hit Clara with the bar. Then the container was closed and I tried to pull Clara to me, all the way to me, hoping that there was some spark of life in her, but she was dead. I am sure of it. Then I don't remember anything else until you arrived,' she said, looking at Daníel. 'And after that I don't remember anything until I was in the hospital.'

Helena's and Daníel's phones flashed at the same moment as a message from Oddsteinn the prosecutor arrived, asking them to leave the room. Daníel got to his feet, and Helena followed.

'One moment,' she told Bisi. 'We're almost finished.'

Oddsteinn and Baldvin stood just outside the door.

'Incrimination consistent with the investigation,' Oddsteinn said. 'This looks ready to go.'

'Yes,' Daníel said.

'I know you were hoping for something to pin on Leonid,' Baldvin said.

'We don't have what we don't have,' Oddsteinn said. This was one of his favourite expressions, apparently drawn from his stock of home-made phrases.

'And we have no information on who could have murdered Clara,' Daníel said. 'We have a reliable witness, but I doubt that Valur or Sergei would incriminate that person. But I've remembered something that Lárentínus the truck driver said when I visited him up at Hólmsheiði.'

'Which is?' Helena asked.

'He said he felt bad because someone had died in his truck. He didn't say he felt bad because he had been driving around with these dead women, but because "someone had died" in his truck. That supports Bisi's testimony that Clara was murdered while the truck was parked in the yard at Auðbrekka. Which means it must have been either Valur, Sergei or this third man who struck her.'

'Or...' Helena didn't finish what she was about to say as an idea began to form in her mind. There was something about Bisi's description of how Sergei had shouted when the man came into the container with him.

'I need to check something,' she said, and left the three men, who looked at her in surprise as she went back into the interview room.

'Bisi,' she said as she sat down. 'When you say this man shouted and shouted' – she pointed at Sergei's picture – 'do you mean he was shouting at Clara, or just shouting in anger, or was he shouting at the man who came in with him?'

Bisi didn't need to think it over.

'At the man,' she said. 'He was shouting at the man.'

'Do you know what language he used?'

'I was so weak and frightened that I didn't understand everything he shouted, but what I heard was in English.'

'English? Not Russian or Icelandic?'

'It was English,' Bisi said. 'He yelled "hit her, hit the fucking bitch", but I don't think the man wanted to kill Clara. But this one,' she said, and her hand again rested on the picture of Sergei, 'he screamed at him, louder and louder, right in his face, until he hit her.'

Helena turned and left the room. The three men still stood in a group outside.

'It was Lárentínus,' she said. 'I believe it was Lárentínus the truck driver who beat Clara to death.'

87

Daníel was unable to conceal how downcast he was when Elín opened the door and invited him into the studio.

'You look like how I feel,' she said, hugging him tight.

'I've just come from Hólmsheiði, where I had to inform a young man that he's being considered a guilty party in this container affair,' he said.

'Ach,' Elín said. 'That can't have been easy.'

Daníel nodded. Lárentínus had fallen to his knees and wept, saying that he had wanted to tell the whole story earlier, but had hoped the police wouldn't piece together an exact picture of what had taken place at Auðbrekka during the little time that the container was open. Daníel felt sorry for the lad. He seemed relieved to have admitted everything. Daníel reminded him that he would need to consult his lawyer and they would speak at greater length during a formal statement process.

'That looks familiar,' he said with a smile. There was a smear of green paint on her cheek, black spots on her forehead, and her hair stuck out in all directions, as it usually did when she was working.

'Trying to paint my way through it,' she said. 'Dad said I ought to work on the sorrow and the anger, and channel them into creativity, and that would help. He's right.'

Daníel looked around and saw that Elín was working on a number of paintings at once, some on easels and others on the floor, and the air was thick with the smell of oil paint. The dominant reds and blacks allowing her to vent the anger inside her.

'Sergei forced him to do it,' Daníel said. 'Sergei stood and yelled at the terrified driver and ordered him to batter the girl around the head.'

Elín dropped onto a stool and dabbed at her eyes with the sleeve of her overall. She shook her head in despair.

'I'm no longer surprised at the things I hear about Sergei. Now I could believe just about anything.'

'And to be honest with you, with good reason, my darling Elín.' He pulled up a stool that appeared to be more or less free of smears of paint and sat down. 'The truth about Sergei is still gradually coming together,' he said. 'His reason for leaving Russia was that his mother died under suspicious circumstances – an overdose of painkillers, which the police suspected he had a hand in administering. He inherited his mother's estate, and of course the estate of his wife in France, who died under such strange circumstances too.'

Daníel fell silent. He took Elín's hand and squeezed it. They were no doubt having the same thoughts. What would have happened to her if she had married Sergei?

Elín sniffed and again patted her eyes dry with her sleeve.

'Just how wrong is it possible to be about someone?' she said.

88

Gurrí was on duty at the refuge, and she hugged Bisi after Helena had accompanied her inside. It had taken a while to get Bisi out of the car and into the refuge as she had been captivated by the snow that was now coming down hard, in huge flakes. She turned her face up to the falling snow and laughed. Helena smiled. It was as if Bisi was welcoming a new future, far distant from sun and warmth, but hopefully a future that would come with freedom and joy. It cheered Helena to see that Bisi seemed to have forgotten the snow that had covered the ground on the day she had been freed from the container. Maybe she hadn't noticed it. Perhaps she hadn't been fully conscious when Daníel had run after her, out onto the moor, and wrapped her in his coat. It was just as well. A positive memory of her first experience of snow would be better.

Bisi said goodbye and went up to her room, and Helena made things clear for Gurrí.

'We don't know how many people are connected to this case, or if any of those who put her in the container are still on the lookout for her, so she absolutely must not leave with anyone unless—' Helena got no further, as Gurrí interrupted.

'The container? Is she the victim in this container case that's been in the news all the time?'

'Yes,' Helena said. 'I thought you knew.'

'I didn't,' Gurrí said, shocked. 'Bisi didn't want to say much, and the police guard just said she was a victim of human trafficking. I hadn't connected the two.'

'She was tricked into getting into a container in France with four other girls. They thought they were only going to be in there for a couple of hours, but ended up days later in Iceland. You've heard on the news how that ended. The other four died. Anyway, if anyone asks about Bisi, then call me or Daníel—'

Gurrí interrupted a second time.

'This isn't the first time I've heard a story like this,' she said. 'The case I know was exactly the same, with a shipping container, but it has a different ending. The woman involved came to us by herself. Now she lives across the street. She wants to be close to us in case she's frightened, in case she suspects the criminals who brought her to Iceland in a container might have found her.' Gurrí led Helena out onto the steps and gestured to a three-storey block across the street. 'It looks like she's at home,' Gurrí said. 'Her lights are on.'

Helena gazed at the building as she fished her phone from her pocket and called Daníel. When he answered, she got straight to the point. This was no time for courteous niceties.

'I think you ought to come down to the refuge right now,' was all she said, making no apology for troubling him when he had just arrived home from work.

89

The woman's name was Rita and she was originally from Albania. As soon as she saw that Daníel and Helena had Gurrí at their side, she didn't hesitate to invite them into her living room. The ceilings were high, and through the tall windows she would be able to see the women's refuge on the other side of the street whenever she looked up.

'I get a feeling of security when I can see over there to Gurrí and the others,' she said. 'I don't feel safe anywhere except at work and here at home. I work for a computer games company called CCP, debugging. I have a skills-based visa.'

Daníel nodded and smiled as the words tumbled out of her. He had no idea what sort of work debugging might be, and whether it was a real job or something that some kind-hearted person had invented for her, but he wasn't here to verify the woman's residence permit.

'You've heard about the container case that's been in the news?' Gurrí asked.

Rita nodded, a grim expression on her face.

'They're still doing it,' she said. 'They're out there somewhere. That's why I'm frightened when I get in or out of the car, and when I go to the shop or to the doctor. I never know when I might run into one of them.'

Daníel took some time to phrase his words as carefully as he could:

'If you could help us put these men in prison, your life would be better and more secure.'

'I'm told that trafficking cases never get to court in Iceland,' she said. 'And if I'm a witness against them, then they'll know I'm involved and that they will be able to find me. I can't let myself fall into their hands again. I can't take the risk.'

Gurrí placed a hand on Rita's arm and gave it an encouraging squeeze.

'I have to be completely honest with you,' he said. 'You're right that trafficking cases are not generally successful, and I can't promise that everyone involved in trafficking will be sentenced. But with this case it's different. Now we are dealing with four dead women.'

'We have to bring these people to account for their actions,' Helena added. 'There's no other option. This case will be pursued until we have all the evidence we need.'

'We have the testimony of the woman who survived the ordeal in the container,' Daníel said. 'If your testimony could confirm what she has already told us, then we have a pretty strong case.'

Rita nodded, as if thinking carefully. Her eyes flitted between Daníel and Helena, and then to Gurrí, who still had an arm around her shoulders. Then she clapped her hands and stood up.

'I think we ought to make ourselves some coffee,' she said.

90

The woman's account mirrored Bisi's in every detail, except that when she entered the container, she believed she was going to Denmark, where she could apply for a work permit and settle. She had paid a woman called Fifi to get her there. Helena's heart was in her mouth as she brought up Sofia's picture on her phone. She showed it to Rita.

She nodded.

'Yes,' she said. 'That's Fifi.'

Helena swallowed repeatedly and felt a pang that reached all the way from her heart to the back of her neck. The unbelievable wrongness of it – making the victims pay. It was as if Daníel sensed her emotions, because he took over the questioning.

'How much did you pay Fifi for this trip to Denmark in the container?' he asked.

'Two thousand euros,' Rita said. 'I had saved for a long time.' Daníel made notes while Rita continued her account. 'I hadn't been in the container for long when I realised I had been tricked. When I spoke to the other girls, it turned out they were all prostitutes. Or, I should say, they had all been forced to become prostitutes. The reality was that they were slaves.'

Helena had more questions than she could ask, but she decided to leave it to Daníel to lead the conversation from this point on. He was better able to remain calm, and when he took people's statements he had this special knack of not asking anything once they had begun to talk, instead making notes for questions he would ask later. That way there was no interrupting the person's flow.

'We were taken out of the container at some garage and then locked in little rooms. There were two girls there already, and we slept two to each room. The rooms were locked every time we were brought back. One time we almost died because a sandwich toaster caught fire when Valur had made himself a snack one night in the kitchen and forgot to switch it off when he left. It was just as well that Timmy came by soon after, because he fancied a fuck. He got us out of the smoke. Two of the girls were coughing for a week afterwards and it took us a long time to clean up.'

'Can you give us a description of Timmy?' Daníel said, and Helena made a note of the name in her pad. This could be the third man who had been there when the container was delivered to the yard on Auðbrekka.

'He's a heavily-built Russian guy with a belly and a shaved head. He wasn't the worst one. He often brought sweets and beer for us, and he was friendly, as if we were all his pals.'

Helena called up the picture of Sergei from the LÖKE system.

'Is that Timmy?' she asked.

Rita shook her head.

'No,' she said. 'That's Sergei. He was Leonid's special friend. They normally arrived together to take us to the club.'

Helena saw how Daníel stiffened in his chair.

'Leonid?' he said.

Helena brought up a photo of Leonid Kuznetsov to show her. 'This Leonid?'

'That's him,' Rita replied. 'They told us to always call him "Boss". My mother was from Russia and I speak some of the language, and I understood a lot of what they talked about. They always had to get Leonid's say-so for everything. I think he was the chief of all this for the whole of Iceland. Fifi was definitely the main person in France.'

Daníel made rapid notes in his pad, so Helena felt it was time for her to take over asking questions.

'You mentioned a club they took you to. What club was that?'

'It was a sort of private club. They fetched us around eight in the evenings, earlier at weekends, and took us down there. They blindfolded us on the way, but if I stood on the toilet I could just see a Hagkaup sign through the skylight, so I know exactly where the building is.'

'Could you describe the place and what went on there?' Daníel said.

'Yes. It's the top floor above a row of shops on Skeifan. There was a stairway going up and a buzzer down below, where customers could call and would be let in if they had a password from the website where we were advertised. There was a red carpet and a circular bar in the middle of the floor, and sofas along all of the walls. At the end were the rooms where the customers took us to fuck. I still get nightmares about those rooms. I wake up sweating and have to pace the floor and sing to myself to try to wipe those memories away. But the other girls said that this wasn't the worst place they had worked. That's because Leonid was very strict, telling the customers they weren't allowed to beat us or "damage the goods" in any way.'

They sat in silence for a while, all the detectives' questions answered for the moment; that or they found themselves struggling to put any new ones into words. Their thoughts brimmed with revulsion at what Rita had told them.

'But it was one of the difficult customers who saved me,' she continued. 'Indirectly, anyway. He was making trouble by the entrance. Sergei had let him in via the intercom, but when he came up he was obviously blind drunk, and Leonid was pissed off with him because the last time, he had given one of the girls a black eye. So Sergei was trying to get him out, and Timmy and Leonid went to help him get a grip on the man and throw him out, and I saw the door was open. So I ran. Down the stairs and out into the street. I didn't look right or left, just ran over roads and through gardens and yards, hid myself away in a rubbish bin and waited until the morning.'

'And then you came to me,' Gurrí said, putting an arm around Rita's shoulders.

'Yes. The old lady who came out in the morning to put her rubbish in the bin found me, and drove me to the refuge.'

Daníel got to his feet and went into the kitchen, signalling with an almost imperceptible jerk of his head for Helena to come with him.

She followed and they stood side by side, and poured coffee into cups. Daníel leaned close to her and whispered with excitement in his voice.

'We have evidence against Leonid. We have a watertight case against every one of them!'

91

'What I find hard to come to terms with is how anyone would even think of shipping people in a container. Over such a long distance. In such cold.'

Daníel's gaze was fixed on Leonid Kuznetsov, who showed not the least sign of remorse. He just shrugged.

'We didn't know it was going to be so cold,' he said, and the lawyer appointed to defend him continued to look down at the table, as he had done the whole time. He seemed to be the one taking the guilt on Leonid's behalf.

'There's a thing called a weather forecast,' Helena snapped.

'With hindsight, it would have been a good idea to have consulted that,' Leonid said. 'But we had no reason to expect it would be so bad.'

'Because you've brought women here in containers before and there were no problems?' Daníel said. At this point the lawyer coughed, a signal for Leonid to speak with care.

'Is that a question?' Leonid asked.

'Yes,' Daníel said. 'But I can put it another way. We have documented evidence that InExport has on two previous occasions shipped containers to Iceland – the same method and route – so I'm asking you straight out if there were women in those containers?'

'Leonid chooses not to answer the question at this point,' the lawyer said. 'We need more time to examine the case files, and I need more time to confer with my client.'

Leonid nodded in agreement with the lawyer's words.

'All right,' Daníel said. 'Let's get back to the basics. According to Sergei, you were the one who had the idea of bringing women to Iceland in a shipping container. How did you get such an idea?'

Leonid shrugged again, as if this were no more than a casual chat about nothing of any importance.

'The cost is about the same as five flights, and there are no visas to bother with,' he said. 'That's about all there is to it. And it seems a good way of keeping up a supply of fresh girls for the customers. They want variety, you see – different girls, different colours, different figures.'

'So the best way to keep your customers happy is to exploit desperate, helpless women with no family support, a long way from home,' Helena said, glaring at Leonid, while he smiled in return and the lawyer looked at her wearily.

This was a tactic they had worked out in advance. Daníel was the patient, impartial policeman, and Helena was the irritating, judgemental cop, in a good cop/bad cop interplay. Helena was somehow in unusually good form as the bad cop. Yesterday's blow to the head had left her genuinely irritated, and Daníel knew that he should have sent her home some time ago. But he couldn't bring himself to do that to her.

'As I said, all these girls were from countries where it's not easy to get a Schengen visa, and in this business it's best not to register them as coming in and out of this or that country. But there's relatively little monitoring of container traffic.'

'So you decided to risk these women's lives?' Helena said.

'I repeat that this was simply the method of transport. There was no intention to harm the girls. You can talk about criminal negligence or deprivation of liberty, but there was never any intention to kill anyone. A dead whore is worth nothing, you see.'

Now Leonid smirked and there was a challenge in his expression. Daníel took a deep breath and was relieved that Helena appeared to have sensed that this wasn't worth a response. Now was the moment to switch roles, however – time to upset the balance.

'What I'm wondering about is the sheer stupidity,' Daníel said, with a snort of disgust. 'We've checked out your background, Leonid. You weren't much more than a small-time errand boy for the Russian mafia before you came to Iceland. But here it seems that you had bigger ideas. You were going to act like you were the big man; a proper *Vor*, as you'd call it. But you're just not smart enough to be the big man, Leonid. And the astonishing stupidity of ferrying living people in a container in the middle of winter demonstrates that you're a hopeless criminal.'

'I feel a little sorry for you, Leonid,' Helena added gently. 'If that's the best you can manage.'

Daníel glanced at Helena, who caught his eye.

'It never fails to take me by surprise...' Daníel said to her.

'Yes, it's true,' Helena replied, shaking her head sadly.

'How stupid small-time crooks turn out to be.'

'That's right,' Helena said.

'But at the same time capable of doing so much damage,' Daníel said.

'And we thought that this was organised crime. I mean, genuine organised crime,' Helena said. 'But it turns out to be one bent cop in France and a few meatheads. And the brains supposedly behind the whole thing are nothing special.'

'That's it,' Daníel said. 'Just amateurs. Bodgers who don't even think to check the weather forecast.' He turned his gaze back to Leonid, leaned forward onto the table and stared into his eyes. 'But stupidity is no excuse,' he said firmly. 'Not when you're so determined to make money, you cause the deaths of four people. So you can expect to be prosecuted for the murder of four individuals, plus deprivation of liberty, trafficking, prostitution, tax offences, money laundering, and anything else we can pin on you. And being a stupid small-time criminal is no mitigation.'

Leonid's fist hammered the table and his face twisted in fury.

'Small-time?' he snarled from between clenched teeth. 'You've no idea what you're talking about!'

Daníel leaned back in his chair and felt the knot of tension inside him unravel. He smiled, and this time it was sincere. They had broken through the wall. He breathed deep and sighed with satisfaction. Then he stood up and Helena did the same.

'Interview with Leonid Kuznetsov closed at 0200. Continued tomorrow.'

Out in the corridor he raised a hand for Helena to give him a triumphant high-five.

'He'll tell us everything,' he said. 'To protect his own self-image as a respectable gangster.'

'Being branded a small-time crook obviously touched a nerve,' Helena said. They looked into each other's eyes and smiled. Their relief was huge, and the way ahead appeared to be clear. It looked as if they had all the documentation and evidence needed to build a case, and after this conversation, Daníel was certain that there would be a confession from Leonid.

'I need to go home and lose this headache,' Helena said. 'Shouldn't we have a drink sometime later in the week to celebrate?'

Daníel nodded.

'Sounds good to me.'

They smiled again at each other and walked together along the corridor. They could hug later. They would raise a glass and hug, and pat each other on the back and celebrate when the case was concluded. Now they had the feeling that often came with the end of a tough case – the need for a long bath.

ONE WEEK LATER

92

Áróra had decided not to call ahead – she didn't want to lose the courage she needed to tell Daníel what was on her mind. But she regretted not calling as soon as a plump little girl came to the door. It hadn't occurred to her that Daníel's children would still be with him – he had said they would be staying for only ten days. She failed to grasp what the child said when she asked after him.

'He's out in the garage with our step-mother,' the girl said. 'Shall I call him?'

Áróra felt her heart sink. Step-mother? Was Daníel in a relationship with some woman? A relationship serious enough for him to introduce this person to his children as their step-mother?

'No, it's all right,' she said, turning away. 'I'll give him a call later.'

The child shut the door, and Áróra couldn't get to her car fast enough. It wasn't as if she had any hold on Daníel or that she intended to claim him for her own. She had been the one who had rebuffed most of his romantic advances, but this still hurt. She got into the car, but hadn't yet closed the door when Daníel came running out of the house and over to her.

'I won't disturb you,' she said. 'If you're with the children and their step-mother.'

'What?'

'Your daughter said you were out in the garage with their step-mother.'

Daníel broke into a shout of laughter.

'Oh. She means Lady Gúgúlú. The queen of the back garden has taken over the running of my household for the last few days while I've been so busy with the case. There's been all kinds of unexpected stuff. Such as the children deciding to refer to her as their step-mother.'

Áróra laughed as well with a surge of relief. All her tension was suddenly released and she felt the blood rush to her head as she flushed.

'Do you have time to chat over a coffee?' she asked, and Daníel gestured for her to come with him. Áróra got out of the car and followed him into the house.

'I've been keeping up with the container case in the news,' she said. 'Is it all over now?'

'More or less,' Daníel replied. 'I just got the DNA results from hair that was found on a length of metal pipe in a pile of rubbish in the yard on Auðbrekka, where the container was delivered. The pathologist has confirmed that it's virtually certain that this was the weapon used to murder one of the girls in the container. So that concludes the investigation. There'll be a press release tomorrow, as soon as the case is handed over to the prosecution service.'

'Is it true what the news reported – that it's the driver, Lárentínus, who murdered her?' Áróra asked.

Daníel nodded.

'Yes. The poor lad gave in to Sergei's pressure and threats, and he hit her. So they thought they had got rid of the only witness. But the girl who survived has identified them both, as well as the Icelandic guy, Valur, and Sofia Ivanova, who you've already seen all over the news. On top of that we have another witness whose testimony has handed us Leonid Kuznetsov and another man on a silver platter. I'm sure you'll be pleased to hear that Leonid is in custody and will be for a good while. But what's interesting is that when the French police went to Sofia's house in Paris, which is actually the house Sergei inherited from his wife, who tumbled off a cliff, they found the passports of some of these girls, all sorts of documents relating to container shipping, and an Icelander hiding there.'

'Valur?'

'That's him. Valur Jón Pálsson. The one who was named on the shipping manifest and who rented the building where the girls were held, and also the place on Skeifan where this so-called club was. The owner of all these properties is of course Leonid, through his Kuzee business.'

'About Leonid—' Áróra began, ready with the speech she had prepared in her mind before leaving to call on Daníel. But he cut in.

'Ach, Áróra. I'm sorry I was unpleasant over this the other day. This case has been a challenging one for me mentally, and I haven't been at the top of my game. And I hadn't plucked up the courage to call you and...' He got no further as his daughter skipped into the living room through the French windows that stood open to the garden in shoes wet with snow.

'Dad, is it true that Lady Gúgúlú hatched me and Tumi like chicks from eggs that she kept in an incubator for twenty-one days?'

Daníel sighed and shook his head.

'You see?' he said to Áróra. 'The information they get isn't always that reliable.' He crouched down and looked into the little girl's eyes. 'No, my love. You're old enough to know that mammals don't come from eggs. And you know exactly who your mum is and where children come from. Lady's just teasing you. Now you can be either indoors or out, but at least take your shoes off when you come inside.'

Áróra watched as Daníel encouraged his daughter back out into the garden and fetched a cloth to wipe up the puddles that had formed on the parquet as the snow had melted from her shoes.

'So,' he said. 'Coffee. Or...' He turned and looked at Áróra. 'Or shall I open a bottle of white wine?'

Áróra smiled and Daníel's eyes brightened into a smile of his own.

'Why not?' she said. 'It's Saturday, isn't it?'

Daníel's smile broadened and he caught her eye. Then he hurried to the kitchen and Áróra heard the fridge open. She followed him and found him standing absorbed in his phone as he tapped at the screen.

'Sorry,' he said, flustered.

'I'm keeping you from work, aren't I?' Áróra said. 'We can always meet later.'

'No, not at all,' he said urgently. 'You ... er ... caught me in the act. I was sending Lady a message, asking if she could take the children for a movie and a burger. So we could get some peace and quiet. You and me, I mean. To talk.'

Áróra felt her heart beat faster and she grinned.

'What you said the other day,' she began. 'About passing the investigation into Ísafold's disappearance to another officer if there were to be anything going on between the two of us.'

'Yes?'

'That would be fine as far as I am concerned.'

Daníel looked into her eyes, hesitating at first, before returning her smile. She felt her heart fill with joy, and for the first time in longer than she could remember, she didn't feel a stab of guilt over a positive emotion, over feeling good. Maybe the wounds were starting to heal, and the effect her sister's fate had on her life was starting to fade.

She went over to Daníel and reached for the bottle of wine on the worktop behind him. She put a hand on his upper arm and experienced the familiar jolt as she felt the warmth of the muscle beneath his shirt.

She picked up the bottle and winked at him.

'Don't you have some glasses we can drink this from?'

93

Although the apartment was small and the furnishings were sparse, this was still her own refuge for the next few months, giving her a real breathing space – time during which she could regain her bearings and decide what she wanted to do next. Bisi took care not to think back – to her apartment at home in Lagos, about Habiba, about her brothers and parents. It would be best for none of them to know where she was. The best thing would be a fresh start and not to think about what she had lost. She had her training, and could always rely on that. There had to be demand everywhere for people who could fix computers, whether she were to settle in Iceland or somewhere else.

She had laid plates on the little coffee table and lit the candles she had planted in empty wine bottles, and now she had her phone play music while she stirred the jollof rice once more, and basted the chicken she had stuffed with beans, shredded carrots and a variety of spices. It wouldn't be as tasty as Habiba's cooking, but she hoped it would be good all the same. When the doorbell rang, she took off the towel she had wrapped around her waist as an apron.

Helena and Sirra stood at the door, their faces alight with smiles. Sirra handed Bisi a large, brand-new steel cooking pot, tied with a ribbon.

'Didn't you need another pot?' she said. 'When someone's settling in, it's better to bring something useful rather than just flowers.'

'But we still brought wine,' Helena said, handing her a bottle of red. 'You can't invite us for dinner without us bringing wine.'

'You speak for yourself,' Sirra laughed.

Bisi showed them in and took the pot and the bottle to the

kitchen. Tears threatened to break out from the corners of her eyes. These women had been so good to her. Sirra had given her a phone, and Helena had taken her through the whole process of applying for asylum as a refugee due to sexual orientation. Sirra had insisted on her lawyer handling everything concerning the Directorate of Immigration, and had no doubt persuaded the poor man to work *pro bono* for her.

'Wow! That smells so good,' Helena said as she appeared in the kitchen. Bisi sniffed hard and Helena was startled. 'Hey, are you all right?'

Bisi nodded emphatically. She was fine. For the first time in too long, everything was fine.

'I'm a little emotional after everything today,' she said.

Helena nodded.

'I understand.'

Earlier that day Helena had accompanied Bisi to say farewell to Clara again. She had been cremated and her ashes were to be sent to her family in Côte d'Ivoire, whom the police had somehow been able to track down. Bisi had whispered to Clara in her coffin that the police would make sure that her murderers would be punished, so now she could let go of the husk of her body, and her anger, and fly home to Côte d'Ivoire to float in the air in the warmth of the sun among her family. She had watched the coffin disappear, to be taken for cremation, and felt the sorrow clutch at her heart. But a moment later her heart had lifted as she knew that Clara would follow her advice. She felt Clara's soul rise, float and dissolve into the air like vapour as her body became dust.

Helena had asked if she wouldn't prefer to put dinner off to another night, but Bisi said no. She felt she needed to have something to do, something to look forward to. Now she served nuts and fried bananas with red wine, and Sirra and Helena said how delighted they were that she had settled in so well. She knew they were being polite, as these were women used to much finer places than hers, but one day she would invite them to dinner at a smart apartment. It would be her own place where she could be just who she wanted to be, where she could mark down her own achievements.

She urged her guests to have more wine then went back to the kitchen to take the chicken from the oven. It had been roasted until it was golden and the aroma of the rice came from the pot. She quickly washed the new pot and transferred the rice into it. It was better to serve it in this than in the battered old pot she had bought from a charity shop. The food looked just fine, but there was one thing she needed to do first. She opened the cutlery drawer and pulled it all the way out. There it was, wrapped in plastic and taped to the back of the drawer, safe and carefully hidden from anyone who might want to take it off her. Her passport. She felt a sense of relief in her heart and shut the drawer again. She knew perfectly well there was no reason to check on it so many times every day. It was always there in its place, but she wanted to be certain. She went to the window and watched flakes of snow flutter to earth. The snowflakes seemed so light and airy that it was soothing to watch them, turning the landscape outside soft and gentle.

She recalled emerging from the container and seeing the snow. At first she had found it so strange. It had been a thin covering, like a layer of dust on the red gravel, and she had thought that she was in another world. She'd been ready to accept that she had died and that this was what the realm of the dead looked like: cold and strange, the ground white.

Now, standing here in her kitchen, she found the snow beautiful, like in a movie. She wanted to try a sledge, or even skis.

Bisi took the pot of rice and carried it into the living room. Helena and Sirra cooed with delight, and then again when she brought the chicken. She sat beside Sirra on the little sofa, took a deep breath and felt the tightness in her middle soften. She was safe to relax. She picked up her glass, sipped and rolled the sweet red wine across her tongue. Then she smiled at her visitors.

'Please, be my guests,' she said, and dipped the ladle into the fragrant rice.

ACKNOWLEDGEMENTS

Being a writer is the best job there is. I get to study the world and its people in a way few jobs allow, and that process feeds my imagination until it creates a story. I take my research seriously, and I diligently study the real-life situations on which I base my books. But very soon after I started studying the background to *White as Snow*, I wished I hadn't. Human trafficking is one of the ugliest crimes there is, and it has been hard to get some of the stories I heard out of my head. It was also hard to believe the scale of this crime in 'innocent little Iceland'. I hope this book gives some insight into the reality the victims of these crimes must deal with.

In the often-unpredictable journey of bringing *White as Snow* to readers, there are numerous individuals whose tireless dedication and commitment cannot go unmentioned. Gratitude is due to the team at my Icelandic publisher, Forlagið, for their unwavering faith in my writing. A particular nod of appreciation is reserved for my editor, Sigríður. Her counsel serves as my beacon, illuminating the often-clouded seas of creativity.

My utmost gratitude also goes to Orenda Books. Their faith in my work and their drive to bring them to the English-speaking audience has been nothing short of extraordinary. Karen, Cole, West, Danielle, Mark, thank you for all your work. And Mary, you are an angel!

A special thanks goes to translator Quentin Bates. Our collaboration over the years has grown from a mere professional relationship into a profound friendship I hope to maintain for years to come. Our conversations, debates, and shared laughter have enriched our journey together in ways that are immeasurable.

To all my readers, both old and new, I hope *White as Snow* offers, in a thoughtful, considered way, a window onto a world you find disturbing to the point that you are inspired to join the fight against human trafficking. At the same time, I hope you enjoy reading the story.

—Lilja Sigurðardóttir, September 2023